EDGE

BLACKWINGS
CROFTRIDGE

TEAGAN
BROOKS

EDGE

BLACKWINGS MC - CROFTRIDGE
BOOK TWO

TEAGAN BROOKS

ISBN: 978-1-951704-26-1

BLURB

Evie

After starting over once again, I thought my life was on the right track, but everything changed in the blink of an eye when my roommate's secrets caught up with him—and me.

I didn't have a choice. I had to hide while I figured out what to do.

I drove until I was almost out of gas and stopped in the next town I came to, which happened to be Cedar Valley. When I walked into the local diner to apply for a job, I had no idea I would walk out with so much more.

Edge

When Byte asked me to watch over Irene's Diner, I was happy to help. He considered Irene to be family, which made her my family.

What I didn't expect was to become fixated on her newest employee. Evie's beautiful face was marred with bruises and swollen eyes. I didn't believe the story she told me, but I couldn't press her for more information.

I was determined to find out what happened to her, but my instincts told me to gain her trust and make her feel safe first. Little did I know—it would come at a significant cost.

ACKNOWLEDGMENTS

Cover Designer: CT Cover Creations

Proofreading and Editing: Tina Workman at Romance Revisions

CHARACTER LIST

- Phoenix Black - Blackwings MC President
- Badger Marshall - Aaron - Blackwings MC Vice President
- Duke Jackson - John - Blackwings MC Sergeant at Arms
- Carbon Walker - Chase - Blackwings MC Enforcer
- Shaker Marks - Jacob - Blackwings MC Road Captain
- Dash Lawson - Reed - Blackwings MC Treasurer
- Byte Fuller - Micheal - Blackwings MC Tech Support
- Patch Vaughn - Blackwings MC Member and Physician
- Ranger Norris - Noah - Blackwings MC Original Member
- Edge Ellis - Jamie - Blackwings MC Member
- Ink - Isaac - Blackwings MC Member

- Dice - Grady - Blackwings MC Member
- Diesel Jackson - James - Blackwings MC Member - Son of Duke and Reese
- Flint Black - Blackwings MC Member - Son of Phoenix and Annabelle; Twin brother of Blaze Black
- Blaze Black - Daughter of Phoenix and Annabelle; Twin sister of Flint Black
- Raven Lawson - Daughter of Dash and Ember
- Falcon Lawson - Son of Dash and Ember
- Harlow Walker - Daughter of Carbon and Harper
- Mason Walker - Son of Carbon and Harper
- Jake Marks - Son of Shaker and Keegan
- Quincy Marks - Daughter of Shaker and Keegan
- Gabriella "Gabby" Marks - Keegan's half sister; Adopted by Keegan and Shaker; Byte's Old Lady
- Copper Black - Blackwings MC - Devil Springs President
- Judge Jackson - Blackwings MC - Devil Springs Sergeant at Arms
- Boar Anderson - Manglers MC President
- Luca Peccati - Friend of the Blackwings; Rumored to have ties to the Mafia
- Evie Sinclair - New employee at Irene's Diner
- Randall Myers - Evie's roommate

- Muzzle Sinclair - Carl - Evie's father; Mad Dogs MC vice president
- Snarl Sinclair - Ken - Evie's half brother; Mad Dogs MC enforcer
- Hound - Mad Dogs MC president
- Mange - Mad Dogs MC member
- Irene Dawson - Owner of Irene's Diner; Close friend of Byte
- Tony - Diner employee
- Bart - Diner employee
- Marcy Wagner - Diner employee
- Walter - Diner customer; Retired professional boxer; Gym owner
- Buck - Diner customer; Retired professional boxer; Gym owner
- Charlie - Cedar Valley Chief of Police
- Roger Pond - Cedar Valley police officer
- Gary Doyle - Former private investigator
- Daphne Clark - Real estate agent

PROLOGUE

EVIE

"I'll see you tomorrow," I said and waved goodbye to my coworker. After picking up some extra shifts, I hadn't had a day off in over two weeks, and I was exhausted.

As I walked to my car, I was going over my upcoming expenses and the money left in my account instead of paying attention to my surroundings like I should have been. The hospital wasn't in a bad area of town, per se, but it was dark, and anyone could be lurking around.

When a dark figure appeared out of nowhere and a hand covered my mouth, I was completely disoriented. It took several seconds for me to realize I was being pulled in the opposite direction of my car.

"No!" I tried to scream when my brain finally caught up to what was going on.

"You better shut the fuck up if you know what's good for you," a gruff voice said.

I struggled to break free from his grip on me, but it

was no use. He dragged me to another vehicle and tossed me inside with ease. As soon as he let go of me, I reached for the door handle, but another set of hands latched onto me before I could make contact.

Moments later, my hands were secured behind my back, and a piece of duct tape was placed over my mouth. Fear like I've never felt before hit me. Whatever was about to happen wouldn't be good.

"Get her keys and follow me to her house," the man with the gruff voice said. It had a hint of familiarity, but I couldn't place it.

I felt someone tug at the purse still strapped across my body. "I can't find them," a new voice said.

"Where are your fucking keys?" Gruff asked.

I mumbled a series of unintelligible sounds from behind the duct tape that was silencing me. Seconds later, the tape was harshly ripped away. "Give me your keys," the second guy demanded.

"I-I dropped them," I stammered, "wh-when he grabbed me."

"Fuck," the guy spat, and slapped a new piece of tape over my mouth.

"Hurry up," Gruff barked.

Second guy got out of the car, presumably to look for my keys and subsequently follow us to my house. I had no idea why they were forcefully taking me to my house, but I planned to use the fifteen-minute drive there to think of a way to get away from them.

"Don't even think about trying anything," Gruff said and turned in his seat to look at me.

My eyes widened in surprise and dread settled in my

gut when I saw his face. The man sitting in the driver's seat was none other than my father, which meant the other man was likely my half brother.

As the pieces started to come together, I had a pretty good idea of why they were essentially kidnapping me. If I was right, there wasn't anything I could do besides cooperate with their demands, and I would. I refused to become collateral damage because of someone else's mistakes.

When we arrived at my house, I was yanked from the car and frog-marched inside. "Where is he?" Muzzle asked. I refused to call him by his given name or refer to him as my father. On the rare occasions I had to use something to indicate him, I used his road name, just like I did when it came to my half brother, Snarl. They were both members of the Mad Dogs MC, and I wanted nothing to do with either of them.

They both stared at me, waiting for me to answer. I stared back at them, wondering how they could be so stupid. When it seemed like they weren't going to realize their mistake, I once again tried to talk with the tape sealing my mouth shut. For the second time that night, tape was painfully ripped from my lips.

Grimacing, I glared at both of them.

"Where the fuck is he?" Snarl snapped.

"I don't know," I reluctantly admitted. I knew it wasn't what they wanted to hear, but it was the truth. "He doesn't tell me where he goes or when he'll be back."

"You better not be lying to us."

"Why in the hell would I lie to you?"

"To protect your little boyfriend," Muzzle said.

"He's not my boyfriend, and I have no interest in protecting him. You want him, you can have him," I said. There was a time when I would have tried to protect Randall, but that was long gone. He'd changed, and not for the better. If it came down to him or me, I was choosing me. The presence of Muzzle and Snarl in my house was proof enough for me that Randall had also chosen himself.

"We don't have all night. You better figure out a way to get him here, or we'll take you back to the clubhouse and let you work off his debt," Muzzle said. His words confirmed my earlier assumption. Randall owed them money, likely for meth, and it was time for him to pay up.

I knew exactly how to get him to come home, but I needed my hands free to do it. "Can you remove the tape from my hands so I can call him?" I asked, trying to keep my tone neutral. I didn't want to do anything to piss them off more than they already were.

Without a single word, Snarl grabbed my arm and cut through the tape that was binding my wrists together. The moment I was free, I located my phone in my purse and called Randall, silently pleading for him to answer.

"What?" he said when he accepted my call.

"I was wondering when you were going to be home," I said. "They gave out surprise bonuses at work today, so I thought we could place an order for delivery from that restaurant you like. The one I can never remember the name of."

"You got a surprise bonus?" he asked, sounding far more alert and interested than he had when he answered. I knew he'd come running at the possibility of getting his hands on some money.

"Yes," I lied. "Our department came in way under budget. They decided to reward the employees by giving us a percentage of the leftover funds. I thought we could celebrate."

"Yep. Great. I'm on my way," he rushed out and ended the call.

I placed my phone on the counter and turned to the two assholes invading my home. "He says he's on his way."

"How long?" Snarl asked.

"I didn't ask," I said. "I never do, and I didn't want to do anything to make him think something was going on." Randall had become increasingly paranoid and suspicious over the last six months.

"You better not be fucking with us."

I wanted to roll my eyes. "You heard everything I said to him," I pointed out. "Trust me, I want him to show up as much as you do."

"What's the matter, sister? Are you not happy to see your family?"

He couldn't be serious. Regardless, I threw caution to the wind and answered him honestly. "Family is not the word I'd use to describe you, and no, I'm not happy to see you. As soon as Randall gets here, I want all of you out of my house. I don't know why you're looking for him, and I don't want to know. I want nothing to do with any of it."

"That's not how this works," Muzzle sneered.

His words sent a wave of fear rolling through me. Randall's mistakes were not mine, but I was beginning to think they felt differently.

Before I could ask how it worked, I heard Randall's car in the driveway. "He's here," I announced, in case they didn't hear him pull up.

Snarl moved to stand beside the front door while Muzzle yanked me to him and wrapped his hand around my throat to keep me in place. Randall walked through the door, saw Muzzle holding me by my neck, and turned to run, but Snarl grabbed him by the back of his shirt and threw him to the ground. Any residual doubts I had about handing Randall over were extinguished when I saw him turn to run. He wasn't even going to try to help me before saving himself.

"Where the fuck do you think you're going?" Snarl spat.

Randall scrambled to his feet and glanced around the room with panic-filled eyes. He shook his head and scratched at his face. "Uh, hey, guys. What's going on?"

"You know what's going on. Where's our money?"

Randall turned to me, where I was still being held in place by Muzzle's disgusting hand. His eyes shifted to Muzzle. "Evie just got a bonus. We can go to the bank and get your money."

"I didn't get a bonus, dumbass. I lied to get you to come home. Whatever you've got going on with them has nothing to do with me," I told him.

"You what?" he asked and started pinching the skin on his arms. "You don't have any money?"

"No, Randall," I snapped. "I don't have money because you stole everything I had!"

"How am I supposed to pay them?" he yelled back.

"I don't know, and I don't care," I said and pulled away from Muzzle. Thankfully, he let me go. My skin was crawling from being so close to him. I just wanted all of them out of what *used* to be my safe space. They were tarnishing it more and more with every second they stayed.

"Are you telling us you don't have our money?" Snarl asked.

"I'll have it soon," he blurted. "She gets paid tomorrow."

"No, I don't," I said. I didn't have time to do anything other than answer honestly and hope it would be enough to save myself. "I don't get paid until the end of next week, and most of that paycheck has already been spent."

Snarl's fist plowed into Randall's face, knocking him to the ground. "We don't like being lied to."

"I'm sorry. I thought it was tomorrow," Randall whined. "I'll figure out something and have it for you next week."

"That's what you said last week," Muzzle said. "And the week before that. And the week before that. Time's up, Randall. I'm going to ask you one last time. Do you have our money?"

Randall pushed himself off the floor and sat on his knees. After a few beats, he exhaled heavily and admitted, "No, I don't."

"When you started selling for us, what did we tell

you would happen if you didn't have our product or our money?"

Randall swallowed audibly. "You said you'd kill me."

"Do you have any of our product to return to us?" Muzzle asked.

"No," Randall said quietly.

"No product, and no money. Seems like there's only one thing left to do."

"No! Please, no!" Randall begged. "Do something, Evie. You have to help me."

It was too late for me to do anything. He and I both knew that. I'd offered to help him months ago, but he wasn't interested. After he stole my phone while I was sleeping and emptied my bank account, I was done with his shit. Instead, I focused my attention on working extra shifts and saving up enough money to get a new place for myself since we were about to be evicted. I didn't care if he had to sleep on a sidewalk somewhere, I was moving out and he was not coming with me. The Randall I once knew was long gone, and I had no desire to be around the meth monster who had replaced him.

I gave Randall an apologetic look and raised my hands in surrender. "There's nothing I can do."

"No!" he screamed. "Don't let them do this. Please. Please!"

I turned my head and closed my eyes. I couldn't stop what was about to happen, but that didn't mean I had to watch it. Or so I thought.

"Oh, no you don't," Muzzle said and roughly grabbed my arm to turn me back around. I struggled to break free from his hold, but was no match for his strength.

Snarl looked at me and grinned maniacally before he plowed his fist into my face. After the second hit, I agreed to comply with whatever they wanted.

"Good," Muzzle said. "Here's how this is going to go."

As I listened to his plan, I tried to disconnect from what was happening. Randall was going to die, and there was nothing I could do about it. The only thing I could do was cooperate in order to save myself.

When he finished explaining, Muzzle looked at me expectantly.

"The knives are over there."

* * *

It took everything I had to keep from vomiting. Twice, I felt bile rise in the back of my throat and forced myself to swallow it back down. I didn't have time to be sick. I needed to get my stuff together and get the hell out of there as soon as possible.

When Muzzle and Snarl finally left, they promised they'd be back and told me to have the mess cleaned up before they returned. The mess they referred to was Randall's dead body and the blood he spilled after having his throat slit. They didn't specify how much time they were allotting me to dispose of the body and clean up the crime scene, but I didn't want to wait around to find out. I also wasn't going to do anything to disturb the plethora of evidence they left behind. Instead, I thought it would be better to pack my stuff and run.

As I was gathering my things, I realized how little I had left. Randall had stolen so much from me. I was partly to blame for letting it go on for so long. It took me a while to realize he had developed a problem. I started to suspect something was going on when he couldn't pay his half of our bills. He hadn't had a major unexpected expense, so there was no reason for him to have no money to contribute.

Then he started taking things from the house and selling or pawning them. First, it was things we didn't use very often, like certain small kitchen appliances and miscellaneous electronics. After he ran out of those, he moved on to things we did use. I caught on when the coffee maker wasn't on the kitchen counter where it should have been. As I started going through the cabinets looking for it, I realized the coffee maker wasn't the only thing missing from the kitchen. When I confronted him later that day, he was very apologetic and admitted he had a problem. I offered to help him in any way I could, but he said he needed to do it himself. Unfortunately, I didn't see that for the red flag it was.

I thought he was doing better and even praised him for his hard work. Little did I know, the only thing he'd gotten better at was hiding his actions. It became clear when my debit card was declined during my lunch break at the hospital. I opened up the banking app to check my balance and almost died when I saw the amount available. Instead of having over two thousand dollars, I only had two dollars. After frantically scrolling through the transactions, I found a Zelle transfer for two thousand dollars to Randall Myers. I confronted him as soon as I got home from work. He denied stealing the money and became extremely defensive. When I showed him the receipt, clearly showing the money was transferred to an account in his name, he tried every trick in the book to blame anyone other than himself. But it didn't matter. I was done. He'd stolen from me. Again. As a result, we weren't going to be able to pay our rent and some of our other bills. When the eviction notice arrived, a part of me was relieved. I could move on without Randall and put the whole mess behind me. Little did I know, that's exactly what I would be doing but in a very different way than I thought.

Carefully avoiding the area on the floor where Randall's dead body lay sprawled in an unnatural way, I glanced around the small house one last time. I hoped I hadn't forgotten anything, but I didn't have time to double and triple check. I needed to hit the road and put as many miles between me and Fairbanks, Georgia as possible before anyone noticed I was gone.

As I drove away from the place that I called home for a large part of my life, my anger grew. I couldn't let them get away with what they'd done. Yes, Randall owed them money, but it was for illegal drugs they shouldn't have been selling in the first place. Two wrongs didn't make a right, and two wrongs certainly shouldn't go unpunished. And I couldn't spend the rest of my life hiding from them. If they were in prison, I would be free to live my life.

Before I could think better of it, I pulled over at a

gas station. Once I found a phone I could use, I called the Fairbanks Police Department and anonymously reported Randall's murder. I identified Snarl as the murderer and Muzzle as the accomplice, as well as where they could find the murder weapon. Then I told them they abducted the other occupant of the house, and they could check the hospital surveillance cameras to verify. After answering a few questions and refusing to give them my name, I got back into my car and drove until I couldn't drive any more.

1

EVIE

Taking one last look at the Help Wanted sign, I took a deep breath and entered the diner. I desperately needed a job, but I could only work under certain conditions, and I hadn't had any luck finding a place willing to meet those conditions. I was quickly running out of options.

Taking a seat at the counter, I pushed my sunglasses closer to my face and glanced around the room. The place was busier than I expected for the middle of the day.

"What can I get ya?" a woman asked, appearing out of nowhere and causing me to jolt in my seat. "Sorry, didn't mean to startle you."

"I saw the sign in the window and would like to apply for a job. Is the manager here?" I asked.

"You're looking at her," she smiled. "I'm Irene, manager and owner."

"Hi," I said and extended my hand. "I'm Evie. What positions do you have available?"

"I need a server. Full-time hours, probably more. Minimum wage plus tips. Are you interested?"

"Yes, but…," I started and paused. I wasn't sure how to ask for what I needed. "I, um, when I asked about a job at the gas station on the corner, uh, they told me to come talk to you."

She gave me an appraising look and lowered her voice. "Let me see what's behind those glasses."

I froze. I didn't want to remove my sunglasses, but something told me it might be the key to getting this woman to employee me. Slowly, I slid the glasses down my nose, allowing her to see my bruised and swollen eyes.

Her eyes narrowed briefly before her face softened. "You're hired. You can start tomorrow."

"But I—"

She waved her hand dismissively. "You don't have to explain. I know why Gus told you to come see me. You got a place to stay?"

"My car," I said quietly.

"Well, it's nothing fancy, but I got a place you can rent," she said and patted my hand.

"I don't have money for rent," I admitted, overwhelmed with shame. I was broke, beaten, and begging for help. Everything I never wanted to be.

"I know, honey. We'll work it out," she said. "Let me get you something to eat while I clear out a few tables. Then we'll go over to your new place and get you settled. You like cheeseburgers?"

"Yes, I do. Thank you," I said.

"Great. I'll be right back."

I sat there wondering what had just happened. It seemed too good to be true. A job and a place to live. I thought I would be living in my car for months, if not longer. And I was okay with that. Anything was better than still being in Fairbanks.

Sooner than I expected, a plate with a cheeseburger and fries appeared in front of me. "I forgot to ask what you wanted to drink."

"Water, please," I said.

She raised and eyebrow. "Is that what you really want? Or did you say water because it's free?"

"Sweet tea, please."

She smiled. "Coming right up."

Who was this woman, and how did she seem to know everything?

"Thank you." I hoped she knew I meant it for more than the meal.

"You're welcome," she said and gestured to the food. "Eat up while it's still warm. I'll be finished soon."

I almost groaned when I took a bite of the cheeseburger. All I had eaten since I arrived in town was vending machine and gas station food. Before I could stop myself, I inhaled the burger, followed by the fries.

"Did you get enough?" Irene asked, seeming to appear out of nowhere.

I nodded. "It was delicious. Thank you."

"Good. Let's go take a look at your new place. Drive around back, and you can follow me there."

"How much do I owe you for the meal?" I asked.

She shook her head. "It's on the house."

"But—" I started to protest.

She held up her hands to stop me. "You can't tell your customers how good the food is if you haven't tried it."

"Okay," I conceded. But I made a mental note to find some way to pay her back.

I climbed into my car and prayed Irene didn't live far from the diner. I had less than a quarter of a tank of gas, and I needed it to last until after my first shift.

Thankfully, it was only a short drive to our destination. Irene pulled into a long driveway that led to a moderately sized one-story house. She continued past the house and came to a stop in front of a cute single-wide trailer at the back of the property.

"Here we are," she said when she got out of her car. "It's not completely furnished, but there's a bed, a small couch, and a kitchen table."

She unlocked the front door, and I followed her inside. As she said, it was minimally furnished, but I didn't need much. Just a safe place to rest when I wasn't working.

"What do you think?"

"It's perfect," I breathed.

"Great," she said and extended her hand. "Here are the keys. Since I'm assuming you need to be paid under the table, how about this? Instead of paying you an hourly rate, you can work for tips only and live here rent free."

"Deal," I said and held out my hand.

She took my hand, shook it, and pulled me in for a hug. "Your shift starts at seven tomorrow morning. I'll see you then."

"What about this?" I asked and gestured to my eyes.

"You had sinus surgery. It went well," she said and nodded once. "See you in the morning." With that, she was gone.

I stood there for several minutes and took in the silence, the peacefulness. For the first time in a long time, I felt safe. I could only hope it would last.

* * *

I TRIED TO COVER THE BRUISES WITH WHAT LITTLE makeup I had, but there was no point. I looked like hell, and there wasn't much I could do about it. Hopefully, people would believe the sinus surgery story.

I arrived at the diner fifteen minutes before seven. There were already a few customers at tables and two at the counter. Irene smiled when she saw me. "You're early. Ready to start?"

"Yes, but I don't really know what I'm doing," I admitted.

"That's okay. You can spend a few hours with me until you get the hang of it. It's pretty simple," she said and gestured for me to follow her. She went to her office, where she rummaged around in a cabinet before she tossed something to me. "I forgot to give that to you yesterday. Remind me to give you a few more before you leave for the day."

I unfolded the T-shirt and held it up to look at it. Irene's Diner was printed across the front with a retro-style design.

"You can change in the employee bathroom across

the hall. There are lockers in the break room for your stuff. A couple of them are empty. You can have whichever one you want," she said.

I hurried across the hall and changed into my new shirt. It was the first new piece of clothing I'd had in a long time. Even though it was a work shirt, I was still excited. I hurried to the break room and tossed my old shirt into an empty locker before returning to the kitchen.

Irene nodded in approval when she saw me and handed me an apron to tie around my waist. Next, she gave me a pen and a small notepad. "Ready?"

"Yes," I nodded eagerly.

"Let's go," she said and glanced at her watch. "It's time for the morning rush."

She wasn't kidding. Within minutes, it seemed, the place was packed with people waiting at the front for a table to become available. I followed along dutifully and paid close attention to everything she did. She greeted many of the customers by name and even knew what most of them were going to order.

"It's not as hard as it looks. These old farts are in here at least four days a week. It doesn't take long to have it memorized," she told me. "It helps if you come up with a system. Like that table over there. I call them the four farts. Then I pair their order with a prominent feature. Bald eggs, hairy pancakes, ear gravy and biscuits, and bearded breakfast burrito."

With a scrunched nose, I burst into laughter. "I may never eat breakfast foods again."

"I know, right? It's a win-win strategy. I remember

their orders without eating myself out of house and home. I mean, my food is delicious, if I do say so myself."

After the crowd died down, Irene sent me off to take care of a few tables on my own. To say I was nervous was an understatement, but I was determined to do a good job. I had to. My survival depended on it.

I'd barely had a chance to breathe when the diner started filling up again.

"Time for the lunch crowd," Irene announced. "It's the same routine as the morning, except with burgers instead of biscuits. We'll tackle the major rush together and split up like we did earlier when it settles down."

We stayed busy taking orders, filling drinks, and serving food. Table after table. Irene definitely wasn't hurting for business.

When she gave me my own tables to wait on, I felt more comfortable than I did at breakfast. The customers were easy-going and pleasant, and that helped put me at ease.

I was behind the counter putting in an order when I heard Irene hang up the phone and curse.

"Is something wrong?" I asked.

"Marcy's supposed to work the evening shift, and she just called in sick," she grumbled. "I know she's not sick. I swear, as soon as I get another server in here, I'm canning her ass."

"I can stay and work," I offered.

"I don't want to wear you out on your first day."

"Please. I'm happy to help," I said sincerely. She'd gone out of her way to help me mere minutes after meeting me. It was the least I could do. Plus, it was an opportunity to earn more money.

"If you're sure," she said reluctantly.

"I am," I promised.

"Well, at least take a break while you have a chance and get yourself something to eat. Order whatever you want on the house," she said. Then she reached into her pocket and pulled out a wad of cash. She counted it out and handed a stack to me. "Here's your half of the morning and lunch tips."

"Thank you," I said and tried to keep my eyes from bulging out of my head. I didn't know how much it was, but I knew it was much more than I'd expected to make. I clutched it in my hand and stared at it for a few long seconds before I shoved it in my pocket and took my first break of the day.

"You did great today," Irene said as she locked the front door and turned off the open sign. "I hope you're still going to come back tomorrow."

With my hand in my pocket, I ran my fingers over the wad of money. "I'm definitely coming back."

"Good," she smiled. "It doesn't take long to close. We'll be out of here in no time."

After we finished, she handed me my cut of the evening tips and two more T-shirts. "I don't have any more in your size. I'll have to order some. If you don't have a clean one, just wear a plain T-shirt that day."

"Is there a laundromat nearby?" I asked. I'd only been in town for a few days and didn't know where anything was.

"My washer and dryer are on the back porch. It's

closed in, so I'll need to give you a key. You can come up to the house and wash your clothes whenever you need to."

"Thank you," I told her, for what felt like the hundredth time that day.

"Happy to help," she said. "You ready to go?"

"I'm ready if you are."

"Let me check on the guys in the kitchen first," she said and disappeared through the swinging door. She returned moments later. "They're good. Let's roll."

I followed her back to her house and waved as I continued down the driveway to my new home. Once inside, I went straight to the bathroom to soak my feet in the small bathtub while I counted my tips.

When I climbed into bed, I was exhausted and thought I'd fall asleep quickly, but I didn't. Every time I closed my eyes, I saw Randall's dead body. When I finally did fall asleep, my dreams were filled with Muzzle and Snarl promising to find me and do horrible things to me before they killed me.

After waking up numerous times throughout the night, I was relieved when it was time to get up and get ready for work. Being awake and tired seemed better than being asleep and terrified.

2

EDGE

When Byte called and asked me to hang out at Irene's diner to keep an eye on things, I was happy to help. Irene was cool as fuck, and her food was some of the best I'd ever had.

Irene smiled and shook her head when she saw me. "I knew he'd send one of you."

"I can't complain. I consider this one of the perks of the job."

"I told him I'd be fine. Tony's in the back, and I've got a shotgun under the counter," she said.

I wasn't surprised. She looked like the kind of woman who would blow a hole through someone who tried to cross her. "What can I say? He worries."

"It must be something worth worrying about if Phoenix has y'all stationed up here."

"Are you fishing for information?" I teased.

"You know damn well I am. Byte told me a little bit, but he didn't have much time to talk and neither did I. You want a coffee or something to eat?"

"Coffee for now, please," I said and took a seat at the counter. "We don't know the details yet, but someone's been harassing Gabby. They thought it was a guy she went out with a few times. Then they thought it was Lauren, the girl she met here to study with last week. Now they think it might be both of them. The problem is the police can't find either of them, and neither can Byte."

"Oh, I bet that's eating him up," she said and placed a mug of coffee in front of me.

"It is," I confirmed. "He's been glued to Gabby's side since all this shit started."

"I don't think he needs to worry about me. Lauren asked about Byte and Gabby, but I didn't have anything to tell her. She said she was worried because she hadn't been able to get in touch with Gabby. I told her I would call Byte after I tended to a few tables, but the guy came in and they started arguing before I had a chance to call. He seemed pretty pissed off about her being here, so I doubt they'll come back," she said.

"Could you hear what they were arguing about?" I asked.

"Not really. He called her stupid and said something about her ruining everything. She said he was an asshole and was overstepping his bounds. He told her to shut up, and that's when I headed for their table. He saw me coming and practically dragged her out the door."

"I'm sure Byte's downloading the video clips as we speak."

"I have no doubt he is," Irene chuckled. "How many Blackwings are in town?"

"Three. Me, Diesel, and Ink."

"Let me know before you leave. I'll send you home with food for them," she said.

"I'll be here until you close," I told her.

"Seriously, Edge. You don't have to stay here all night."

"It's either sit here or sit at Gabby's house. Personally, I'd rather be here," I told her. I didn't mind hanging out at Gabby's house, but after a few days, it was nice to have a change of scenery.

"Well, make yourself comfortable. Let me or Evie know if you need anything."

"I don't think I've met Evie," I said.

"Oh, you probably haven't. She's new."

Irene disappeared around the corner and came back with a woman in tow. She looked to be in her early thirties with long, dark blonde hair, and two black eyes. Possibly a broken nose. Someone had done a number on her. Rage instantly filled me at the thought.

"Edge, this is Evie. Evie, this is Edge," Irene introduced.

Evie reached out to shake my hand. When she glanced at my cut, her entire body stiffened, and her face paled. "Nice to meet you," she rushed out, while her eyes darted around the room like she was looking for a way to escape.

"Nice to meet you, too," I said.

"He's a family friend. Be sure to take good care of him," Irene said before leaving the two of us at the counter.

"Can I get you anything?" Evie asked, keeping her eyes on the floor.

"What happened to your face?" I blurted. I didn't mean to ask, but the question had been on repeat in my mind since I saw her.

She cleared her throat and shifted from foot to foot. "Sinus surgery."

She was lying. It was written in every aspect of her body language, from the way she was nervously wringing her hands to the way she wouldn't make eye contact.

"Did it help?" I asked.

"Did what help?"

"The surgery," I said.

"Oh, uh, it's too soon to tell. There's still a lot of swelling."

"It looks painful. I hope it helps so you didn't go through all of that for nothing," I said and took a sip of coffee.

"It's getting better every day."

It would continue to get better if I had anything to say about it. I made a mental note to ask Irene about her. There was no way Irene believed her story about sinus surgery. I knew what a face looked like after it had been punched a few times, exactly like Evie's. *Surgery my ass.*

I wanted to demand she tell me the truth and give me the name of who did that to her, but I couldn't. Something about me scared her. I wasn't as scary as some of my brothers, but I didn't look like a pushover either. I was tall and muscular and had more than my fair share of tattoos. Add in my cut and a little facial hair, and I was the portrait of a typical biker.

"I need to check on my tables," Evie said quietly. "Let me know if you need anything."

"Thanks," I said and wondered what I should do next. I wanted to get her talking, but I had to proceed carefully. One wrong move would scare her off for good.

I tried to read a book on my phone, but I gave up after I read the same paragraph five times and still didn't know what it said. I couldn't stop thinking about Evie. It was hard to keep myself from staring at her while she worked.

Finally, Evie was busy with customers, and Irene was behind the counter. "What's the story with Evie?" I asked quietly.

"What do you mean?"

"Oh, come on. You and I both know those bruises aren't from sinus surgery. Somebody did that to her."

Irene frowned. "I honestly don't know what happened to her. She showed up yesterday looking for a job. Said she was new in town and was living in her car. So, I gave her a job and a place to stay."

"That's sort of your MO, isn't it?" I asked.

"I guess so. It's just a feeling I have when people need help."

"You think she's running from someone?"

"That'd be my best guess. She was looking for a job that would pay her off the books. Poor thing barely had any money. I didn't hang around while she unloaded, but it didn't look like she had much in her car," she said.

"Do you know her last name?"

Irene shook her head. "I didn't ask. I figured she'd tell me when she was ready."

"I know you don't want to pry, but it might be a good idea to know what she's running from in case it shows up here."

"I hear you, but she'll bolt if she gets scared, and then I won't be able to do anything to help her." She glanced at something behind me. "Do you want fries or a different side?"

I wrinkled my forehead in confusion until I looked over my shoulder and saw Evie approaching. "Fries, please."

"Got it. It'll be out soon," Irene said and turned to Evie. "You doing okay?"

"I'm good. I have three tables about to leave, two are waiting on orders, and the others are enjoying their meals."

"Good. You let me know if you need any help or want to take a break. I don't want you getting burned out and leaving me," Irene said.

Evie smiled. "I'm not going anywhere."

"What happened to Marcy?" I asked.

"She's been out sick. Evie worked a double shift yesterday and is doing it again today to cover for her. As soon as I find another server, I'm kicking Marcy's ass to the curb."

"For calling in sick?" I asked.

"She's not sick," Irene snapped.

I held my hands up in surrender. "My mistake. Marcy's bad. Evie's good. I got it."

Irene swatted my hands. "Where is your food? You

need something to keep you occupied for a while."

"It's right here," Evie said and placed a plate in front of me.

"Thanks," I said. "It looks great."

"I don't care how it looks," Irene teased. "I want to know how it tastes."

"You're doing a lot of fishing today."

"I'm going to smack you. I am not fishing for compliments," Irene snapped, though I could tell she was enjoying our banter. She always did.

I picked up my fork and took a bite. "Mmm, this is delicious," I said, exaggerating every word.

"Keep it up, and I'll banish you to the table in the corner."

I laughed. The table in the corner was a running joke with Irene. She didn't want to waste any space in the diner, so she had a table made to fit specifically in the corner of the room. The tabletop was triangular, and the attached booths tapered to a point. It could only seat two people, and it was uncomfortable if said people were larger than an average-sized ten-year-old.

"Fine. I'll behave."

"You're distracting," Irene said and pointed an accusatory finger at me.

"You can't blame me for my charming, good looks. I was born this way," I said.

Irene laughed and shook her head. "What are we going to do with you?"

I shrugged. "Feed me."

She feigned exasperation. "I'm trying."

I returned to my food and covertly looked at Evie.

She was standing off to the side, watching me. She reminded me of a scared animal, wanting to come closer, but too afraid to do so.

"Irene's good people," I said and kept my eyes on my plate.

"Yes, she is," Evie agreed.

I wanted to say more, but waited to see what she would do. Much to my disappointment, she left me to my meal and went to check on her other customers.

I tried not to let it bother me. There was plenty of time for her to warm up to me.

3

EVIE

A biker. Irene was friends with a biker. A beautiful biker with piercing blue eyes and a killer smile, but that wasn't the point. I was already rattled by the couple who got into an argument with each other during the middle of the lunch rush. The way he grabbed her arm and started yelling in her face was very similar to the way Muzzle manhandled and yelled at me. Irene assured me things like that rarely happened, but I couldn't shake the anxiety they had caused. So, when Irene's biker friend walked in, it took everything I had not to freak out and run away screaming. Instead, I tried to maintain my composure and draw as little attention to myself as possible while telling myself he would eventually leave. I just had to wait him out. But he didn't leave. By the time the dinner rush was over, he'd already been there for hours and showed no signs of going anywhere.

"Can I get you anything else?" I asked.

"More coffee, please."

I picked up the carafe and refilled his mug. He'd already had multiple cups, and I briefly wondered if he planned on ever sleeping again.

"Thanks," he said and picked up the mug to take a tentative sip. "Hot."

"It usually is," I blurted without thinking. Anticipating his reaction, I tensed and braced myself. "I'm sorry," I said quickly. "I didn't mean to be rude."

"Relax," he chuckled. "It's fine."

It wasn't the reaction I expected, but I'd take it. "Let me know if you need anything else." I hurried away and tried to stay busy with the other customers for the rest of the night. Maybe I was being paranoid, but it felt like he was watching me. I didn't want his attention on me, or anyone else's, for that matter.

Finally, it was time to go home. Surprisingly, Edge stayed at the counter while we closed. Then he watched Irene and me walk to our cars before he left.

"I'll see you tomorrow," Irene said and waved goodbye.

"See you tomorrow." The entire way home, I kept wondering if Edge would be at the diner again. What really unnerved me was I wasn't sure if I wanted him to be there or not.

* * *

Edge wasn't at the diner the next day. I tried to ignore the slight disappointment I felt at his absence. Thankfully, Marcy showed up for her shift, and I was able to leave at the regular time. I didn't mind working extra, and was grateful for the additional income, but I desperately needed to run a few errands. I hadn't had time to do anything except work since I met Irene.

My first stop was the grocery store. While the trailer was furnished, it was not stocked with groceries. I thought it would be a simple trip to the store, but I found myself frequently looking over my shoulder and darting around corners. By the time I was finished, my heart was pounding, and my hands were shaking. Even though I knew there was only a slim chance of anyone finding me, I couldn't convince myself that I was safe. I felt marginally better when I returned to my little home hidden away on Irene's property.

Three weeks passed before I saw Edge again. By that time, I'd fallen into a routine and was feeling more settled. I worked five or six days a week and picked up extra shifts when I could. On my days off, I took care of my errands and did my laundry. Otherwise, I stayed at home and kept to myself. During my second week in Cedar Valley, I found a discount bookstore and bought a stack of books to help keep myself occupied when I wasn't working. Since I didn't have a television, and the phone I had couldn't play videos, there wasn't much to do when I wasn't working but boredom was much better than the situation I could have been in.

When Edge showed up at the diner again, I spotted him as soon as he came through the door, and my stomach did a little flip at the sight of him. My face was completely healed, but I still felt self-conscious around him. I couldn't figure out why he unnerved me so much, but he did, and I decidedly didn't like it.

"Hey, Evie. How's it going?" he said and took a seat at the counter.

"Good. What can I get you?" I asked, keeping my eyes downcast.

"A cup of coffee for now."

"Coming right up."

"How are your sinuses?" he asked.

I wrinkled my forehead in confusion. "My what?"

"Your sinuses. Looks like you're all healed up from your surgery."

"Oh," I said, suddenly remembering the lie I told him. "So far so good."

"I'm glad you're doing well."

"Thanks. Let me know if you want to order something," I said and got away from him as fast as I could without being too obvious.

I spent the rest of my shift trying to stay busy and act normal, even though I could feel him watching me. Finally, it was time for me to leave, and I was more than ready to go, but Marcy wasn't there.

"Where in the hell is she?" Irene asked as she stared at the clock. "Do you mind staying while I try to get a hold of her?"

"Of course not," I said. Truthfully, I wouldn't have minded at all if Edge wasn't there. To make matters worse, he was the only customer in the diner, so there wasn't much I could do to avoid him.

"How do you like working here?" he asked.

"It's great," I said. I opened my mouth to say more but thought better of it. Engaging him was not something I needed to do.

"Irene's a nice lady. If you're good to her, she'll be good to you," he said.

Irene came back to the front, shaking her head. "She's sick again and forgot to call. The least she could do is try to sound sick. Maybe throw in a fake cough or two."

"Do you want me to cover her shift?" I asked.

"If you want to," she said. "If not, I can always get Bart to help me run plates." Bart worked in the kitchen with Tony. He didn't talk much, but he seemed like an okay guy.

"I can stay."

She smiled. "You're the best."

I smiled in return, though I was jumping up and down on the inside. I cherished every compliment she gave me.

Before long, the dinner crowd had arrived, and I was running around trying to stay on top of my tables. I'd almost forgotten about Edge until he called my name. I turned to him and stopped short when I realized another biker had joined him. "Did you need something?" I managed to ask.

"Yeah. This is my brother, Ink. He needs to place an order to go."

"Sure thing," I said and fumbled for my notepad and pen. "What can I get you?"

He placed an order for two meals, and Edge also ordered something for dinner. Was there a third biker around somewhere? And why were they hanging around Cedar Valley? Irene told me they were from Croftridge, which was a smaller city about thirty minutes away.

I handed Ink his order. "Here you go."

"Thanks, Evie," he said and handed me a fifty-dollar bill. "Keep the change."

My mouth dropped open in shock as I stared at the money in my hand. The change he referred to amounted to well over twenty dollars. When I looked up to thank him, he was already gone.

"I think your friend gave me the wrong bill."

Edge grinned. "No, he didn't."

"Order up," Tony called from the back.

"Please thank him for me," I said to Edge as I placed his meal in front of him.

"Will do," he said and turned his attention to his food.

Once again, he stayed until we were ready to leave for the night. As he watched us walk to our cars, I wanted to ask Irene why he was there. It was none of my business, but there had to be a reason he was hanging out at the diner for hours at a time.

The next day, he came in shortly after breakfast and was still there when I finished my shift. He didn't talk as much, but he was polite when he did. There were so many things I wanted to ask him, and even more that I wanted to ask Irene about him, but I didn't. It was better to keep my distance.

I waved goodbye before I left, not knowing that was the last time I would see him for months.

4

EVIE

"I'm not taking no for an answer," Irene said. "In the time that you've known me, when have I taken a day off? Never. So we shouldn't waste this rare opportunity. And it's a party. Who doesn't love a party?"

"Me," I told her. It wasn't that I didn't like parties, per se. It was that the party was in Croftridge, and she'd already told me Edge would be there. Since I highly doubted he would be the only biker in attendance, I was more than reluctant to attend. But I also didn't want to hurt Irene's feelings. She was excited about the party, and it seemed like she really wanted me to go with her.

"Oh, come on. You've got to get out and live a little. Meet some people your own age and make some friends."

I didn't want to meet anyone or make any friends. I was doing just fine on my own, and I wanted it to stay that way.

"Just agree to stay for an hour. Then, if you're not having a good time, we'll leave."

"I guess that'll be okay," I said.

"Great!" she said excitedly. "I'll pick you up in an hour."

An hour would barely be enough time for me to shower and get ready. I could do it if I hurried and did my makeup in the car. I was in the middle of washing my hair when it dawned on me that I didn't know what to wear to the party. The options I had to choose from were limited, and they weren't what I would call party clothes. "Crap, crap, crap. Why did I agree to this?"

I hastily rinsed the conditioner from my hair and hopped out of the shower, slipping on the floor and almost busting my ass as I ran across my trailer to get my phone. "What are you wearing?" I said between breaths when Irene answered my call.

"Why is that question always accompanied by heavy breathing?"

"Sorry, I just got out of the shower."

"Must've been some shower," she laughed.

"I don't know what to wear," I confessed.

"You don't need to dress up or anything. A black T-shirt and jeans will be fine. Really any color T-shirt except red. That's what I'm wearing, and we don't want to be all matchy-matchy."

"Got it," I said. "See you in a bit."

When she knocked on my door, I was dressed and my hair was dry, but I was also sweaty and flustered. "You ready to go?"

"Yeah, let me just grab my stuff," I said. I also got a paper towel and used it to dry my face. "Sorry, I always get hot after I dry my hair."

"Well, it's no wonder. You've got so much of it," she said.

"Yeah, I probably should cut it. It's a lot to manage."

"Don't you dare. Plenty of women would kill for hair like yours. Keep it like it is for as long as you can," she said.

"Thank you," I said sincerely and followed her out to her car. Once inside, she put the AC on full blast, and I wanted to thank her again. "Do you mind if I do my makeup?"

"Go right ahead," she said and pulled out of her driveway.

By the time we reached Croftridge, I was much more put together and felt sort of okay about the party. Then she pulled up to a gate and rolled down her window. A man in a leather vest stepped out of the booth and asked for her name. "Irene. I'm Byte's friend."

"You're good to go. Have you been here before?"

"A few times," she said.

He nodded. "Have a good time."

"Where are we?" I asked and tried to hide the trepidation in my voice.

"The Blackwings MC clubhouse," she said, like it was no big deal. Meanwhile, I was internally freaking out. I didn't want to go inside. In fact, I wanted to run as far away as I could and never look back.

"Are you okay?" she asked.

"I don't think I can go in there," I admitted.

"You don't have anything to worry about. I wouldn't have brought you if it wasn't safe. Some of them may look a little rough, but they're all big teddy bears."

"I don't know." I hated how scared I sounded, but it couldn't be helped.

"You're really scared, aren't you?"

I could only nod. My throat felt thick, and I was on the verge of tears.

"I would never put you in harm's way. I promise. When we go inside, stay right beside me. I won't leave you for a second. They're the good guys. You'll see."

"Okay," I whispered. I trusted Irene. If she said it was safe, then it was safe, but I was still scared to go inside.

Steeling myself as best as I could, I got out of the car and walked inside, glued to Irene. A tall man with reddish brown hair and kind eyes immediately came over to greet her. "You made it," he said and wrapped her up in a hug. "And who's this?"

"This is Evie. She works at the diner with me. Evie, this is Byte. I've known him since he was a kid."

"Evie," he said, like my name sounded familiar to him. "Nice to meet you."

"Nice to meet you, too." I blurted the words so fast they almost ran together.

"She's a little nervous," Irene said, causing me to almost die on the spot.

"First time at a biker clubhouse?" he asked.

No, it wasn't, which is why I was terrified to be there. "Uh, yeah," I said.

He gave me an appraising look. "We're not like some of the other clubs."

When I only blinked in response, he added, "That's a good thing."

"That's what Irene tells me," I said.

"Make yourself comfortable and help yourself to drinks and snacks. Gabby should be here soon," he said and excused himself to the kitchen.

"Gabby's his girlfriend," Irene explained. "She just finished college, and this is a surprise party for her. Her brother-in-law and grandfather are also club members."

"What did she get her degree in?"

"She's a nurse and just finished the requirements to become a nurse practitioner. I think Byte said she has one more exam to take before she gets her license."

"Really? That's impressive." From what I knew of motorcycle clubs, the women weren't exactly career oriented.

"Yeah, it is. She had a rough go of it for a bit. A girl was stalking her and shot her and the doctor she was training with. It was a mess, but they both survived and got right back to work."

"When did that happen?"

"Around three months ago. Not long after you started working at the diner," she said. "Do you remember the couple that came in and caused a scene? The one I was going to kick out, but they left before I could."

"Yes, I remember them. That happened on my second day at the diner."

"The girl is the one who shot Gabby. You want something to drink?"

"Sure," I replied distractedly. *So that's why Edge was at*

the diner. He showed up not long after the arguing couple left and stayed for the rest of the day.

"He was watching over you," I accidentally said out loud.

"Yeah. Byte sent him. I told him he didn't need to worry about me, but that boy is protective as hell over the people he cares about." She laughed. "Listen to me. He's been a man for a long time now, but I suppose I'll always think of him as a boy."

"Seems like he's special to you."

"He is," she confirmed. "I met him right after my husband died. I took one look at him and knew he needed help. Little did I know, he helped me as much as I helped him."

"How did you help him?" I asked.

"I had a feeling he had just come from a bad situation. I gave him a job and a place to stay. Helped him get on his feet. I never asked him what happened, just like I'll never ask you, but I'm happy to listen if you ever want to tell me."

I stared at her in shock.

"What?" she said and shrugged. "After Byte, it sort of became my thing. Actually, he helps out from time to time." She glanced around and lowered her voice. "He can make IDs and do all kinds of stuff with a computer. If you ever need anything in that department, he's your guy."

"Like a new identity?"

"Yep," she confirmed. "I don't know how he does it, but he's pulled it off many times. I mean, he's not going to help a cold-blooded killer get away with murder, but he'd help an innocent woman running from an abusive husband or boyfriend."

"You're serious?" I asked.

"Oh, yeah. They don't put up with that kind of crap around here. These fellas cherish their women and children, and they'll rain hell on anyone who tries to hurt them. Like that girl that was stalking Gabby. Well, Gabby actually handled her. But the guy that was in on it. He went after the president's son and got himself killed in the process."

"How?"

She nodded to an older man across the room. "That's Gabby's grandfather. Technically, he's her great-grandfather, but that's not the point. Anyway, the crazy guy was holding the president's kid at gunpoint. Ranger shot and killed him. He may be the oldest one here, but he's a crack shot with a rifle."

Ranger's head turned, and he noticed us looking at him. Smiling broadly, he sauntered over. "Irene," he chuckled. "Were you telling stories about me?"

She laughed. "Of course I was. You have the best stories to tell."

He pulled her in for a hug. "It's good to see you. I don't suppose you brought any burgers with you?"

"I would have, but no one asked me to cater this shindig."

"I'll have to file a complaint with the management," he said, though I could tell he was joking.

He turned his attention to me. "Forgive my manners," he said and extended his hand. "I'm Ranger."

"I'm Evie," I said and shook his hand. "I work with Irene."

"It's a pleasure to meet you. We've got a number of single fellas around here, and you're a pretty girl. If you get tired of them peacocking for you, come find me."

I couldn't help but smile. Something about Ranger put me at ease. "I will. Thank you."

"I told you. Big teddy bears," Irene said after Ranger excused himself.

As the evening progressed, I was introduced to countless people, including the guest of honor, Gabby. She was kind and friendly, much like the other women I'd met. It seemed like maybe Irene was right about the bikers after all. The entire place had a warm family vibe.

Irene and I were sitting at a table near the back of the room when Edge approached with two slices of cake. "I thought I'd take the opportunity to serve you for a change," he said and placed a slice of cake on the table for each of us.

"Where's yours?" Irene asked.

He grinned. "Are you asking me to join you for dessert?"

"Of course I am. And for the record, you're supposed to flirt with her, not me."

"Yes, ma'am," he said and left to get another piece of cake.

I nudged Irene with my elbow. "What are you doing?" I whisper-hissed.

"Helping," she said and shoved a bite of cake into her mouth.

"That is not helping."

"Honey, that boy hasn't taken his eyes off you since we arrived. And you turn into a jumping bean every time he's around. Y'all might not see it, but I do."

She couldn't be serious. Yes, Edge made me nervous, but not for the reason she thought. Hell, every biker in the room made me nervous. That didn't mean I had chemistry with all of them. As for Edge staring at me, well, I didn't have an explanation for that.

Edge returned to the table and sat in the chair directly across from me. He glanced at Irene's plate. "You started without me."

"You took too long," she returned.

He laughed. "It's been a while since I've seen you. How have things been?"

"Are you asking me or her?" she asked and pointed to me with her icing covered fork.

"Both, I suppose."

"Same old, same old. The diner keeps me busy."

"And you?" he asked.

"Good," I said. "Same as Irene. Busy with work."

"That's why I brought her here," Irene added. "She needs to meet some people and make some friends."

I was going to die of embarrassment before the night was over. I just knew it.

"You came to the right place. We're a friendly bunch, and there are plenty of people here," Edge said.

I didn't know what to say, so I focused on my cake, or tried to. Edge seemed determined to get me to talk to him.

"I remember Irene saying you were new in town. Where did you move here from?"

Well, damn. He was the first person to ask me that question since I moved to Cedar Valley. It hadn't even occurred to me to think of a cover story to tell people. I swallowed the bite in my mouth and lied the best I could. "I'm from Florida." It wasn't entirely a lie. I was born in Florida while my mother was visiting her parents and moved there to live with my grandmother when I turned eighteen, but I grew up in Georgia and moved back there after my grandmother died.

"How did you end up in Tennessee?"

I couldn't tell him the truth—I stopped in Cedar Valley because I was almost out of money and gas. "I had distant relatives who used to live in the area. I loved visiting them and moved here once I had the chance." To stop his casual interrogation, I turned the questions back to him. "What about you? How did you end up in a motorcycle club in Croftridge?"

"I grew up here. The Blackwings have been around for a long time and are well known in the area. I started prospecting for the club as soon as I graduated from high school. In fact, I went to high school with Ember and Reese," he said and pointed to two women at a table nearby. "Actually, Reese and I went to prom together."

"I heard my name. Are you talking about me?" Reese asked as she approached our table.

"I was telling Evie that I went to prom with you."

The other woman, presumably Ember, came over to

join us. "Did you tell her about the time I broke your nose?"

Edge sighed. "You're never going to let me forget that, are you?"

She shrugged. "It was your own fault. You offered to spar with me when you knew I was worked up."

"I was trying to be nice," he said. It was obvious they'd had this friendly argument many times before.

"So, I'm going to skip the how and why, but I was trained in hand-to-hand combat from an early age. I was in the middle of a rather intense situation, and Edge was tasked with protecting me while my man went to slay my dragons. Anyway, I was a nervous wreck, and Edge here offered to spar with me to help me work off some of my nervous energy. Long story short, I accidentally broke his nose."

"What happened to you?" I asked.

Her brows narrowed in confusion. "What do you mean?"

Suddenly, I realized what I asked and wanted to cover my face with my hands. "What happened with your situation? Were you okay?"

"Oh. Yes, I was fine. We went to the hospital, and they fixed him right up," she said and reached out to tweak Edge's nose. He dodged and gently swatted her hand away.

"Don't you have children to tend to?"

"My children are grown," she returned. "Well, one is. The other's not far behind. Why? Are you trying to get rid of me?"

"Possibly," Edge said.

"I'll come back to hassle you later," she said and got up to leave.

"She has grown children. How old is she?" I asked. She looked like she was in her late twenties.

"Thirty-eight. Same age as me. Reese is a year older." Edge turned in his chair to survey the room. "See that girl over there? That's Ember's daughter, Raven. The girl to her left is Ember's sister, Blaze. Blaze and her twin brother, Flint, are only a few weeks older than Raven."

"So Ember and her mom were pregnant at the same time?" I asked.

"Yep," he confirmed. "We have lots of fun stories like that around here. Reese is married to Duke, and Reese's brother, Carbon, is married to Duke's sister, Harper. Their kids are super cousins. I'm not sure where Duke is, but Carbon is the huge guy lurking behind Harper."

I was happy to have the focus off me, so I listened intently and asked questions when I could. Irene chimed in from time to time but let us do most of the talking. Before I knew it, the party was winding down, and it was time to leave.

"We're going to head out," Irene said to Edge. "Thanks for keeping us company."

"Anytime," he smiled. "It was good to see you again."

"He's talking to you," Irene stage whispered.

"It was nice to see you, too," I said, completely ignoring Irene.

She looped her arm through mine. "Come on, I need to find Byte to say goodbye before we leave."

She dragged me along with her until we found Byte and Gabby talking to a group of people. "Congratulations, honey," she said to Gabby and gave her a hug. Then she wrapped her arms around Byte. "Come see me when you have a chance."

"I will," he promised.

I awkwardly waved goodbye to the crowd and thanked them for inviting me. Once we were in the car, I breathed a sigh of relief.

"That wasn't so bad, was it?" Irene asked.

"No, I suppose it wasn't," I reluctantly admitted.

"You and Edge seemed awful chatty."

"Edge was chatty. I was being polite."

"Mmm-hmm," she said, as if she didn't believe me.

I did enjoy talking with Edge, but I didn't want to admit it to myself or anyone else. He was exactly the kind of guy I needed to steer clear of.

5

EVIE

"Shit!" I yelled and slammed my hands on the steering wheel. "Why are you doing this to me now?"

I tried several more times to get my car to start, but I was out of luck. I knew it was going to give out on me sooner rather than later, but I'd hoped I had more time.

Exhaling heavily, I leaned back in my seat and tried to figure out what to do next. I was pretty sure I couldn't afford to have whatever was wrong with my car fixed, so that left me with walking or asking Irene for a ride to and from work. Since she worked all day, every day, I'd have to find a way to occupy myself for almost eight hours each day after my shift.

As I stared out the windshield contemplating my next move, someone rode by on a bicycle, and an idea hit me. I could ride a bike to and from work. I knew I could afford one, I just needed to find out where to buy one. After a quick search on my cheap little phone, I found a place within walking distance of the diner.

Thirty minutes later, I was the not so proud owner of my new two-wheeled transportation.

I didn't know the exact mileage from the diner to Irene's house, but it felt like I'd biked across the entire state by the time I made it home. I looked at my phone to check the time and groaned. It took me almost forty-five minutes to get home. I tried to look on the bright side. At least I didn't have to pay for gas and would get plenty of exercise.

* * *

"WHY WAS YOUR CAR STILL IN THE PARKING LOT WHEN I left last night and already here when I arrived this morning?" Irene asked as soon as I walked through the door.

"I'm sorry about that. It wouldn't start when I got off work yesterday, and I wasn't sure what to do with it."

"How did you get home yesterday and get to work this morning?"

"I bought a bike from a shop a few streets over," I said.

"Well, that explains why you look like you just ran a marathon."

"Sorry," I apologized and reached for a paper towel to wipe the sweat from my face. "I'll get myself cleaned up."

"Don't apologize for coming up with a solution to your problem. I admire your determination," she said and headed out to the front.

I stepped into the employee restroom to wash my

face and change into my work clothes. Once I was somewhat presentable, I went to the front and started waiting on customers.

At the end of my shift, I got my clothes from my locker and started for the bathroom to change into my riding clothes, but Irene called out for me to come into her office. I entered her office and came to a sudden halt when I saw Edge sitting in a chair in front of her desk.

"Hey, Evie," he said with a slight smile.

"Uh, hello," I stammered.

"Okay, don't get mad," Irene started. Her words caught me off guard. I couldn't imagine ever being mad at her. "I probably should've talked to you about it first, but I didn't want you to say no."

"Say no to what?" I asked carefully.

"I can't go into the details, but the Blackwings owe me a favor or two. Since they own a garage, I cashed in one of my favors to get your car fixed. Edge is here to drop off a loaner car and take yours back to Croftridge," she explained.

I was at a loss for words. "I don't know what to say."

"You don't have to say anything. Just give him your keys," she said.

"Thank you," I finally said. I didn't like being a charity case, but I knew I needed the help, so I didn't make a fuss about it.

Quickly retrieving my keys, I returned to her office and handed them to Edge.

"Do you need to get anything out of it before I take it?"

"No, I don't keep anything in it."

"All right," he said and extended his hand. "Here are the keys to the loaner. It's parked out back."

"Thank you," I said.

"Do you have any idea what's wrong with your car?"

I shook my head. "It was making a weird noise for a few days before it wouldn't crank. I don't think it's the battery because the lights and radio came on."

He nodded. "I'll get it back to Croftridge and take a look. I'm not sure how long it'll take. It all depends on what's wrong with it."

"I really appreciate it."

"Happy to help," he said and headed out the door.

I turned to Irene, who was eyeing me cautiously. "So, you're not upset with me?"

I opened my mouth to speak, but suddenly burst into tears.

"Oh, honey," she said and wrapped her arms around me.

"I don't know what I did to deserve you."

"You're a good person. Everybody needs some help at some point or another."

"I can't thank you enough."

"Sure you can. Pay it forward when you're able. Help make the world a better place."

Stepping back, I wiped the tears from underneath my eyes. "Are we going to break out in song and dance now?"

Irene threw her head back and laughed. "There's the spunk I've been waiting for. I knew you had it in there."

I smiled. "I really do appreciate this. More than you know."

"I know," she said and made a shooing motion with her hands. "Go on and get out of here."

I did as she said and walked outside to find a shiny SUV sitting in the space next to where my car was previously parked. "Holy shit," I breathed. It was nicer than anything I'd ever driven. I was almost afraid to touch it. "There's no way this is a loaner car."

I climbed inside and marveled at the interior. There were more buttons and controls than I'd ever seen in a car. When I went to put the key in the ignition and realized it didn't have a key, I wondered if I needed a class on how to operate it.

It took me several minutes to figure out where everything was before I finally got going. The vehicle was bigger than what I was used to, but it glided along the road as if the streets were made of clouds. It was going to suck when I had to give it back.

6

EDGE

I forgot to ask Evie for the details about her car, so I opened the glove box, hoping to find the car's manual inside. Thankfully, it was there with the information I needed. What was also there was the car's registration, with Evie's full name and previous address on it. I wasn't intentionally snooping, but I'd already read it before I realized I might be invading her privacy. Once the damage was done, I couldn't stop myself from trying to find out more. I truly believed she was running from something, or someone, and wanted to help her. If I was right and those black eyes came from a person instead of a surgery, she needed more than help; she needed protection. I also didn't want her troubles to become a problem for Irene. And that's how I rationalized what I did next.

I knocked on Byte's door. "Hey, man. You got a second?"

"Yeah. Come on in," he called through the door.

I let myself in and took a seat in an empty chair.

"What's up?" he asked.

"I wanted to see if you would look into Evie Sinclair," I said. "She's from Fairbanks, Georgia."

"As in Evie from the diner?" he asked.

"Yes."

"What am I looking for?"

"I don't know," I admitted. "She showed up in Cedar Valley with no money and no place to stay. She was living in her car and looking for a job that would pay her under the table. And she had two black eyes. She said she just had sinus surgery, but I'm not buying it."

"You think she's running from something," Byte mused.

"She has to be."

"Does Irene know about any of this?"

"Sort of. She knows something's going on with Evie, and that the sinus surgery story was bullshit, but she said she didn't want to pry and scare her away," I explained. "Hell, Irene doesn't even know her last name."

"How'd you find out what it was?"

"Evie's car broke down. Irene called and asked if we'd fix it. Phoenix sent me to pick it up and drop off a loaner. When I got her car back here, I was looking for the manual and came across her registration."

"What are you going to do if we find something?" he asked.

"I don't know," I admitted. "I haven't gotten that far yet. I guess it depends on what it is."

"Well, let's go down the rabbit hole," Byte said and rubbed his hands together before he started typing.

Twenty minutes later, he abruptly stopped typing and turned to me with a look I couldn't interpret. "Oh, brother. I think we might have a problem on our hands."

"Fucking hell," I grumbled. "I wanted to be right, but at the same time, I really didn't. What did you find?"

"Evie Sinclair is the daughter of Carl Sinclair," he said.

"Carl Sinclair," I repeated. The name sounded familiar to me, but I couldn't place it. And then I did. "Wait. Carl Sinclair, as in the vice president of the Mad Dogs MC?"

"Yep. And her brother Ken is the enforcer," Byte said.

"Oh, this doesn't sound good." The Mad Dogs weren't good people. They were one of the clubs that gave the rest of us a bad name. Honestly, their club's name was fitting as they weren't much better than rabid animals.

"There's more," Byte said. "Not long before Evie arrived in Cedar Valley, her dad and brother were arrested for murder. It looks like the charges against them have been dropped, but the original reports say the guy owed them money."

"Does it say who the guy was or why he owed them money?"

"His name was Randall Myers. It doesn't say, but the Mad Dogs make their money selling drugs, so I would assume that's why."

"Can you find an address for Randall?" I asked.

"Yeah, one sec," he said and started typing. "Here it is."

I looked at his screen in disbelief. "That's the same address that's on Evie's registration."

"What are you thinking?"

"The same thing you are. That Evie's boyfriend was doing drugs and racked up a tab with the MC. When he couldn't pay, her dad and brother killed him. Evie got caught in the crossfire and took off when they were arrested."

"I bet they were expecting her to pay off what he owed," Byte said. "Probably still are."

"Son of a bitch." No wonder she looked like she was scared to death whenever she was around me or any of the Blackwings. "What the hell am I supposed to do now?"

"Talk to Phoenix," he said simply. "He needs to know and so does Irene."

"If Evie finds out, she's going to run."

"That'd be a stupid move on her part. She's in a safe place, and it'd be hard for anyone to locate her. The only giveaway is her car, and they don't know where to look for it."

"Maybe I can talk to her and convince her to let us help her."

"Let's talk to Phoenix first," he said. "I believe he's in his office."

I followed him down the hall to Phoenix's office in a slight daze. Of all the things Evie could have been running from, I never once thought it would be another motorcycle club.

"Damn it," Phoenix said when he saw us. "It's never

good news when one of you shows up with Byte holding his laptop."

"Sorry, Prez," I said and closed the door behind us.

"Let's hear it."

I started at the beginning and told him everything I knew about Evie. Then Byte showed him the proof on his laptop.

"Evie's the one who came to Gabby's party with Irene, right?" he asked.

"That's the one," I confirmed.

"Aw, hell. She seemed like a sweet girl. It's hard to believe she's related to those jackasses."

"What can we do to help her?" I asked eagerly.

Phoenix sat back in his chair and gave me a pointed look. "Does she want our help?"

"I don't know."

"This is probably not what you want to hear, but you need to talk to her first. Make sure the assumptions you've made about her life are correct. If it turns out they are, and she is running from them, we can talk about our options if she wants our help," he said.

"She is not going to be happy about this."

"Just tell her you saw her registration and recognized the name and town she was from. Ask her if she's related to the vice president of the Mad Dogs MC and see what she says. She might tell you everything herself. Then you won't have to admit to having Byte snoop into her background."

"And what if she doesn't?"

Phoenix chuckled. "Then you'll have to own up to it

and tell her why you did it. If you're offering to help her, chances are she'll forgive you."

"This could end up causing problems for the club."

"I'm not worried about that. This isn't the first time one of you little shits brought home a woman with a shit ton of problems, and I'm sure it won't be the last."

"She's not my woman," I protested.

"Oh, please," Phoenix laughed. "You don't take your eyes off her when she's around. You're fixing her car for free, and you were so worried about her you had Byte run a background check on her. You might not know it, and she might not know it, but she's your woman."

"He's got you there, man," Byte laughed.

"You can both piss off," I grumbled.

"Let me know how it goes when you talk to her. Like I said, if she wants our help, we'll do what we can."

7

EVIE

I almost jumped out of my skin when someone knocked on my door. The only person who ever stopped by was Irene, and I knew she was still at work.

Quietly getting to my feet, I tiptoed across the room and looked through the peephole to see Edge standing on the front steps. Assuming he was there about my car, I opened the door and gestured for him to come in.

"That was fast," I said. "What was wrong with it?"

"Oh, I'm not here about your car," he said.

"You're not?" I asked and turned to look at him. He seemed different. Nervous maybe.

"No. I came to talk to you about something else. Can we sit?"

"Sure," I said and took a seat at the end of my couch, leaving the other end available for him. Suddenly, I was nervous.

He sat and clasped his hands together. "I'm not really sure how to begin."

"Did something happen to Irene?"

"No! She's fine," he insisted. "It's nothing like that."

"Then what is it?"

"When I was getting started on your car, I opened the glove box to get your manual and I saw your registration, particularly your last name and the town you're from. Are you related to the vice president of the Mad Dogs MC?"

Everything inside me froze. I couldn't move. I couldn't breathe. I couldn't do anything but stare at him with unmasked terror on my face.

"Evie?" he asked, sounding worried. "Are you okay?"

My fight-or-flight instincts kicked in, and it was at one hundred percent flight. "I have to go," I blurted and got to my feet.

He rose from his seat and blocked my path with his enormous body, though he didn't reach out to touch me or physically stop me. "Please, wait," he said urgently. "I'm only asking because I want to help you if you need it. I know they're bad news."

"You have no idea," I said quietly.

"Pretty sure I do. I know they sell drugs and treat their women like shit. I know they wouldn't think twice about putting their hands on a female or killing someone who owed them money," he said.

He only thought he knew. There were no words to describe how awful they really were. "I can't do this."

"You don't have to do anything. Just tell me if they're the reason you're hiding in Cedar Valley."

I wanted to trust him and tell him everything. No one knew what happened besides me, and it weighed heavily on my soul. But I couldn't quite bring myself to do it. Then a tear slipped out of my eye and rolled down my cheek.

"Fucking hell," Edge said quietly and pulled me against his chest. His big arms wrapped around me and held me close. "I didn't mean to make you cry. You don't have to tell me anything you don't want to. But I want you to know I'm here if you need me."

And that did it. I couldn't hold it back anymore. The dam broke, and I burst into tears, crying all over his shirt. He continued to hold me, rubbing my back and whispering words of reassurance against the top of my head.

It took longer than I cared to admit, but I finally pulled myself together and took a step back while wiping the tears from my face. "I'm sorry," I whispered.

"You don't have anything to be sorry about. I'm sorry I upset you."

I shook my head. "You're not the reason I'm upset," I said and exhaled heavily. I was about to take a huge leap, and I hoped I wasn't making a colossal mistake. "I am related to the vice president. He's my father."

"And Ken is your brother?"

I involuntarily shivered at his name. "Yes," I said disgustedly. "He's my half brother."

Edge waited patiently for me to continue. I took a few moments to decide where to start. "Ken and I have different mothers. My mother divorced Carl when she found out he cheated on her and had a kid with a club whore. I was six years old at the time, and I think Ken was around three. After we left, I didn't see Carl again until I was an adult. Shortly after I moved back to Fairbanks, I ran into them at a gas station, which was the first time I met Ken. I was upset with my mom and wondered if maybe she lied to me about what kind of person Carl was. So when he invited me to have dinner with them at the clubhouse, I went. During the short time I was there, I saw two different women get hit in the face by a man and another one was bent over a pool table and fucked by three different men in front of everyone. I got out of there as fast as I could and made it a point to avoid the Mad Dogs. If I was going somewhere and there was a motorcycle in the parking lot, I went somewhere else. I didn't see either of them again until several years later when they came looking for my roommate." I paused for a few moments before starting the next part of the story. "I met Randall when I started working at the hospital. One day, I mentioned something about looking for a new place to live. He was also looking for a new place, so we ended up finding something together. Everything was fine for a while, but then Randall started staying out to all hours of the night. He'd come home stumbling and slurring his words. Then he'd pass out and sleep all day. Eventually, he got fired for missing work. We had a big fight about it, and he promised he'd find a new job and do better. I kept waiting for things to improve, but they only got worse. He was different. It took me longer than I care to admit to figure out things were much worse than he said. He'd started using meth and didn't seem to have any intentions of stopping. Since he didn't have a job, he started taking things from the apartment and pawning them. By that point, I was trying to move out and get away from him. I almost had enough money saved up for a deposit on a new place when he broke into my phone and transferred all the money in my account to himself. We were on the verge of being evicted when everything came to a head. Apparently, he'd been getting his meth from the Mad Dogs with a promise to pay. When he couldn't give them the money he owed, they came to collect." I stopped abruptly and tried to swallow past the emotions clogging my throat. I wasn't sure if I could actually say the words to the next part.

"And they killed him," Edge said.

I couldn't speak, so I wordlessly nodded.

"Oh, Evie," he said sympathetically.

The tears had started again, but I didn't bother to wipe them away. "I tried to stop them. That's how I got the black eyes. They told me they'd kill me, too, after they took me to their clubhouse and let all the members fuck me to pay off his remaining debt. So, I didn't say anything as Randall's throat was slit with one of my kitchen knives. When they left, I packed up my shit and got the hell out of there. I stopped a few towns away and called in an anonymous tip. I told them about the murder and where they could find the murder weapon. I made sure they knew Ken's fingerprints would be on the knife and both of their prints would be all over the apartment. Then I got back in my car and didn't stop until I made it to Cedar Valley."

"Evie," he said quietly and once again pulled me against him. "I'm so sorry you had to go through that."

I was too tired to resist any longer and relished in the comfort he offered.

"I feel bad that I don't feel bad," I admitted.

"What do you mean?"

"About Randall's death. I feel like I should feel guilty for not doing more to stop them, but I don't. They were going to kill both of us if I didn't comply, and he wasn't the same person I once knew. That person had been gone for a long time. In a way, I feel like it put him out of his misery." It felt like a weight had been lifted off my shoulders when I uttered those words.

"It's okay to feel however you feel. You were put in a bad situation by no fault of your own. You did what you had to do to save yourself. There's no reason to feel guilty about that," he said.

"Thank you," I said, and let him hold me for a little while longer before I stepped back. "Where are my manners? Would you like something to drink?"

"Coffee, if you have some."

"I should've known that." It seemed like coffee was all he ever drank.

Edge leaned on the counter while I started making his coffee. "I think you should talk to Byte about getting a new ID."

"Irene mentioned something about that when we were at the clubhouse."

"You might not need it right now, but you will if you ever want to do anything requiring identification, like opening a bank account. And you should probably consider trading your car for another one and registering it in your new name," he said.

"Why do I need to do that?"

"The tags are going to expire soon. When you pay the taxes, you'll have to give them an address to send the sticker to. Anyone who knows how to get their hands on that information could find you."

"I don't think Muzzle or Snarl are smart enough to know how to do that," I said.

"Maybe not, but I'm sure they could pay someone who is," he countered.

I swallowed thickly. He was right. They could easily do that. But would they?

"I don't even know if they're looking for me."

"You reported them to the police and got them arrested for murder. They're looking for you," he said confidently.

"It was an anonymous tip."

"You may not have given your name, but they knew who the tip came from. Who else besides you would know about their fingerprints and where the murder weapon was?"

"Yeah, that was the only part of my plan I couldn't figure out how to get around. At least their arrest bought me some time. Once they're found guilty and sentenced, I won't have to worry about them anymore," I said.

Edge grimaced.

"What?"

"I told you I recognized your last name and the town you were from. Before I came up here to talk to you, I had Byte search your father's name to see if I was right," he said and paused. "The charges were dropped against your father and brother."

I nodded in acknowledgment and took a few moments to process his words. "I shouldn't be surprised. People have always said the cops in Fairbanks were dirty."

Edge was quiet for a few moments while he sipped his coffee. "Do you have a gun?"

"What?"

"A gun," he repeated. "Do you have one?"

"No."

"You need one. And you need to know how to use it. I have one you can hang onto for a while. Are you free to go target shooting tomorrow?"

"Hold on," I said. He was moving too fast. "You want to give me a gun and teach me how to shoot it tomorrow?"

"Yeah," he said simply. "You need to be able to defend yourself if something happens. If you're comfortable with a gun and know how to use it, you'll be able to do that."

"You mean if my father and brother find me," I clarified.

He nodded. "Would you be able to shoot them if you had to?"

I didn't even have to think about it. After what they did to me and what they threatened me with, it was a no brainer. "Oh, yes."

Edge chuckled. "Thought so."

"I was wrong about you," I admitted.

He grinned. "I know."

"You do?"

"You were terrified of me, and you didn't hide it well."

"I'm sorry," I apologized.

"It's okay. I knew something was going on with you, but it makes more sense now."

"I almost died when Irene pulled up to your clubhouse for Gabby's party."

His face softened. "I know you've heard it before, but we're not like the Mad Dogs. We're not angels by any means, but we don't hurt women and children, and we don't kill people unless we're defending ourselves or protecting someone else. That's why I've been pestering you since I met you. I wanted to know who hurt you and what I needed to do to make sure they didn't do it again."

"That's…," I started and reached out to gently squeeze his hand. "Thank you. I didn't appreciate it then, but I do now."

"You're welcome," he said and placed his other hand on top of mine. "You should let me take you out for dinner."

"I couldn't."

"Oh, come on. You've had an eventful afternoon. It's the least I can do."

"Okay," I conceded. "Where are we going?"

"There's this great little diner on Main Street," he teased.

"Yeah, I think I've heard of it," I said and started putting on my shoes.

"Do you like hibachi? There's a really good Japanese steakhouse downtown."

"I do if it's real hibachi. I don't like the fake hibachi."

He chuckled. "What is fake hibachi?"

"If they serve it with zucchini, mushrooms, and onions, it's real. If it's served with broccoli and carrots, it's fake and usually tastes like Chinese food."

"This place serves zucchini."

"Sold. Let's go," I said.

When we walked outside, I was surprised to see a truck parked in the driveway. "Where's your bike?"

"It was raining in Croftridge when I left. Some brothers don't mind riding in the rain, but I'm not one of them."

"I've never ridden on a motorcycle before."

He grinned. "We'll have to change that." Then he walked to the passenger side of his truck and opened the door for me. I couldn't recall the last time, if ever, someone had done that for me.

"Thank you," I said quietly.

Suddenly, I was nervous and couldn't think of anything to say. Thankfully, Edge didn't seem to have the same problem and continued to make small talk until we arrived at the restaurant.

After we were seated and placed our orders, Edge looked at me like he wanted to say something but seemed hesitant.

"What? Do I have something on my face?"

He laughed. "No, it's nothing like that. I'm honestly just curious about you, so if you don't want to answer, tell me to mind my own business."

"Okay," I said slowly.

"When you and Irene came to the clubhouse, you told me you were from Florida, but earlier, you mentioned moving back to Fairbanks. What happened there?"

"Oh," I sighed. "I told you I was from Florida because I didn't want you, or anyone, to know I was from Fairbanks for obvious reasons. The truth is, I moved to Florida to live with my grandmother after I graduated from high school. My mother remarried when I was twelve, and I never got along with my stepfather. So, when I was old enough to leave, I did."

"What made you decide to come back to Fairbanks?"

"It's a long story that doesn't have a happy ending. Are you sure you want to hear it?"

"I want to get to know you. If it's your story, good or bad, I want to hear it."

I wasn't ready to admit it, but regardless of how hard I tried to keep him at arm's length, he was worming his way in.

"When I told my mother that I was moving in with Grandma, she wasn't happy about it and refused to help me pay for college. It wasn't a huge deal to me since I wasn't sure what I wanted to do anyway. So, for the first two years I was in Florida, I worked as a housecleaner for a company that cleaned vacation rentals. Once I had enough money saved, I paid for my classes and became a certified phlebotomist."

"You're a phlebotomist?" he asked in surprise.

"Yes," I said and reached out to run my finger over one of the many prominent veins in his forearm.

"Sorry, I've been dying to do that. You have juicy veins."

He chuckled. "Was that supposed to sound dirty? Because it did."

"It did, didn't it?" I laughed.

"You can poke my juicy veins later," he teased. "How'd you end up back in Fairbanks?"

"This is where the story goes downhill. I'd been working at the hospital drawing blood for about six months when I met Austin. We started dating and things became serious. A year later, we got an apartment together. We'd been living together for almost two years when my grandmother started showing signs of dementia. As things progressed, I started spending more and more time at her house, sometimes staying the night two or three times a week. One night, I told Austin I was staying with Grandma and wouldn't be home. Later, I realized I didn't have any clean clothes with me and needed to run home to get something to wear to work the next day."

"Oh, no," Edge said knowingly.

"Oh, *yes*. I walked in on Austin screwing some girl on our couch."

"What did you do?"

"Honestly, nothing. I got what I needed and left. He tried to talk to me, but I refused to speak to him. I didn't want to have that conversation in front of the stranger he was cheating on me with, and I didn't want to leave my grandmother alone for the time a conversation of that nature would take. So, the next day at work, I told my boss what happened, and she gave me the following day off to move out. Austin came home from work while I was loading the last of my stuff into my car and asked if we could talk. I agreed, even though there was nothing he could say to change my mind. Basically, he said he was lonely and blamed me for spending so much time taking care of my grandma." I started to laugh and paused for a moment to get myself under control. "I'm sorry, but I can laugh about this part now. He actually thought his actions were justified, *and I was the one being unreasonable*."

"You're not serious."

"Yes, I am. He was right, and I was wrong. When I told him how ridiculous he was, he doubled down. I told him we'd have to agree to disagree and left."

"What an asshole."

"I completely agree."

"Then what happened?"

"I spent the next few years working and taking care of my grandma. Her condition progressed, and she eventually needed more care than I could provide. The handful of facilities my grandmother could afford were awful. My mom claimed she couldn't afford to help pay for her care, so I used what savings I had and got a second job so she could go to one of the nicer places. For two years, I lived at her house, worked my ass off, and spent whatever free time I had with her."

"So, you decided to move back after she passed?" he asked.

"Not exactly. I probably would have stayed in Florida if things happened differently, but they didn't."

"You don't have to tell me the rest if you don't want to," he said sincerely.

"It's okay. I'll just give you the highlights."

"Sounds good."

"The town we lived in got hit by a hurricane. The nursing home moved the residents to another facility that was in a safer location. Or so they thought. That town flooded, and the building my grandmother was in collapsed. She was one of the residents who didn't make it."

"Oh, Evie, I'm so sorry."

"Yeah, me, too. I wasn't ready to let her go, but I'm glad she's at peace now."

"You said your town got hit by the hurricane. Was your house okay?"

"Nope. The house was completely destroyed. Since my grandmother was dead, the insurance payout went to the next of kin—my mother. She kept the money instead of rebuilding, leaving me without a place to live. I'd spent everything I had paying for the nursing home, so there wasn't much I could do. My mother was gracious enough to allow me to move back in with her until I could get on my feet again. Her words, not mine. So, that's how I ended up back in Fairbanks."

"And you moved in with Randall to get out of your mother's house as fast as possible," he finished for me.

"Pretty much. And you know what happened after that. It feels like I keep having to start over every couple of years, and it's exhausting," I admitted.

"Maybe this time will be the last time."

"One can only hope."

"How were things with your mom after you moved out?"

"Pretty much nonexistent. She's always been a negative and critical person. It was hard for me to voluntarily subject myself to that, so I kept my distance. I also never forgave her for the way she handled things with my grandmother. Maybe one day, but I'm not there yet."

"That's understandable."

"Thanks. I've never really talked about my relationship with her with anyone, and a part of me has always wondered if I was being too harsh."

"I don't think you are. Being a part of someone's life is a privilege not a right. If their presence isn't positive for you, revoke their privileges," he said simply.

After dinner, he drove me back to my trailer and walked me to the door. "I'll pick you up around four tomorrow for target practice."

"I'll be ready," I said. "And thanks again for dinner. I'm sorry I spent the whole time telling you my crappy story."

"You don't need to be sorry. I wanted to know," he smiled. "See you tomorrow." He got back into his truck and waited for me to go inside before he left.

I found myself slightly disappointed that he didn't kiss me. Then I shook my head. He wasn't interested in me. He felt sorry for me, especially after I overshared at dinner.

I needed to remember that.

8

EDGE

The next day, I stopped by the clubhouse to see Byte before I got started working on Evie's car.

"Sorry to bother you again. I should've asked yesterday," I started. "Can you find out what's going on with the investigation of Randall's murder?"

"Sure," Byte said. "Is there something specific you want to know?"

"Since they dismissed the charges against Carl and Ken, I want to know if they have anyone listed as a suspect. I also want to know if Evie's name is mentioned anywhere." As I was lying in bed the night before thinking about her situation, it occurred to me that Evie's disappearance immediately after her roommate's murder wouldn't go unnoticed and would likely be interpreted in one of two ways—she was guilty and ran, or she was also a victim.

"I should be able to find that out for you. Not sure how long it will take, though. Do you want to wait, or do you want me to call you with the info?"

"Call me," I said. "I need to head over to the garage and take a look at her car."

"Will do," he said and opened his laptop to get started.

When I arrived at the garage, I made myself a cup of coffee and began inspecting her vehicle. Based on her description of the problem, there were a few things that could be the culprit. I started with the most common issue and worked my way through a mental checklist of possibilities.

By the time I was finished, I wondered how the damn thing lasted as long as it did. She had not kept up on the maintenance whatsoever. The oil was basically sludge, her air filter was caked in filth, and the ends of her spark plugs were burned to a crisp.

I was pretty sure I knew what the problem was, but I hoped I was wrong. After trying and failing to rotate the crankshaft pulley with a breaker bar, I knew I was right. She had a seized engine.

"Damn it," I swore and tilted my head toward the sky.

"Something wrong?" Dice asked.

"There's nothing I can do," I said. "This engine's toast."

"You sure?"

"Oh, yeah," I said and told him the steps I'd already taken. Then I showed him the oil.

He let out a low whistle and grimaced. "Yeah, no one's fixing that."

I'd been hoping for an easy repair so Evie could trade her car for something else. With the seized engine, she was more or less screwed. It wouldn't be cost effective to replace the engine and then trade the car. She'd be better off just buying another vehicle, but I knew she couldn't afford to. Not without taking out a loan, which I also knew she couldn't do.

Before I could think of a solution, Byte called.

"I don't have great news," he said without preamble. "She's been named as a person of interest."

"Fucking hell," I grumbled.

"There's more. They issued an APB for her. It has her picture, physical description, the make and model of her car, and her tag number."

"Thanks, man."

"No problem. I'll let you know if I find anything else."

After Byte's phone call, one thing was certain—her car had to disappear. Even though I would have advised her against it, repairing the engine and trading it was no longer an option.

Exhaling slowly, I leaned against the hood of her car and tried to think of a solution that would work for her, as well as one she would agree to. After two more cups of coffee and a solid hour of brainstorming, I finally came up with something that might work.

* * *

Evie smiled when she opened the door for me. "Hey, Edge," she said and gestured for me to come inside. "I'm almost ready to go."

"Take your time." I struggled to keep my face

neutral, knowing I was about to wipe the smile off her pretty face. Figuring it was best to get it over with, I cleared my throat and said, "I need to talk to you about your car."

"That doesn't sound like good news."

"I'm afraid it's not."

"What's wrong with it?" she asked hesitantly.

"The engine needs to be replaced."

"Are you serious?"

I nodded. "It looked like the oil hadn't been changed in a while and that caused the engine to seize. Once that happens, it can't be repaired."

She closed her eyes and used one hand to rub her forehead. "Damn it. Whenever my car needed something done, I gave Randall the money and he took care of it. It never occurred to me he was lying to me and keeping the money for himself."

"There's sort of a silver lining," I said. "Well, it's more of a tarnished silver lining."

"I'm not sure I want to know."

"Maybe not, but you need to know," I said and paused to choose my words carefully. "I was thinking about your situation and asked Byte to see what else he could find regarding Randall's death." There was no easy way to break the news, so I just told her like it was told to me. "You're listed as a person of interest. An APB was issued with your picture and a description of you and your car, including your license plate number."

Her mouth dropped open in shock. "A person of interest? What does that even mean?"

"In this case, it probably means they think you're a

suspect, but they don't have enough evidence to prove it yet. They want to bring you in for questioning to see what they can get out of you."

"Great. That's just fucking great," she said and began to pace. "What am I going to do now?"

"You don't have to do anything. They can't question you if they can't find you."

Exhaling heavily, she said, "Yeah, I guess you're right." She stopped pacing and turned to face me. "Wait. What's the silver lining you mentioned?"

"You might have been found if your car hadn't crapped out on you."

"I see what you mean about it being tarnished," she sighed. "I can't afford to buy a new car right now, even if it's a bottom of the barrel used one. And since I can't get a loan for one, I guess it's back to the bike."

"About that," I said and held up one finger to stop her protest. "Hear me out first. What if Irene put the loan for the car in her name and you made the payments?"

"I couldn't ask her to do that," she said. "She's already gone above and beyond to help me."

"What if she offered without you asking? What would you say then?"

She narrowed her eyes at me. "What did you do?"

I held my hands up in surrender. "I didn't do anything. I merely told Irene what was going on with your car. She suggested getting a loan for you. She was going to call you herself, but I told her I'd talk to you about it after I gave you the news about your car." My explanation wasn't entirely honest. In truth, I was going to pay for her car. Since I knew Evie wouldn't go for that, I asked Irene if she had any ideas. That prompted Irene to volunteer herself as the middleman. Evie would pay Irene, and Irene would, in turn, pay me.

Evie's eyes suddenly widened. "Does she know about what happened with Randall?"

"No," I assured her. "She obviously knows you came from a bad situation, but that's your story to tell if and when you choose to."

She nodded in acknowledgment, but remained silent for several minutes. Finally, she said, "I guess I should figure out what I can afford and start looking for a new car."

"Do you want to go look at some used car lots instead of going to the shooting range?" I asked.

"Yes, if you're sure you don't mind."

"Mind? I work on cars for a living. I'd be offended if you didn't ask me to go with you," I teased.

"Thank you," she said softly. "I really appreciate everything you're doing for me."

"It's not a hardship," I said honestly. I enjoyed being around her and genuinely wanted to get to know her better. "Are you ready to go now?"

"As ready as I'm going to be."

Once we were in my truck, she pulled out her phone and started tapping away. "What are you doing?" I asked.

"Trying to figure out my price range," she said distractedly.

"Keep in mind, Irene's not going to charge you interest," I told her.

"She's not?"

"Of course not," I laughed. "You have met her, right?" Even though I was the one who wouldn't be charging her interest, I knew Irene wouldn't either if she were the one behind the loan. She was out to help people, not make a profit off them.

"She really is a saint. I'll never be able to repay her for everything she's done for me."

"Yes, you will. Getting on your feet and living a happy life is all she wants in return," I said. "Bonus points if you're able to do some good for someone else down the line."

"Is that why Byte does the things he does?"

"I never really thought about it like that, but it probably is. I mean, most of the stuff is club related, but he does more than is expected of him," I said.

When I pulled into a used car lot a few minutes later, I turned to her and said, "No matter what you're thinking, try to act neutral while we're looking. If you act overly excited about a vehicle or seem desperate, they might be less inclined to negotiate on the price."

"How about I let you do the talking?" she suggested. "As long as it will get me to and from work, I'm good."

"I think we can do a little better than that," I said. I was going to make sure she had something reliable and safe, even if I had to work on it myself.

The first place was a bust. The lot was full of vehicles with mechanical problems hidden behind shiny exteriors and immaculately clean interiors.

"And that's called putting lipstick on a pig," I said once we were on our way to another dealership.

"I'm glad you came with me. I had no idea and probably would have tried to buy the first one that looked okay to me," she said.

"That's what they were counting on."

We went to dealer after dealer, but we didn't find anything suitable for her. I watched Evie's disappointment grow each time we left a car lot with no prospects.

"You okay over there?"

She sighed heavily. "This is beginning to seem like a pointless endeavor."

"Car shopping isn't easy. It can take a while to find the right one."

"I don't want to monopolize so much of your time."

I waved my hand dismissively. "It's fine. I knew what I was getting into when I offered to help."

"It seems like we've been all over Cedar Valley. How many more used car places can there be?"

"Not many, but there's still all the cars for sale by owner, and we can always look in areas nearby, like Croftridge. There might even be a police auction coming up."

"Oh, no," she said. "While I'm willing to drive around in almost anything with wheels, I draw the line at some drug dealer's confiscated car. With my luck, one of his cronies would see me rolling around town in it and come after me."

"My initial response was to say that wouldn't happen, but you have had some pretty shitty luck lately. So, yeah, we'll cross the police auction off the list," I laughed.

We stopped at two more car lots before calling it a day. She was tired, and I didn't think I could exchange fake pleasantries with one more salesperson without losing my shit. They were like mosquitoes at a bloodbath, flocking to us the moment we stepped out of my truck.

"You hungry?" I asked.

When she turned to me, I knew exactly what she was thinking by the look on her face.

"For fast-food. Something with a drive-thru. I don't want to go in anywhere," I clarified.

She exhaled in relief. "Then, yes. I could eat."

"Taco Bell?"

She smiled broadly. "Yes, please. I love Taco Bell."

We went through the drive-thru and ordered a ridiculous amount of food that we took back to her place to eat.

"I haven't had Taco Bell in a long time. Please don't judge me for how much I'm going to eat."

I laughed. "No judgment here. I'm about to eat my weight in tacos."

When she took a bite of a burrito and moaned in delight, I had to quickly look away before she caught me staring at her. The pure unadulterated pleasure on her face from something as simple as a fast-food burrito was one of the sexiest things I had ever seen.

"This is so good," she said around a mouthful of food.

"Yes, it is," I agreed and focused on my own food, so I didn't stare at her and inadvertently make her self-conscious.

After we finished eating, I helped her clean off the table while trying to think of a reason to stay, because I wasn't ready to leave.

"Do you want to look online and see if we can find some used cars to look at?" I asked.

"Sure, if you have time. I don't want to keep you from anything."

"You're not," I assured her and pointed toward the door. "I'm going to grab my tablet from the truck. I'll be right back."

"I don't have Wi-Fi," she said apologetically.

"Not a problem. We can use my phone as a hot spot, but I need a bigger screen to see what I'm looking at."

She laughed. "I know what you mean. I have to squint and hold my phone at just the right angle if I want to read anything on the screen."

When I returned with my tablet, we settled on the couch and started browsing through the classified ads. In order for both of us to see the screen, we had to sit so close together that we were touching from shoulders to thighs. It was awkward and uncomfortable. I tolerated it for as long as I could before I raised my arm and wrapped it around her shoulders. She automatically settled against my chest and continued scrolling through the listings as if it was the most natural thing in the world. She didn't seem to notice the minor position change, and I didn't point it out.

I'm not sure when it happened, or who was first, but at some point, we both fell asleep.

9

EVIE

I was hot. Really hot. And slightly uncomfortable. I was also on my stomach, which was odd because I usually slept on my back or on my side. I moved my hand to push myself over and froze when it landed on something that felt more like a person than the mattress it should have been.

Slowly lifting my head, I opened my eyes to find myself looking at Edge's sleeping face. Seconds later, internal panic ensued. I didn't know what to do. Getting up might wake him, but I couldn't exactly stay there and go back to sleep. Could I?

Before I could make a decision, the arm resting across my back tightened around me while he brought his other hand up to cradle the back of my head. "It's okay, baby. Go back to sleep," he said sleepily.

Ignoring the way my heart fluttered when he called me baby, I rested my head against his chest and closed my eyes. We were just sleeping. Nothing more. I had almost convinced myself that was the case when he slightly shifted his position and I felt him gently kiss the top of my head.

That little kiss did a better job of waking me up than any cup of coffee ever had. While he drifted off to sleep, I laid there wondering what, if anything, it meant. Did he mean to do it? Was it a sleepy accident? Would he even remember?

Then I moved on to the self doubt portion of my internal debate. Why would he even be interested in someone like me? I wasn't like other women. And not in the stereotypical "I'm not like other girls because I'm unique and special" way. In the very real "my life is a mess and I have a boatload of problems with even more baggage" way.

Finally, after who knows how much time had passed, I reached the "I have to pee but don't know how to get up without waking him" stage. Furthermore, I had another slightly pressing issue. If I had known he was going to spend the night, I wouldn't have agreed to Taco Bell for dinner. But I did, and well, I really needed to fart. At least, I hoped that's all it was. I also knew there was no way I could pee without passing gas, but I was running out of time.

Carefully extracting myself from his arms, I got to my feet and tiptoed down the hall to the bathroom. Closing the door behind me, I used a towel to fill the small gap under the door and turned on the water in the sink as high as it would go. Then, with every muscle clenched as tightly as possible, I sat down and took care of business, praying for a whoosh of air instead of a thunderous reverberation. After all was said and done, the universe had smiled in my favor, but I learned my lesson. No more Taco Bell unless I was alone.

When I came out of the bathroom, Edge was awake and sitting up on the couch. "Morning," he rasped.

"Good morning. Would you like some coffee?" I asked and immediately held up my hand. "Never mind. I know the answer."

He grinned. "Thanks. Mind if I use your bathroom?"

"Not at all. It's right through there," I said and pointed toward the bathroom door while silently thanking the powers that be for my odorless morning gas. Meanwhile, I tried to make as much noise as possible while he was in there so I didn't hear anything that might or might not be happening.

I was so focused on being loud that I didn't hear him come out of the bathroom and startled when he spoke behind me. "Sorry about last night. I didn't mean to fall asleep."

"You don't need to apologize," I said and handed him a mug of coffee. "I fell asleep, too."

"I blame all the carbs from dinner," he said, grinning as he took a tentative sip of coffee.

"You're probably right," I agreed and finished making my own cup of coffee. I felt awkward and didn't know what to do about it. It was like the morning after sleeping with someone for the first time, but without the sex.

Edge didn't seem to have the same issue. He made himself comfortable at the kitchen table and started looking at his tablet. "Do you want to check out some of these cars today?"

I didn't exactly want to, but it was my day off and needed to be done. "Sure," I said with a little too much excitement.

He laughed. "I hope you don't think that was believable."

I shrugged and told him the truth. "I don't want to spend the day shopping for a car, but I have the day off, and you've offered to help, so I don't want to waste the opportunity."

"I have a feeling today will be better than yesterday."

I was glad he thought so, because I didn't. I didn't have much faith in anything anymore, and if it weren't for Irene, I probably wouldn't have any at all.

He finished his coffee and rinsed out his mug before placing it in the sink. "We can get started whenever you're ready."

"Do I have time to take a shower?"

"Do whatever you need to do," he said. "There's no rush."

Still, I felt bad for making him wait, so I hurried through my regular routine and opted to braid my wet hair instead of drying it. I was quite proud of myself when I managed to be ready in record time. He seemed surprised when I told him I was finished, but he didn't comment.

Thirty minutes later, it was my turn to be surprised when he briefly stopped in front of an iron gate before it opened for him to drive through. "Where are we going?" I asked and continued to survey my surroundings.

"To my house so I can shower and change," he said.

"You live here?" I asked in surprise. We were driving through what appeared to be hundreds of acres of farmland.

He chuckled. "Yes, but it's not what you're thinking. Phoenix owns the property and everything on it. There are numerous businesses scattered throughout the land, including a dairy farm and a counseling center, but there's also quite a bit of housing. Phoenix lets club members live here for free, so I have a house here and a room at the club."

"Like a compound?" I asked.

"Yes, but there's nothing fishy going on. All the businesses are on the up and up, and we're free to leave whenever we want," he explained.

I continued to stare out the window while he drove through the property to his house. The place was huge. I'd never seen anything like it. "What's that?" I asked and pointed to what looked like a red barn in the distance.

"That's the horse stables. They board and train horses, give riding lessons, and offer equine therapy. There's another barn behind it you can't see from here. That's where Keegan breeds and raises racehorses."

"Really? That sounds amazing."

"After we get your car situation squared away, I'll be happy to give you a tour of the place," he said and pulled into the driveway of a beautiful Cape Cod style house.

"You get to live here for free?" I blurted.

"Yes," he said. "Some members bought their own homes elsewhere, but I thought it was too good of a deal to pass up."

"No kidding," I agreed. "Can I become a member?"

He laughed, but I was only partially joking. I would totally join a motorcycle club if I got to live in a house like his for free. Well, if it was a club like the Blackwings.

I followed him inside and had to consciously keep my mouth from falling open when I saw how nicely decorated his home was. "Wow," I breathed. "Your house is gorgeous."

"Thanks," he said. "But I can't take credit for it. Shortly after Phoenix took over the property, Ember took it upon herself to have all the homes upgraded and redecorated." He waved his hand around the room. "This is all her doing."

"She did a great job."

"I'll be sure to tell her," he said and gestured to the large sectional sofa in the living room. "Make yourself comfortable. I won't be long."

I sat down on the plush sofa and fought the urge to get up and explore his house. It was the kind of home I'd only ever dreamed of having, and I wanted to see more of it. The entire compound seemed like something out of a fairytale.

I was staring off into space daydreaming about rolling green hills and fields of wildflowers when Edge reappeared downstairs, freshly showered and looking sexy as hell with his messy wet hair.

"You ready?" he asked.

"Uh, yeah, sure. I mean, yes, if you are," I stammered, mentally slapping myself and telling myself to get it together.

"I am," he nodded and opened the front door. "After you."

As we were walking to his truck, a black SUV came to a stop at the end of his driveway. Instinctively, I stopped walking forward and stepped behind Edge to shield myself. I held my breath as the car door opened and closed.

"Hey, Edge," a familiar voice called. "Is that Evie with you?"

Edge moved to the side and placed his hand on the small of my back. "It's okay. It's just Ember," he said before answering her. "It is."

"I thought so," she smiled and waved as she came closer. "What are you two doing today?"

"Evie's car died, so I'm helping her find a replacement."

"Are you looking for anything in particular?" she asked.

"No. Just something reliable and affordable," I said.

She looked at Edge and cocked her head to the side. "What about my old car?"

"How much do you want for it?" he asked.

She turned her attention to me. "If you want it, you can have it."

I blinked at her in surprise. "Are you serious?"

"Yes," she nodded. "It just sits in the driveway, taking up space and costing us yearly taxes. No one ever drives it, so it probably needs a tune up and a new set of tires, but it's in good condition. Do y'all want to come over and take a look at it?"

I was at a loss for words, so I deferred to Edge. "Sure. When's a good time?"

"We can go now if that works for you." When we both nodded, she pointed to her SUV. "Hop in. If you don't drive away in your new car, I'll bring you back."

"Thank you," I said and climbed into the back seat. It didn't take me long to realize her SUV was the same kind as the loaner I was driving. As she drove to her house on the property, I noticed several more of the same exact SUV parked in various driveways. "Do you guys get some kind of deal on these SUVs?" I asked. "It seems like there's a lot of them around here."

Ember laughed. "Sort of. My dad buys them in bulk. Most of them are business vehicles, but he adds extras to his order for anyone who wants to buy one. Usually, they're white, but he chose black the last time, and now we look like a fleet of federal agents at any family gathering."

She pulled into her driveway a few moments later. She also had a Cape Cod style house, though hers was much bigger than Edge's. I was torn between gawking at her house and watching her walk to the covered vehicle parked at the end of her driveway.

"Here it is," she said and started removing the cover. Edge went to the other side of the car to help her. Moments later, the cover was off, revealing a shiny, white sedan that was much nicer than I was expecting. In fact, it was so nice that I couldn't possibly accept her offer to give it away for free.

"Before you say no, I want you to know I didn't pay anything for this car. It was given to me. So, I'm not losing anything by giving it to you. Actually, I'll be saving money because I won't have to pay the taxes on it anymore," she said.

"But you could sell it and get a decent amount for it," I countered.

"I could, but I don't need the money. I'd rather give it to someone who needs it and maybe make a difference in their life."

"That's very kind of you."

"There was a time in my life when the help of strangers saved me from a horrible future and changed my life in ways I never thought possible. If I can do something like what they did for me, even if it's on a smaller scale, I'm going to do it," she explained. "So, shall I go inside and get the keys?"

My vision blurred as my eyes welled with tears. "If you're sure," I said, my voice clogged with emotion.

"Of course I'm sure," she said and pulled me in for a hug.

"Thank you," I whispered and tried to get a handle on my emotions.

She went inside to get the keys, leaving Edge and me alone in the driveway. "I can't believe this," I said.

He smiled. "I can. Ember's one of the nicest people I know. She's like Irene in a way. Helping others is something she genuinely enjoys and it comes naturally to her. Years ago, she convinced her dad to let her grow hydroponic plants and organic fruits and vegetables to create jobs for a large group of people who had recently become unemployed."

"I feel like this is too much," I admitted.

"I understand why you feel that way, but as far as Ember's concerned, it's not. She wants you to have it. If you don't take it, she'll have someone park it outside of your trailer and leave the keys on your doorstep."

"He's right," Ember said, reappearing with the keys in her hand. "I would totally do that."

"Thank you doesn't seem like enough," I told her.

"The smile on your face is all the thanks I need," she said and held out the keys. "Here. Take these and go enjoy your new car."

I took the keys from her and hugged her once more before I nervously climbed into the driver's seat. Although she said the car had been sitting in her driveway for a long time, its interior was clean and it had a fresh smell inside. Evidently, someone took care of the car even though no one was driving it.

I was still in a state of disbelief when I started the car and backed out of her driveway. Edge had to direct me back to his house, but it was a smooth ride the entire way. I highly doubted the car needed much work, and I was beyond grateful for the gift.

"Can I ask you something?" I asked when we pulled into Edge's driveway.

"Sure."

"Ember is Phoenix's daughter, right?"

"She is," he confirmed.

"What did she mean when she said she had to rely on the kindness of strangers to help her?" It was none of my business, but for my own sanity, I needed to know why strangers helped her instead of the MC.

"It's a long story, but she didn't know Phoenix was her father until she was eighteen. He didn't know about her either. Annabelle was told Ember was stillborn. Phoenix thought Annabelle was dead. It was a mess. The strangers she referred to were actually the Blackwings. She met Reese in high school, and Reese brought her to the clubhouse to get help. Phoenix agreed to help her, and they figured everything else out shortly after," he explained.

"Thank you. I know it's not my business, but I had to ask."

He reached over and squeezed my hand. "I know. Normally, I wouldn't share those details so freely, but I figure if we keep showing you we're the good guys, you'll eventually believe us."

I felt my cheeks heat with embarrassment. "I don't think you're bad guys."

"I know, but you shouldn't blindly trust us, either. And I don't expect you to, especially after what you've experienced with the Mad Dogs."

I shivered involuntarily at the sound of their name and fought the urge to gag. Just thinking about them and what happened that night made me sick to my stomach.

"On a different note, how do you want to handle the registration?" he asked.

"What do you mean?"

"If you want to stay under the radar, I don't think you should register it in your name," he said. "If you want, you can put it in my name until you get your situation settled."

"I don't know," I said hesitantly.

"If you're worried about me running off with your car, we can sign a contract that says the car belongs to you. Then we'll transfer it into your name whenever you're ready," he offered.

"I don't think that's necessary. I'm more concerned about insurance," I said.

"I'll add it to my current policy, and you can pay the difference."

"Why would you do that for me?"

He shrugged. "Because I'm in a position to do so. Everyone needs help at some point or another."

"When have you needed help?"

"When I was younger. My older brother was headed down the wrong path, and I started to follow. At first, I didn't realize he was dragging me down with him. Soon after I began prospecting for the MC, I realized the error of my ways, and they helped me get back on the right track."

I wanted to know more, but I was hesitant to ask. Apparently, my face did the asking for me.

He chuckled. "What is it you want to know?"

"I was going to ask what kind of path your brother was headed down, but now I'm wondering how you knew I wanted to ask something."

"You tend to kind of chew on the corner of your bottom lip and your eyebrows wrinkle a little when you're reluctant to say something."

I nodded thoughtfully. "I'll try to be more conscious of that in the future."

"Only the people who know you well would notice."

I laughed. "Those are the ones I'm worried about. I don't really care what strangers think of me."

"So, to answer your question, my brother fell in with the wrong crowd. Before long, he was selling drugs and joined a gang. My parents tried to intervene, but there wasn't much they could do since he was an adult."

"Is your brother still involved with the gang?" I asked carefully. Edge mentioned joining the Blackwings after high school, indicating he'd been a member of the club for around twenty years. I was by no means an expert in gang statistics, but I was pretty sure most of them didn't live long enough to celebrate twenty years of membership.

Edge shook his head solemnly. "No, he isn't. He was shot and killed fifteen years ago. I assume it was a drug deal gone wrong or something to do with a rival gang. Back then, my parents and I never asked for details or tried to find out. Jared was dead. The story of how it happened wouldn't make it any less painful."

I reached over and placed my hand on top of his. "I'm sorry your family had to go through that. Watching a loved one slowly slip away and destroy their life while feeling completely helpless isn't something anyone should have to experience."

"It destroyed our family. My parents couldn't come to terms with his death. I guess they needed someone to blame, so they pointed the finger at each other. They got divorced, Dad moved to a cabin in the middle of nowhere and became a recluse, and Mom also isolated herself and died a few years later. The doctors said it had something to do with her heart, but I believe she grieved herself to death."

"They just left you?" I blurted, before I could stop myself. "I'm sorry. I don't mean to sound insensitive, because I can't imagine the pain of losing a child, but the death of one son doesn't give them the right to abandon the one that's still living."

"I don't disagree. It felt like I had a family one day, and they were gone the next. During that rough time, my MC family helped me through it. I'm not sure how I would've handled things if I didn't have them, but I'm glad I never have to know."

"I know what you mean. I don't even want to think about what would've happened if I hadn't met Irene when I did. Even though she wasn't aware of the specifics, she knew I was going through something and stepped in to help. For someone with no one, her willingness to help was life changing, and likely lifesaving."

Edge slipped his hand out from underneath mine and patted it twice. "I think that's enough of the heavy emotional stuff for today. Since we have your car situation taken care of, do you want to learn how to shoot?"

"Um, sure."

"You don't sound sure."

"If I'm being honest, it's not something I want to do, but I need to do it. Maybe I'll sleep better with a gun in the house."

Edge's face quickly filled with concern. "You're having trouble sleeping?"

"It's nothing new. I haven't slept well since Randall started coming home at all hours of the night. I hoped it would get better once I got settled somewhere new, but it hasn't. It seems like every little noise wakes me up. I tried wearing earbuds one night, but that only made things worse. I kept thinking I heard something and would take them out to listen, over and over, until I finally left them out. Another night, I tried barricading the doors, but then I convinced myself I would die in a fire and had to remove the barricades before I could go to sleep."

He reached out and gently cupped my cheek. "You don't feel safe. I'm going to help you fix that."

"Thank you," I said softly. I wanted to close my eyes and lean into his hands. I felt safe when I was with him.

Before I was ready, he removed his hand and stepped back. "We can go to the clubhouse and shoot outside, or we can go to one of the indoor ranges. It's up to you."

"Which place will have less of an audience?"

"Definitely the indoor range. We'll have at least three brothers come out and join us if we go to the clubhouse."

"Indoor range it is." Since I'd never shot a gun before, I preferred to have as few onlookers as possible in case I made a fool of myself.

"You want to stop for lunch first?"

I smiled. "Yes, please."

10

EDGE

After lunch, Evie was unusually quiet while I drove to the gun range.

I waited until I pulled into the parking lot to ask, "Are you okay?"

"I guess I'm a little nervous," she admitted.

"I'll be with you the whole time. We'll go over everything before we start shooting," I assured her.

And that's exactly what we did. I showed her how to load and unload the gun and how to chamber a round. Then I had her do it a few times. After that, we talked about gun safety and went over the current gun laws for our state.

"I don't need a permit for this?" she asked in surprise.

"As of right now, no, but gun laws tend to change frequently, so keep that in mind. Are you ready to give it a try?"

"I'm as ready as I'll ever be."

After we put on our ear and eye protection, she

followed me into our assigned lane. Once we were all set up, I stepped to the side and gestured to the target hanging in the distance. "You can go first."

She glanced at the gun, the target, and then back at me. "I'm not sure about this."

"It's okay. I'll help you. Come stand right here." When she was in front of me, I moved in behind her. "Pick up the gun and point it at the target, but don't pull the trigger." Wrapping my arms around her, I put my hands over hers and helped her correct her aim. "When you're ready, squeeze the trigger to fire."

It took her a few seconds before she fired her first shot. "Holy crap! I didn't expect it to feel like that."

"That's why it's good to practice. So you know what to expect."

"Should I go again?"

"Yes. We'll empty this magazine and then you can shoot by yourself if you feel comfortable."

I hoped like hell she felt comfortable, because I didn't know how long I'd be able to stand being pressed up against her without losing my mind. I'd been trying to keep things platonic between us because I knew she had a lot going on, but I'd be lying if I said I didn't want her. She was beautiful, but she also had a great personality and was fun to be around. I genuinely enjoyed spending time with her.

"Well, what do you think? Do you want to try by yourself?" I asked as she reloaded while I replaced the target.

"I think so," she said nervously.

"I'll be right here if you need me."

She was doing fine until the sixth or seventh round. Suddenly, she put the gun down and jumped back. "Hot! Hot! Hot!" she shrieked while shaking her shirt. When a brass casing dropped to the floor, I understood what happened and started laughing.

"I'm sorry," I chuckled. "Are you okay?"

"Yeah, I'm fine. But holy crap, that was hot. Why didn't you tell me that could happen?"

I held my hands up in surrender. "Because it didn't occur to me. If you were wearing a low-cut shirt, I might've thought of it, but you're dressed fine for shooting." She looked at the gun warily. "It was a fluke. I doubt it'll happen again."

"Are there any other *flukes* I should know about?"

"Not that I can think of." I gestured to the gun. "Do you want to keep shooting?"

She wrinkled her nose. "Not really, but I know I need to."

"I don't know. It kind of seems like you're a natural," I said and pointed to the target. She'd hit the target each time she fired. "If that was a real person, you would've stopped them."

"It's probably just beginner's luck."

"Well, keep shooting and we'll find out."

After reloading and shooting three more times, we determined it wasn't beginner's luck. "You did great! Look at these targets!"

She grinned. "I have to admit, I'm a little proud of myself."

"You should be. Are you ready to go or do you want to keep going?"

"I'm good, but what about you?"

"What about me?"

"You haven't had a turn yet. Aren't you going to shoot?"

"I wasn't planning on it."

"Oh, come on. I want to see what you can do."

"If I didn't know better, I might think you were trying to secretly compete with me."

She laughed. "Compete? No. Honestly, I want to see your targets because I don't have anything to compare mine to."

"Oh, well, I think I can help you with that." Hers were good, but she obviously thought I was just telling her that to boost her confidence.

When I finished shooting, we collected our targets and cleaned up after ourselves before leaving the store. In the parking lot, we stood at the back of my truck and compared our targets. My shots were mostly concentrated in one area of the target while hers were wider spread, but all of her shots had pierced the torso printed on the paper.

"See? I wasn't lying. You did real good."

"Maybe, but I'm nowhere near as good as you are."

"This was your first time. I've been shooting for over twenty years. You did a hell of a lot better than I did my first time."

"Really?"

"Yes, really. I think I missed the target more times than I hit it the first time I went to the gun range."

She grinned. "Since I have no way to verify your story, I'm going to choose to believe you."

"Good. Do you want to get something to eat before I take you home?"

"Sure, but you don't have to take me home. I have a car at your house. Remember?"

"Oh, right." I was slightly disappointed at the thought of not being able to drive her home. Then something occurred to me. "After dinner, I can ride to Cedar Valley with you and drive the loaner back."

"That'll work, but I have one condition."

"What's that?"

"I want to take you to dinner." She held up her hand to stop me when I opened my mouth to argue. "You've done so much to help me, and I'd like to thank you."

"You don't have to do anything to thank me. I was happy to help."

"I know, but I want to."

It went against everything in me to let her pay for my dinner. I wanted to take care of her and do things for her, not the other way around. But I could see that this was something she really wanted to do, so I obliged. "Okay. Where do you want to go?"

She laughed. "I was hoping you'd know of a place."

"We'll figure something out. Let's get going."

Once we were on the way to Cedar Valley in her car, we decided on having pizza for dinner. "I'll place the order online. What kind of pizza do you like?"

"I'm not picky when it comes to pizza. I'll eat anything except sardines."

"So pineapple pizza would be okay?"

"Yes. I know it's one of those things people love to argue about, but I think the real issue with Hawaiian pizza is the thinly sliced meat they try to pass off as ham, not the pineapple."

"I've never had it, so I can't agree or disagree, but it sounds like you have a valid point."

"Well, now you have to try it. Order a pizza with cheese on one side and pineapple on the other for me. Then get one with whatever you want. And breadsticks."

We picked up the order and took it back to her place to eat, where I tried pineapple pizza for the first time.

"What do you think?"

"It's definitely not what I expected, but it's not bad," I said and continued eating the slice of pizza. Before I realized what I was doing, I picked up another slice and started eating it.

Evie laughed. "I'm guessing that means you like it."

"Oh, sorry. Here. Have some of mine."

She waved her hand dismissively. "It's fine. I can't eat an entire pizza in one sitting."

"I can, but I'm not going to."

"Don't hold back on my account. Eat what you want."

When we finished eating, I helped her clean up and put the leftover pizza away. I really didn't want to leave, but I didn't have a reason to stay. I was also tired of holding back and hiding my feelings from her. Deciding it was time to let her know how I felt, I turned toward her and reached out for her waist to pull her to me.

Her eyes met mine and I could tell she was in agreement. Leaning forward, my lips had barely brushed hers when a loud crashing sound startled both of us.

Evie fisted my shirt with both hands and pressed herself against me. "What the hell was that?" she whispered.

"I don't know. I'll go look. Stay here."

"No. Don't."

"If someone's out there, we need to know."

She reluctantly released her grip on me and stepped to the side. "Fine, but be careful."

Pulling my gun from its holster, I checked the chamber before I quietly walked to the front door and looked through the peephole. When I didn't see anyone or anything, I moved to the nearest window to peer outside.

"Do you see anything?" Evie whispered.

"No." I continued moving from window to window until I found the cause of the noise. Exhaling in relief, I returned my gun to its holster and turned back to Evie. "It's fine. A couple of trash pandas knocked over your trash can."

"A couple of what?"

"Trash pandas. Raccoons."

She briefly sagged with relief before she squared her shoulders and marched toward the back door. Flinging it open, she stepped outside and started yelling. "You little shits scared the crap out of me! Shame on you! I toss out plenty of scraps for you, and this is the thanks I get!"

Evie was staring them down with her hands on her hips while the two raccoons were standing on their hind legs with their hands raised in the air. After snapping a picture with my phone, I doubled over laughing.

"It's not funny. They scared me."

"Yes, it is. Look," I said and held out my phone. "They're surrendering. This picture is meme worthy."

She tried not to laugh, but she only lasted a few seconds. "Okay, fine. It's funny." Walking back inside, she grabbed two breadsticks from the refrigerator.

"What are you doing?"

"Feeding them. They're obviously hungry."

"You know you're not supposed to feed them, right?" I asked carefully.

She sighed. "I know, but they kept getting into my trash can and making a huge mess. I thought it would save all of us some trouble if I left the food out for them."

"I'll help you secure the lid so they won't be able to get into it anymore. Once they realize there's no food, they'll stop coming around."

She scrunched her nose. "I know you're right, but I kind of like them."

"They are cute," I admitted.

She made a shooing motion with her hands. "Go on. Get out of here." The raccoons stared at her for a few seconds before they ran off into the wooded area.

Once we were back inside, I pulled her to me and kissed her. I didn't want to give anything else a chance to interrupt us. Wrapping her arms around my neck, she melted into me.

"I've wanted to do that for so long," I said against her lips.

She threaded her fingers through my hair and pulled me closer. "Well, don't stop now."

We stumbled our way to her bedroom, bumping into walls and furniture. I couldn't take my hands off her.

When we made it to the bed, I was struggling to contain myself. I didn't want to scare her, but I wanted her with an unprecedented ferocity.

I tore myself away from her long enough to rip her shirt over her head before I did the same with mine. Then I reached behind her and quickly divested her of her bra.

"Fucking hell," I breathed. With a gentle push, she fell back onto her mattress, and I followed her down. Cupping her breasts with my hands, I captured one nipple with my lips and used my fingers to toy with the other one.

While I continued to lavish her breasts with attention, she pushed her jeans down her legs and kicked them across the room. Sitting back on my knees, I took in the sight of Evie's gorgeous body, only clad in a skimpy pair of panties.

She started to sit up, but I pushed her back down and removed the last bit of clothing from her body. I couldn't wait any longer. I had to know what she tasted like.

Pushing her legs farther apart, I dropped down to my stomach and captured her clit with my mouth.

"Edge," she moaned and clasped a handful of my hair.

I continued licking and sucking while she writhed

and moaned. Then I added two fingers to my ministrations, pumping them in and out.

"Edge," she panted. "I'm going to come."

"Yeah, you fucking are," I said and continued with what I was doing.

Moments later, I felt her tense before her pussy tightened around my fingers and pulsed with pleasure. The sounds she made were music to my ears, and I was eager to hear more from her.

When I was certain she was finished, I looked up to find her staring down at me. She reached for my arms and pulled me on top of her. "I need you to fuck me," she said and started undoing my jeans.

I grabbed a condom from my wallet before I pushed my jeans and boxer briefs off. I made quick work of rolling the condom down my shaft and lining myself up with her entrance. Then I met her eyes and pushed inside.

"Fuck," I breathed. She felt amazing. I was torn between staying still to relish in the feeling and fucking her into another dimension. She made the decision for me when she wrapped her legs around my waist and silently urged me to move.

I don't know how long it lasted, but it wasn't long enough. I knew right then and there that I would never get enough of her. I held out as long as I could and made her come again before I found my own release.

After we had a few minutes to catch our breath, Evie said, "I hope this doesn't change things between us."

"I do."

"What?"

"I don't want to be your friend, Evie. I want to be more than that."

"Oh," she said and smiled softly. "I want to be more than friends, too."

"Good. I'm glad we got that settled." With that, I pulled her to me and proceeded to show her how much I liked being more than friends.

11

EVIE

I was thinking about Edge and replaying everything that had happened the night before when I walked into the diner.

"It's about time," Irene said when she saw me.

Glancing at the clock to make sure I wasn't late, my brows furrowed in confusion. "For what?" I asked.

Irene grinned. "If that goofy smile is anything to go by, I'm guessing you and Edge finally figured out y'all are more than the friends you claim to be."

"Yes," I said, and for the first time in my life, I truly understood what it meant to swoon.

Irene stepped closer and lowered her voice. "Don't keep an old lady waiting. How was he? On a scale of limp dick to wild ride?"

"You are by no means an old lady."

"Nice try, but you can't distract me with flattery. Now, spill. I've always wondered if those bikers lived up to the expectations of every woman who's ever gawked at them."

I couldn't help but laugh at her antics. "There's no need for you to wonder. I'm sure Ranger could satisfy your curiosity."

She arched an eyebrow and pointed one finger at me. "No."

"What?" I laughed.

Our banter was interrupted by the first two customers of the day. Walter and Buck were regulars who ate at the diner three times a week, though they usually came in for lunch instead of breakfast.

"Hey, guys," I greeted and looked at the clock. "It's a bit early for you two, isn't it?"

"Somebody wants to go fishing today, even though it's a diner day," Buck said and gestured to Walter with his thumb.

"You would've thought I asked him to reschedule his vacation with all the bellyaching he did about missing his usual lunch," Walter said.

"You could've picked another day."

"No, I couldn't. They're calling for rain for the rest of the week."

"What's wrong with next week?" Buck asked.

"You said you wouldn't complain if we had breakfast here."

Buck shrugged. "We haven't had breakfast yet."

"Can I get you a cup of coffee or something else to drink?" I asked, interrupting their back and forth. They were lifelong friends, and they bickered nonstop. It was entertaining and somewhat exhausting.

"Two coffees, please. And we'll need a couple of menus," Walter said.

"Here you go." I handed them two breakfast menus and gestured to the empty diner. "Sit wherever you like."

"Perks of being the early birds." Walter lowered his voice and leaned forward like he was going to tell me a secret. "He's less grumpy after coffee."

"I heard that," Buck said. "And for your information, I'm less grumpy later in the day."

"The early bird gets the worm."

"But the second mouse gets the cheese," Buck countered, causing me to laugh.

"I think he's got you there," I said as I brought their coffees to the table.

"Please don't encourage him," Walter teased.

"Wink twice if he's making you uncomfortable," Buck said. "I'll shove him out of the boat when he's not looking."

"You two are something else," I laughed and shook my head. "I'll be right back with your orders."

By the time they were finished eating, the diner was in full swing, and I barely had a chance to wish them good luck on their trip.

"Thanks, sweetheart," Walter said. "We'll see you at our regular time, the day after tomorrow."

"See you then," I said and headed back to the kitchen to pick up the next order that was ready. Halfway there, a commotion at the front door had me turning around to see what was going on.

Walter had his finger pointed at another man. "Watch where you're going, buddy."

"Fuck off, old man."

Buck shook his head. "What you should've said was, 'I'm sorry. Please excuse me.'"

"Is that so?" the rude man asked and straightened to his full height.

"Yeah, that's so. Want us to show you?"

I turned to look for Irene and found her standing a few feet behind me, watching the scene.

"Should we do something?" I asked.

"We don't need to," she said without an ounce of worry in her tone. "That dipshit is about to get his ass handed to him."

"Are you serious?" I asked in disbelief.

Irene nodded with a sly smile. "They used to be professional boxers. That's how they met. After they retired from fighting, they teamed up, bought a gym, and started coaching."

I turned my attention back to the front when the man balled his fists and took a step forward.

Walter clapped his hands together and grinned. "Come on, boy. Let's see what you got."

I gasped when the man pulled his arm back and threw a punch at Walter. In the blink of an eye, Walter dodged the punch and plowed his fist into the man's face. He went down like a sack of bricks.

Buck looked down at the man and stuck out his lower lip, pretending to pout. "I didn't get a turn."

Walter ignored him and focused on the man on the ground. "Are you going to get up and leave on your own, or do you need a police escort?"

The man grumbled something I couldn't hear and got to his feet. Buck held the door open for him and waved at his back as he left.

When the door closed, the customers in the diner clapped and cheered. Walter made a show of bowing for the crowd.

Buck held up his hand. "Okay, folks, the show's over. Sorry about the disruption, Irene."

She waved her hand dismissively. "There's no need for apologies. I saw the way he almost ran you over coming through the door. He obviously needed a lesson in manners, and I'm glad he got it."

Walter nodded. "We'll get out of your hair now."

"Stay out of trouble," Irene said.

Buck winked. "We try, but trouble has a way of finding us."

"Does that happen often?" I asked Irene after the breakfast rush was over. I had witnessed no altercations between customers, with the exception of the arguing couple, since I'd been working at the diner, but Irene didn't seem surprised by the interaction.

"Not really," she said. "Most of my customers are local and know I won't put up with bullshit from anybody. Occasionally, we'll get somebody who wants to cause trouble. More often than not, the customers will intervene and show them the door."

"What happens if the customers don't intervene?" I asked, even though I wasn't sure I wanted to know the answer.

Irene grinned. "You'll call the cops while I introduce them to the business end of my shotgun." I'm not sure what kind of expression was on my face, but it prompted Irene to pat my shoulder gently. "Don't look so worried.

I've only had to do that a handful of times, and the last time was years ago."

Despite her attempt to reassure me, I felt uneasy for the rest of the day. Every time the door opened, I stopped what I was doing and looked to see who was coming in. The last time a man showed up at my place of employment and caused a problem didn't end well for me. Granted, the scenarios were very different, but panic and fear only needed minor similarities to make a connection.

Even though the rest of my shift was uneventful and the customers were pleasant, I was more than ready to leave when Marcy arrived. Surprisingly, she actually got there a few minutes early for once.

"Hey, Evie," she said while obnoxiously smacking her gum. "Can you cover my shift tomorrow night?"

"I'm sorry. I already made plans with someone."

She huffed and crossed her arms over her chest. "But you always cover my shift when I need you to."

That was true. Unfortunately for Marcy, my priorities had changed. When I first started working at the diner, I took every opportunity I had to make extra money. By doing so, I'd been able to save up a decent amount and didn't need the extra hours with the same desperation I once had. I'd also met Edge and enjoyed spending time with him.

"I'm sorry," I said again, even though I really wasn't. Marcy had an unprecedented sense of entitlement and little to no work ethic. "If you can give me more notice next time, I might be able to help you."

"I thought you didn't know anyone in town," she said snidely. "How do you have plans?"

"My personal life is none of your business. I appreciate the opportunities you've given me to pick up some extra hours, but going forward, I need more than one day's notice."

"Whatever," she snapped and walked away from me.

"What was that about?" Irene asked, startling me.

"She asked me to cover her shift tomorrow and didn't like it when I said no."

"You said no?" Irene asked, feigning surprise.

"Shocking, right?"

She laughed. "Get out of here and enjoy the rest of your day."

"I'll see you tomorrow," I said and headed out to my car.

I'd briefly forgotten about the morning incident, but quickly remembered when a shiver ran down my spine as I walked across the parking lot. I felt like someone was watching me and was going to pop out to grab me at any moment, but I didn't see anyone around when I carefully surveyed my surroundings.

"No one's going to get you," I whispered to myself. "This isn't like before."

My efforts to calm myself were futile. I picked up my pace and practically dove into the front seat of my car, scrambling to close and lock the door. Shaking my head, I sighed. I'd always been good at freaking myself out.

Unfortunately, my nerves didn't settle after I got home. Every random sound had me tiptoeing to the nearest window to carefully peek outside. Even though I knew I was safe at the back of Irene's property, I couldn't seem to relax. I was on the verge of driving to the grocery store to buy a bottle of wine when Edge called. He immediately realized something was off.

"What's wrong?" he asked.

I briefly considered lying but decided to tell him the truth. If he couldn't handle what I considered justified paranoia, I wanted to know sooner rather than later. "A man showed up at the diner this morning and got into a fight with two of the regulars. They put him in his place and showed him the door, but the whole thing rattled my nerves."

"Did he say or do anything to you?"

"No. He barely made it in the front door."

"Did Irene call the police?"

I shook my head before I realized he couldn't see me. "No. Walter and Buck hung around for a little while to make sure he didn't come back."

"What time did this happen?"

"About thirty minutes after we opened. Why?"

"I'm going to have Byte pull the camera feed and save the video clips. If he comes back, we'll have proof of the previous incident. Irene really should have filed a police report."

"She probably still can. Should I call her?" I asked.

"No, don't worry about it. Irene knows what she's doing. If she didn't think she needed to involve the police, then she probably didn't."

I didn't like the way he said "probably didn't" but I tried not to overthink it and moved on to tell him about Marcy.

"It's okay if you need to work tomorrow," he said.

"Thanks, but I'm looking forward to our plans," I said. "And I really enjoyed telling Marcy no. You should've seen her face. She couldn't believe I said no. Then she got mad."

"Why is she still working there?"

"Because Irene hasn't been able to find anyone to replace her. Well, that's not entirely true. She's hired a few people, but they've all quit after a few days of training."

"Is Marcy the one training them?"

"Yes," I said slowly as realization dawned. "She's running them off, isn't she?"

"That'd be my guess. She probably knows Irene will fire her once she has a replacement, and she won't be able to come and go as she pleases if she has to get a job somewhere else."

"I bet you're right. I'll mention it to Irene tomorrow morning," I said and changed the subject. I needed to get my mind off work if I wanted to get any sleep that night.

In all honesty, I would've loved for Edge to spend the night, but I couldn't bring myself to ask him. Even though it didn't take too long to drive from Croftridge to Cedar Valley, we both had to be up early for work, and I couldn't rationalize asking him to drive out to my place just so I could sleep.

Later that night, as I stared at the ceiling while lying in bed, I regretted not asking him to come over.

12

EDGE

As soon as I got off the phone with Evie, I called Byte and asked him to save the surveillance footage from the incident at Irene's diner.

"Oh, man," he laughed. "This is great. You can tell the dude has no idea he's about to get his ass kicked. I'll send it to you."

I watched the video, but I didn't find it as funny as he did. Something about it bothered me. I wasn't sure if it was what happened between the unknown man and Walter, or if it was the fact that it happened when Evie was there, but whatever it was, I decidedly didn't like it.

Even though she wouldn't say it, I knew the incident bothered Evie, and rightfully so. Given her past experiences with her father and brother, it was understandable for her to be upset when an angry man showed up at her workplace. I waited for her to ask me to come over and found myself disappointed when she didn't. Still, I sensed she needed me and wanted to be there to comfort her, even if she didn't ask. I wanted her to feel safe.

After giving it some thought, I called Byte for the second time that evening. "What time are we leaving?" he asked after accepting my call.

I laughed, not at all surprised that he knew why I was calling. "I'd like to be there when they open," I said.

"That's what I thought you'd say. Is this an open invitation?"

"Yeah. Whoever wants to join us is welcome to." I wasn't sure how Evie would react if half the club showed up for breakfast at the diner, but I hoped she'd appreciate the show of support. If for some reason the guy returned to the diner, he'd have more than Walter and Buck to contend with.

* * *

"What are you doing here?" Evie asked when I walked into the diner the next morning.

"We came to have breakfast," I said and stepped to the side so the rest of my brothers could enter. Phoenix, Badger, Carbon, Shaker, Ranger, Diesel, Flint, Dice, and Ink joined Byte and me for our early morning excursion.

She smiled shyly and placed a kiss on my cheek. "I think I know why you're here," she whispered.

"We all need to eat breakfast," I replied innocently.

"Mmm-hmm." Turning her attention to the group, she motioned toward two large tables. "Right this way."

When she started to push one table toward the other,

everyone chimed in to stop her, including me. At the various sounds of protest, she lifted her hands and stepped back.

"We got this," I told her and kissed her cheek.

"I can move a table."

"I know you can, but as long as one of us is around, you don't have to."

"Thank you," she smiled. "Is everyone having coffee?"

Everyone nodded, except for Phoenix and Badger. Phoenix gestured to the two of them. "We'll have water."

"For fuck's sake, you can have coffee," Badger grumbled.

"My wife asked me to be supportive. This is me doing that," he said.

"I have an ulcer," Badger explained. "Patch gave me a list of things I shouldn't have, and coffee is one of them."

Evie smiled. "Got it. Nine coffees and two waters coming up."

We took our time eating breakfast, hanging around a lot longer than we normally would. We wanted to be there long enough for people to notice our presence, even if it was just our bikes in the parking lot as they passed by. After a few hours, the troublemaker hadn't reappeared, and it seemed to be business as usual.

"We're going to head out," I told Evie. "I'll see you tonight."

"I should be there around five. I'll let you know when I'm leaving."

"Can't wait," I said and pulled her to me for a quick kiss.

* * *

EVIE ARRIVED AT MY HOUSE AT A QUARTER AFTER FIVE. She was wearing a pair of jeans that perfectly molded to her ass and a shirt that clung to her body in a way that made me want to ask her to change.

"You look great," I said.

She tugged at the hem of her shirt. "Thanks. I wasn't sure what to wear."

"It really doesn't matter," I said, repeating the same thing I told her when she originally asked what she should wear. "No one is going to judge you."

She gave me a skeptical look.

"Well, if you're dressed like a club whore, then yeah, the women are probably going to judge you. But you're not, so it's not an issue."

She laughed lightly. "Thanks for your honesty."

"If you want me to be completely honest, I wouldn't mind you dressing like that, but we'd be staying home instead of going to the party."

"I'll keep that in mind," she winked. "Are you ready to go?"

"Ready if you are," I said.

"Do the Blackwings have a lot of club whores?" she asked once we were on our way.

I wanted to laugh, but I knew she didn't realize how off base her question was. "No. Not in the way you're thinking. There are girls that hang around and come to parties to hook up with a brother, but we don't keep women around specifically for that purpose like some clubs do. Most of the brothers are married with families, so our parties and gatherings are tame in the MC world."

"That might not be a selling point for some, but it is for me. I prefer tame to wild and crazy."

"Me, too."

When we arrived at the clubhouse, the party was already in full swing. Evie turned to me with a look of concern on her face. "Did I cause you to be late?"

I shook my head. "There wasn't a specific start time, but it looks like they got started a little earlier than usual."

"Edge!" Dash called from across the room. "Over here!"

I chuckled. "I guess Ember wants to talk to you."

"What? Why?" Evie asked in surprise.

I placed my hand on her shoulder. "Relax. She likes you. She probably just wants to make sure you feel comfortable."

We joined them at their table, where Ember had a seat for Evie right beside her. "Told you," I whispered before she sat down.

"It's so good to see you again," Ember said cheerfully, and hugged Evie.

"She's a friendly drunk, and she's already had a few drinks," Dash explained.

"I'm friendly all the time," Ember said and turned her attention back to Evie. "How are things? Is the car doing okay?"

"Yes, it's perfect. And thank you again," Evie said sincerely.

"Would you like a drink?" I asked.

"Just a Coke for now," she said. "I should probably eat something before I have anything stronger."

Ember reached back and rapidly patted Dash's arm. "Babe, Evie needs food."

Dash chuckled and looked at his wife. "I think Evie's man can handle that."

Ember nodded once. "Right. Edge, Evie needs food."

"Are you trying to get my woman drunk?" I asked.

Ember grinned. "Maybe."

"Do you want a burger or hot dog?" I asked Evie.

"A burger sounds good, but I can get it," she said.

"I got it. I'll be right back," I told her and placed a kiss on the top of her head.

When I returned with our food, Reese was at the table, and the three women were engaged in a conversation about Evie's hair. "You okay?" I asked quietly.

Evie laughed. "Yeah, they're trying to convince me to let Reese do my hair."

"No," Reese said and pointed to Ember. "Drunky's trying to convince her. I just got here."

Ember dramatically placed her hand over her heart. "I'm allowed to be drunk. My baby boy received his prospect patch today. I'm officially old."

"Talk to me when your grandchild joins the club," Phoenix said from behind her, causing everyone to laugh.

"You don't look old enough to have grown kids," Evie said.

Ember smiled and put her arm around Evie's shoulders. "I knew I liked you."

"So, your son joined the club?" Evie asked.

"Yes. Our son and Carbon and Harper's son joined today. Well, they're prospects, but that's really just a formality," Ember said and went on to explain the process of joining the club to Evie.

"How long do you think she'll last?" I asked Dash.

He chuckled. "I'd say about two hours. Less if she doesn't eat."

Harper walked over to the table with her arms wide open. "I can't believe our babies are prospects!" She wrapped Ember in a hug while they both pretended to cry. At least, I thought they were pretending.

"Is that real?" I asked Dash.

"I honestly don't know."

"It's real emotion being disguised as humor," Carbon said.

"You sound like your wife."

"I've picked up a thing or two over the years."

"At least you have some left. He was my last one," Ember cried.

"Fucking hell," Dash grumbled. "She's been dropping hints about wanting to have more kids all week."

"Get your hands off me, you stupid bitch!" a female screamed, drawing everyone's attention.

I turned to see Raven dragging a girl by her hair

down the hallway toward the front door, and Blaze was right behind them.

"You can go fuck someone else's brother with your disease-infested coochie," Raven spat.

"Raven," Dash called.

She didn't miss a step at the sound of her dad's voice. "I warned her, Dad. I told her not to come here, and she did anyway."

Before Dash could respond, Flint appeared with a look of concern on his face. "Raven, stop! I think she drugged him."

The common room erupted in a flurry of activity at his words. Patch and Gabby sprinted down the hall toward Falcon's room with Dash and Ember on their heels.

Phoenix calmly walked toward the girl standing frozen in Raven's grip. "What did you do to my grandson?"

I could hardly believe what I was seeing when the girl hocked a loogie from her soul and spit it at Phoenix.

A sickening crunch filled the air as Blaze's fist made contact with the girl's face. She covered her face and fell to her knees with Raven still firmly gripping her hair.

Phoenix wiped the spit from his face and looked at his daughter and granddaughter. "Keep her where she is until the cops get here. If she spits again, cover her mouth with tape."

"You can't do this!" the girl screamed. "Let me go!"

He glanced at Carbon. "Gag her."

Carbon grinned like a maniac and walked toward the girl with a bandana in his hand. "Don't even think about spitting on me. I'll slip and fall and break every bone in your body when I land on you."

The girl's mouth dropped open, and he had her gagged in seconds. Then he zip tied her hands behind her back so Raven could release her. "Go check on your brother. I've got her."

Raven hocked her own loogie and spit it on the girl. "My papa has manners, but I don't give a fuck."

I looked over to see Evie watching the scene with wide eyes. Since the situation was under control, I made my way over to her. "You okay over here?" I asked quietly.

To my surprise, she waved me away. "Don't worry about me. Do what you need to do."

"There's nothing for me to do right now," I said and dropped into the seat beside her.

"I can't believe she spit on Phoenix," Harper said.

"Me either," I agreed.

"I can't believe he didn't react," Evie said.

"That's what she wanted," I said. "And he knew it."

"Why would she want that?" Evie asked.

"To take the focus off her. If he hit her, that's all anybody would remember. Not what she did."

"Cops and EMS are at the gate," Dice announced.

"Where's the bathroom?" Evie asked.

"Right over there," I said and pointed to a door near the corner of the room.

Harper gently smacked my arm. "Take her to yours. That one is gross."

"You're right," I said and got to my feet. "Follow me."

When I led Evie to my room and pointed to the bathroom door, she turned to me with the corner of her bottom lip tucked between her teeth. "So, I don't actually need to use the restroom. I thought it might be a good idea if I was out of sight while the police are here."

"Oh," I said as realization dawned. "We can stay in here until they leave."

"I'll be fine," she said and made a shooing motion with her hands. "Go find out what's going on so you can fill me in later."

"You sure?"

"Yes. Go on."

"I'll be back soon," I said and closed the door behind me.

When I returned to the common room, two police officers were talking to Phoenix beside the girl who was still bound and gagged on the floor. I resumed my seat at the table with Harper and Reese. "Did I miss anything?"

"Not yet," Harper said and tossed a few pieces of popcorn into her mouth.

"Popcorn? Really?" I laughed.

Harper pointed an accusatory finger at Reese. "She did it."

Reese shrugged. "It's going to be a good show. You want some?"

"Why the hell not?" I chuckled and helped myself to their very inappropriate snack.

A few minutes later, two paramedics came through the common room pushing a stretcher with a semiconscious Falcon. Ember was walking beside them, holding Falcon's hand while Dash, Raven, Patch, and Gabby were right behind them.

"We'll meet you there," Dash said to Ember.

"Dad?" Ember asked without taking her eyes off Falcon.

"I got this," Phoenix assured her. "I'll be there as soon as we're finished here. Your mom went to get her purse. She's riding with Flint."

Once they were gone, we watched as the stupid girl continued to make poor decisions. First, she refused to tell them what she gave Falcon and continued to deny having given him anything, even after drugs were found in her purse. Then she accused Raven and Blaze of kidnapping her, saying she had been brought to the clubhouse against her will. As if that wasn't enough, she said Phoenix was the one who hit her and broke her nose.

Phoenix genuinely laughed at the accusation. "Look at the size of my hand. If I was the one who hit you, I would've done a lot more damage than a busted nose." He held his hands out for the cops to see. "Does it look like I recently hit anybody?"

"Did someone hit her?" the officer asked.

Blaze stepped forward. "I did. I was standing beside my dad when she lunged forward like she was going to attack us, so I stopped her."

The officer nodded. "All right, let's get her down to the station. Phoenix, we'll be in touch."

With that, they escorted the girl out of the clubhouse while she continued to yell threats and obscenities.

"She's not a smart one, is she?" Harper observed.

"Hey, where's Evie?" Reese asked.

"She's in my room. She wanted to take a quick nap while all this was happening," I said. "I'll go check on her."

To my surprise, Evie actually was asleep on my bed. "Evie," I said quietly and placed my hand on her shoulder to gently shake her.

She slowly opened her eyes and glanced around the room. "Oh, crap. I didn't mean to fall asleep. What happened out there?"

"They took Falcon to the hospital, and the girl was arrested. The cops just left with her."

"Is Falcon going to be okay?" she asked.

"I'm sure he will be. They found whatever she gave him in her purse. Hopefully, they'll be able to reverse it or manage the effects of it until it's out of his system."

"I assume that means the party is over."

"Yes, and no. Most of the people will hang around for a while, but it'll be much more low key than it was before. Ember and Dash went to the hospital, but Harper and Reese are still here. Do you want to go back out to the common room, or would you rather call it a night?"

She glanced at the time. "We can go back out there. Let me use the restroom and run a brush over my hair first."

The rest of the evening was spent shooting the shit with the rest of the club while we waited for an update on Falcon. At one point, Ranger came over and tried to get Evie to play a game of pool with him before Keegan intervened.

A few hours later, Badger turned off the music and announced that Falcon was going to be fine.

"It sucks that their party was ruined," Evie said.

"It does," I agreed. "But I bet they'll reschedule it."

"They already have," Harper said. "It's tomorrow night."

Evie frowned. "I won't be able to come. I'm working the dinner shift tomorrow."

"I thought you told Marcy you weren't going to cover for her."

"That was for tonight. She asked for tomorrow night off last week," she explained.

We hung around for a little longer while Evie helped clean up, despite Harper's protests.

"Well, that was an interesting evening," Evie said when we were on the way back to my house.

"I still can't believe that girl spit on Phoenix. Who in the hell spits on the president of a motorcycle club?"

Evie crossed her arms over her chest and seemed to shiver. "That would've ended very differently if she'd done that with the Mad Dogs."

"I told you we were different."

"Yes, you did, and your club continues to prove it."

13

EVIE

When I walked into the diner fifteen minutes before my shift started, it was quiet. Too quiet. Usually, the guys were banging pots and pans around in the kitchen while Irene made coffee and rolled silverware.

I bypassed the break room and went straight to the front to see what was going on. None of the coffee machines were going and most of the lights were still off. "Irene?"

My skin prickled with fear, and my stomach filled with dread when she didn't answer. "Tony? Bart?"

I turned to go to the kitchen and stopped short when I saw Irene sprawled on the floor with a small puddle of blood seeping out from underneath her. "No! No, no, no," I chanted and ran to her, dropping to my knees beside her. The bag I carried to work slipped from my shoulder and made a sickening splat sound when it landed in her blood.

Reaching into my bag, I felt around for my phone with one hand while I gently tried to rouse Irene with the other.

"It's about time you showed up."

I froze while chills ran down my spine at the sound of Muzzle's voice. "What did you do?" I gritted out while keeping my eyes on Irene and praying that she was still alive.

"I found a way to entertain myself while I waited for you," he said, as if he'd been playing a card game instead of terrorizing innocent people.

The rage that surged through me was almost overwhelming. He'd already taken someone from me and scarred me for life, and he was trying to do it again, if he hadn't already.

"Why are you here?" I asked, hoping to buy myself the few seconds I desperately needed.

Carefully moving my hand, I let go of my phone and wrapped my fingers around Edge's pistol and removed it from the holster. With slow and steady movements, I got to my feet and kept my hands in front of me.

He snorted derisively. "To make you pay for trying to pin Randall's murder on me and your brother."

When I turned around to face him, I raised the gun and fired, hitting him in his torso. I wasn't sure exactly where, but I felt a brief sense of relief when he stumbled backward and fell to the ground.

For several long moments, he didn't move, and neither did I. Then his eyes popped open, and he shifted to reach behind his back. I didn't warn him or tell him to stop before I shot him again, hitting his shoulder. His arm fell limply to his side as blood appeared on his shirt.

"Do not fucking move," I said, sounding more confident than I felt.

I didn't want to give him an opportunity to get up and overpower me by taking my eyes off him to find my phone, so I kept the gun trained on him and slowly moved toward the landline mounted on the wall behind the front counter.

"Hello," Edge answered, sounding sleepy and slightly confused.

"I just shot my father, and I don't know what to do," I blurted. "He hurt Irene, and she needs help. Maybe Tony and Bart, too."

"Is your father dead?"

"No, he's not. I hit him twice, and he's on the ground, but he's very much alive."

"Keep your gun aimed at him and shoot him again if he moves," he said. "Stay on the phone with me. I'll have someone there to help you soon."

Using my shoulder to keep the phone pressed to my ear, I focused on the piece of shit lying on the floor. I desperately wanted to check on Irene, but I knew he'd kill us both if I gave him the chance.

I could hear Edge shouting, followed by a lot of activity on the other end of the line, but I wasn't paying any attention to what he was saying. In fact, I was so focused on making sure Muzzle didn't so much as twitch that I screamed like a banshee and almost fired another shot when a voice sounded behind me. "Evie, I'm here to help."

I risked glancing over my shoulder, but I didn't see anyone and briefly wondered if I had imagined the voice. "Where are you?"

A well-dressed man slowly stepped around the corner with his hands raised in front of him. "Edge requested my assistance," he said and gestured to the phone dangling by its cord. I must have dropped it when he startled me.

I brought the receiver to my ear and heard Edge's frantic voice. "Evie! Can you hear me? Is Luca there?"

"I'm here," I said into the phone and looked at the man with his hands still raised in front of him. "Are you Luca?"

"Yes," he said calmly. "Luca Peccati."

Evidently, Edge heard him answer me. "Let him help you. Do what he says, okay? I'll be there soon."

"Irene," I whispered.

"Evie," he said firmly. "Listen to Luca."

"Okay," I promised and turned to Luca. "He said I should listen to you and do what you say."

Luca lowered his hands and moved toward me hesitantly. "My associates and I are going to remove Muzzle from the premises and clean up behind him. Once we're gone, you will call nine-one-one and tell them what you found when you arrived. Muzzle was never here. You don't know who did this or what happened. How many shots did you fire?"

"Two," I said weakly. Thoughts swirled in my mind, leaving me in a daze.

Luca snapped his fingers and two men materialized seconds later. One of them kicked Muzzle in the head before they lifted him from the floor and carried him away. Two other men, or maybe it was the same guys, started cleaning Muzzle's blood from the floor.

"I have the casings, sir," one guy said.

"I'll need your gun," Luca said to me.

"What? Why?" I asked, feeling and sounding somewhat panicked.

"As a precaution. To prevent unnecessary questioning," he said. "It will be returned to either you or Edge after everything is finished."

"Okay," I reluctantly agreed and placed the gun on the counter. My hands were shaking so badly I didn't think I could safely hand it to him.

"Do you remember what to tell the police?" he asked.

"I found Irene like this when I arrived at work. I don't know who did it or what happened."

"Correct," he said with a curt nod. "Don't say any more than that and don't volunteer any information. Edge will be here soon."

"Okay," I said. I felt lost and unsure of what to do next.

Luca's face softened. "You'll be okay. We're leaving now, so go ahead and call for help."

"Thank you."

"There's nothing to thank me for. I was never here." With that, he disappeared around the corner.

I quickly dialed nine-one-one and rushed to Irene's

side. I regurgitated the words Luca told me to say and begged her to hurry.

"Officers are on the way," the operator said and started bombarding me with questions. I answered what I could, but I was losing my patience. They could interrogate me later.

"Are the intruders still in the building?"

"I don't know. I didn't go look for them," I snapped. "Why aren't they here yet?"

"Officers should arrive soon, ma'am."

"That's what you said the last three times I asked! I need help right now!"

Three sharp knocks on the front door had me sighing in relief. "Cedar Valley Police," a man announced.

"I'm coming!" I yelled and rushed to unlock the front door.

Police officers flooded the diner with guns drawn. To my utter shock, one of them grabbed my arm and had me face down on the floor with my hands behind my back before I knew what was happening.

"What in the hell are you doing?" I shouted.

The officer didn't answer me. Instead, he secured my hands behind my back and left me on the floor.

"Irene's behind the counter!" I yelled. "She needs help! And there might be two injured guys in the kitchen. Is anyone listening to me?"

Tables and chairs blocked my view, so I couldn't tell what was going on. I tried to get to my feet to see for myself, but someone stopped me from moving by placing their booted foot on my shoulder.

I couldn't take it anymore and started sobbing. Irene was going to die because none of them would listen to me. They were treating me like a criminal instead of an innocent bystander. Of all the outcomes I imagined, none of them involved me being restrained and left on the floor to sob uncontrollably while the so-called help let my friend die on the floor several feet away.

14

EDGE

I reached for my ringing phone and sleepily answered without looking at the screen. At the sound of Evie's panicked voice, I was instantly awake.

"Is your father dead?"

"No, he's not. I hit him twice, and he's on the ground, but he's very much alive."

"Keep your gun aimed at him and shoot him again if he moves," I said. "Stay on the phone with me. I'll have someone there to help you soon."

As I ran down the hall banging on closed doors, I'd never been so glad I slept at the clubhouse. "Get up! I've got an emergency!"

Byte opened his door and stepped into the hallway. "What happened?"

"Muzzle is at the diner. Evie shot him, but Irene's hurt. We need to get someone there right the fuck now. And somebody needs to call Phoenix."

"I'm here," Phoenix said. I whirled around and opened my mouth to fill him in, but he held up one finger to stop me. With his phone already pressed to his ear, he spoke quickly and efficiently before ending the call. "Is Evie still on the line?" he asked.

"Yes."

"Tell her Luca and some of his men are on their way."

I moved my phone back to my mouth so she could hear me clearly. "Did you hear Phoenix? Help is on the way."

"Okay," she said, but she didn't sound like herself.

"Help will be there soon," I repeated.

"Okay."

I tilted the phone away from my mouth and looked at Phoenix. "I think she's in shock."

"She probably is," he said. "There's nothing we can do about it from here. Let's get on the road."

I put the phone on speaker and ran back to my room to get dressed and grab my keys. Then I hurried to the forecourt while reassuring Evie that help would be there soon. I'd just reached my bike when I heard a blood-curdling scream, followed by what sounded like the phone falling to the floor.

"Evie!" I yelled. "Evie! Answer me!"

I could hear voices, but I couldn't tell who they belonged to or what was being said. After what felt like an eternity, I heard movement near the phone, followed by the sound of someone breathing.

"Evie! Can you hear me? Is Luca there?"

"I'm here," she said, and I sagged with relief at the sound of her voice. "Are you Luca?"

"Yes," I heard Luca say. "Luca Peccati."

I'd never been so happy to hear another man's voice. "Let him help you. Do what he says, okay? I'll be there soon."

"Irene," she whispered. She sounded distracted, or maybe confused.

"Evie," I said firmly, hoping to snap her out of her haze. "Listen to Luca."

"Okay," she promised, but I truly didn't know if she was processing what I was saying or if she was responding by rote.

"I'm on my way," I promised and fired up my bike. The call transferred to my helmet, and I stayed on the line even though I couldn't hear anything over the sound of my bike. When we got disconnected, panic briefly surged through me. I reminded myself that Luca was there and was just as capable of handling the situation as we were.

My mental pep talk did little to nothing to calm my nerves. The only thing that would ease the fear and turmoil churning inside me was getting to the diner and seeing for myself that Evie was okay. The need to reach her was overpowering. I broke formation and sped ahead, leaving my brothers in the dust. I knew they'd understand. Any one of them would have done the same if it was their woman in need.

When I pulled into the diner's parking lot, it looked like every cop in Cedar Valley was there. Maneuvering around the chaos, I parked my bike on the sidewalk right outside the front door.

"Whoa! This is a crime scene. You can't go in there,"

an officer said and moved to block me from entering the front door.

"The hell I can't! My girlfriend's in there," I told him and continued forward.

His hand moved to his belt, and then he was pointing a taser at me. "Don't move!" he shouted. "Put your hands above your head."

Any other time, I would have pointed out that I had to move to put my hands above my head, but I had one singular goal, and that was getting to Evie.

I held my hands up in front of me. "Look, man, my girlfriend is the one who called you. I know she's in there, and I need to make sure she's okay."

"You need to do what I told you and put your hands on your damn head."

"And you need to let me see my girlfriend!" I yelled and quickly moved past him.

Scanning the area, I completely lost my shit when my eyes landed on Evie. She was on the floor with her hands zip tied behind her back and tears pouring from her eyes. But the thing that had me seeing red was the motherfucker holding her down with his foot on her shoulder.

"Get your fucking foot off her!" I bellowed and started for the shithead who was virtually standing on my woman.

Suddenly, a force hit me from behind and tried to take me to the ground. Logically, I knew I was supposed to cooperate with the police, but logic went out the window when I saw what they were doing to Evie. My fury was no match for the officer who tackled me. I shook him off and continued moving toward Evie. Three officers rushed over to help like they'd been waiting their whole lives to pounce on a biker. I finally went down when the fourth cop jumped in.

They were trying to get my hands behind my back when I heard Phoenix's angry voice. "Who the fuck is in charge here?" he roared.

The room fell silent and a man with a very punchable face stepped forward. "I am," he sneered. "And you've got two seconds to get the hell out of my crime scene."

"Wrong," Phoenix said and pointed to one of the cameras mounted in the corner of the room. "You've got two seconds to get your boss on the phone for me before I send the videos of this shitshow to every media outlet in existence." Phoenix crossed his arms over his chest and stared at the little weasel. "The cameras record in high definition and include audio."

He brought his phone to his ear and glared at Phoenix. "And who, shall I say, is calling?"

"It doesn't matter since you haven't actually called anyone," Phoenix said and tapped at the screen on his own phone. "You might be new, but I'm not."

He stared at the guy while he waited for his call to be answered. Then he smiled, but it wasn't friendly. "Hey, Charlie. I'm down here at Irene's Diner. There was a break-in this morning, and the guy running the show has got innocent people and victims restrained on the floor. And by people, I mean *my people*. Pretty sure he's delayed care for victims with critical injuries."

Even I could hear the man on the other end of

Phoenix's phone yelling and cursing. Phoenix covered the mouthpiece with his hand and leaned toward the shitshow runner. "What's your name?"

Shitshow grimaced. "Roger Pond."

Phoenix relayed the man's name, followed by, "Thanks, Charlie. See you in a few."

As soon as Phoenix's call ended, Shitshow's phone rang. Once again, I could hear Charlie yelling through the phone. Shitshow said, "Yes, sir," and "Sorry, sir," about fifteen times before the call was over. Then he said the words I'd been waiting for. "Let them go."

"And be quick about it," Phoenix added.

I was on my feet and pulling Evie into my arms seconds after they released me. She melted into me and buried her face against my chest. "Are you okay?"

"I'm not hurt, but I'm not okay," she said.

I tightened my hold on her. "I won't let anything else happen to you."

"Is Irene alive?" she asked, and the despair in her voice broke my heart.

"Can you find out about Irene?" I asked Phoenix.

Byte appeared next to Phoenix. "She was taken to the hospital, but I don't know anything other than that," he said.

"Who'd you talk to?" Phoenix asked.

"No one," Byte said with disgust. "After the third fucker refused to tell me anything, I looked at the surveillance footage and saw the paramedics leave with her. Tony and Bart were also taken to the hospital."

Phoenix gently placed his hand on the back of Evie's

head and leaned down to speak softly to her. "Do you want to go to the hospital to be with Irene?"

"Am I allowed to?" she asked.

"Oh, yeah. This bozo has screwed up so badly that you can do whatever you want. They will be kissing your ass for the remainder of this investigation."

"Yes, I want to go. I don't know what's wrong with her or how badly she's hurt. They wouldn't tell me anything," she cried.

"And they're going to pay for that," Phoenix said and stepped back. "Go ahead and take her to the hospital. Byte and Dice will go with you. I'll handle everything here. We'll discuss dinner plans later. I was thinking Italian."

"Sounds good," I said and directed my attention to Evie. "You ready to go?"

She nodded and wiped the tears from her eyes.

I tossed my keys to Phoenix. "My bike's out front."

Phoenix chuckled. "I saw it."

With Evie's hand in mine, I led her to the SUV one of the brothers had driven to the diner. Once we were inside, she asked, "Why was Phoenix talking about dinner?"

I smiled at her question and almost laughed. It was so unexpected. "He was referring to Luca," I explained. "He was covertly telling me we'd meet up with Luca later today."

"Why?"

"To deal with Muzzle."

"Oh," she said and remained quiet for several moments. "How are you going to deal with him?"

"At this point, I don't know," I said honestly. "But I probably won't be able to tell you once I know. What I can do is promise you he will no longer be a problem for you."

"The only way that'll happen is if he's dead."

I gave her a pointed look. "He won't be a problem for you," I repeated.

She nodded once. "Good. He's nothing but pure evil, and so is his son."

I hadn't thought much about Muzzle's son or their club, but we'd have to handle both before it was over.

"I don't want you going anywhere without one of us with you until we get a handle on this situation," I said.

"What do you mean? You have Muzzle."

"I was referring to your brother and the Mad Dogs," I clarified.

"Please don't call him my brother," she said, though it wasn't a request.

"It won't happen again," I said apologetically.

She pinched the bridge of her nose and sighed. "I'm sorry. I didn't mean to snap at you. I just—"

"You don't need to explain," I interrupted. "I get it."

She was quiet for a few moments before she asked, "Do you think Snarl will be an issue?"

"Oh yeah," I said, not bothering to soften my response. "I'm not sure how long it will take for him to realize something happened, but he'll start looking for Muzzle once he does."

"I truly hate them."

"I know you do, but let's focus on Irene right now," I

said and pointed to the hospital as Dice pulled into the parking lot.

"I hope she's okay," Evie said nervously. "I don't even know what was wrong with her."

"She's a tough lady. If anybody has a chance, it's her." I didn't know what kind of injuries Irene suffered or what her chances of survival were, but I couldn't think of anything else to say to comfort her.

As soon as we walked through the sliding glass doors, Evie bolted for the registration window to ask about Irene. "Are you a family member?" the woman asked.

"No. I'm her friend and employee," Evie said before I could intervene.

"I'm sorry. We can only give information to the patient's family."

"You don't understand. I'm the one—"

Byte cleared his throat and stepped up to the counter. "I'm her son," he said and told the woman his name. "I'm listed as her emergency contact."

"What's her security code?"

Byte rattled off four numbers and crossed his arms impatiently.

"I'll buzz you in," she said and pointed to the door beside her window. "She's in room three. Only you and one other person can go back to see her."

"It'll be me and her," Byte said and placed his hand on Evie's shoulder.

Evie glanced back at me with a look of uncertainty on her face. "Go with Byte. The rest of us will wait out here."

15

EVIE

I didn't want to leave Edge in the waiting room, but I desperately wanted to see Irene.

"Go," he said when I hesitated.

Inhaling deeply, I nodded once and turned to follow Byte back to Irene's room. He gestured for me to lead the way, but I shook my head. "I don't think I can go first," I admitted.

His eyes softened. "You don't have to go first, but I need you to at least walk beside me so I can see you."

"Oh," I said. "Sorry, I've never had to…um, I'm not sure what to call it."

"Be protected?"

"It seems weird to call it that, but I guess that's what it is."

"It is," he said. "Just think of it like the buddy system. Don't go anywhere alone. It doesn't matter where you are or how safe you think it is, make sure one of the brothers is with you."

"What about work?"

"We'll figure out all the details later, but work won't be a problem," he said. I wanted to ask him to explain, but we had arrived outside Irene's room.

He stepped inside first and immediately moved to the side so I could enter the room.

"Oh, thank goodness!" Irene said and placed a hand over her heart. "I've been so worried, and no one would tell me anything! What happened? Did he hurt you?"

"You've been worried? I thought you were dead!" I blurted, as tears of relief ran down my face.

She waved her hand dismissively. "I'm fine."

"You're not fine," I countered. "You were unconscious and bleeding when I found you."

She grimaced. "Okay, I'm a little banged up, but I'll be okay. Now, tell me the rest of what I missed."

"Have you said anything to the police?" Byte asked.

Irene shook her head. "I haven't seen any to say anything to."

"Good. When you talk to them, tell them what happened, but you don't know who the man was or what he wanted. Give them a vague description of him," Byte said.

"That won't be hard. I don't know who he was or what he wanted," she said and furrowed her brow. "Why? Was I supposed to know who he was?"

I frowned and looked at my feet. I didn't want to tell her the man who attacked her was my father and that he was there looking for me, but I knew I had to.

"He's my father," I blurted before I could chicken out. "I'm so sorry. I don't know how he found me, but this is all my fault."

Irene held up her hand to stop me. "Is he the reason you showed up in Cedar Valley looking for a job with a busted-up face?"

"Yes," I said so quietly it was almost a whisper.

"Then I don't want to hear any more nonsense about it being your fault. He's the one to blame, not you," she said and turned her attention to Byte. "What are you boys doing to make sure my girl is safe?"

Byte grinned. "You know I can't tell you the specifics."

"Listen here, if y'all don't kill him, I will," she said vehemently.

"I already knew that," he said and reached out to place his hand on top of hers. "We'll take care of it."

"What about Evie?"

"One of us will be with her at all times," he said and smiled. "Which means we'll be able to help run the diner while you're recovering."

"Oh please," Irene said and grimaced when she tried to move her arm. I hadn't noticed the way her arm was positioned until that moment. "I'll be back to work in no time."

"I don't know," I said skeptically, and pointed to her arm. "Have they even said what's wrong with you yet?"

She shook her head. "They're supposed to X-ray my arm and shoulder, and they said something about wanting to scan my head since I was unconscious when they brought me in."

"I think it's safe to assume you'll need a few days off at the very least," Byte said. "I'm not sure when the police will be finished, but I figured you'd want to stay closed for the rest of today and open for business as usual tomorrow."

She sighed. "Maybe I should close for a few days. Even though I'm willing to limp around the kitchen and hobble to tables, Tony and Bart probably need a few days off."

"If you want to open tomorrow, we'll open tomorrow. I know how to run the place, and we have plenty of people willing to pitch in and help until you're back on your feet. You can even sit at the counter and boss people around if you want to."

Irene chuckled. "You know me so well."

It felt like we had been there forever when they finally took Irene for her X-rays and scan. I didn't want to leave her, but I was surprisingly hungry, and I also wanted to see Edge. I didn't like being separated from him when so much was going on.

As if reading my mind, Byte said, "It'll be a while before she's back. Let's get the guys from the waiting room and grab a bite to eat while we have some time."

I nodded in agreement and stayed by his side until we met up with Edge and Dice.

"How is she?" Edge asked as soon as he saw us.

"Better than expected," I said. "They just took her for some tests, but she's awake and talking."

"I'm pretty sure her collarbone is broken," Byte added. "She's going to need some help at the diner for a few weeks."

"We can help out as long as she needs us to," Edge said.

"That's what I told her," Byte said with a smile. "Any word on Tony or Bart?"

Edge shook his head. "No. I asked, but they won't tell me anything. I've been watching for someone to come in and ask about either of them, but so far, no one has."

"We can ask Irene if there's anyone we should call for them when she gets back," Byte said and turned to me. "Unless you know."

"I don't. Neither one of them is very chatty. But someone should call Marcy and let her know she doesn't have to work tonight."

When no one volunteered, Byte scrunched his nose and sighed. "I'll do it."

"What's with the face?" I asked.

"I've never liked her," he admitted.

"Me either."

16

EDGE

"Thanks again for your help," Phoenix said when we arrived at Luca's estate.

"We were happy to help," Luca said. "But I'm afraid I have some bad news."

"He's dead, isn't he?" Phoenix asked.

Luca nodded resolutely. "He lost consciousness in the car and died a few minutes after we got him downstairs."

"Did he say anything of value?"

"Possibly," Luca said. "He was spouting off the usual threats. 'You'll pay for this,' and so on. During his tirade, he mentioned his son knew where he was, and their club would come looking for him if he didn't return."

"Yeah," Phoenix said. "I figured as much. Well, if you'll show us where he is, we'll take him off your hands."

"Right this way," Luca said and led us to a basement that was set up similar to the one at the clubhouse.

Muzzle's body was resting on a metal table and haphazardly wrapped with a tarp.

"Let's get him ready to transport."

Carbon and Duke moved to the table. Carbon dropped his backpack on the ground and pulled out a roll of duct tape and another tarp. They made quick work of wrapping the body and sealing the ends to prevent any leakage of blood or other body fluids.

When they finished, they picked up his body and carried him out through a different exit, placing him in the covered bed of a truck one of the brothers had driven to Cedar Valley.

Luca handed a large envelope to Phoenix. "These are the personal belongings we found on him—wallet, keys, cell phone, etc. I turned his phone off as we were leaving the diner."

Phoenix took the envelope and extended his hand to Luca. "Thanks, man. We owe you one."

Luca chuckled. "I believe you owe me two, but who's counting?"

It took me a moment to realize he was referring to providing a safe place for Byte and Gabby to stay as the other favor we owed him.

"You're right. It is two. We'll be happy to fulfill that debt whenever needed," Phoenix vowed.

"I hope it's never needed, but I have no doubt that I can count on you."

Phoenix nodded in acknowledgment before he turned his attention to the rest of us. "Let's roll. We've got a busy night ahead of us."

I headed for the truck with Muzzle's body and offered to drive. Since he was technically my problem, I felt like I should take responsibility in case we got pulled over or somehow discovered on the way back to Croftridge.

Phoenix shook his head. "I don't think so. You may not realize it, but you're too wound up to drive." He handed the keys to Carbon and clapped me on the shoulder. "But you can ride with us."

Before we left Luca's property, Phoenix reached into the envelope with Muzzle's things and pulled out his keys. "Looks like he was driving a Ford. I need two of you to go by the diner, locate his vehicle, and drive it back to Croftridge."

"What about the cameras?" Shaker asked.

"Depending on where he's parked, it might not matter, but I'll text Byte and make sure they're off."

"We'll go," Dice said and gestured between himself and Ink.

"Ride with Dash and Duke and follow them back in Muzzle's car," he instructed. "I want everyone else to head back to the clubhouse. And for fuck's sake, don't speed."

With that, everyone dispersed while I got into the truck with Phoenix, Shaker, and Carbon. Once we were on the road, Phoenix turned in his seat to talk to me. "Obviously, Evie's going to find out her father's dead. Do you think she can handle knowing she's the one who killed him?"

"I don't think she'll have any issues with it. There was no love lost between them, and she acted in self-defense. He wasn't there to make amends with her, and she knows that."

"I'm not sure how we'll end up handling this, but I know for damn sure we won't be delivering him to the Mad Dogs and telling them the truth. Will she be able to keep this to herself and lie to the cops if necessary?"

"I think so," I said. "I can't say for certain without talking to her, but I think she'd do whatever is needed to protect herself and the club."

"Talk to her and be sure before you tell her any details," he said.

I nodded in understanding. "Will do, Prez."

He opened his mouth to say something else when his phone dinged with a text message. "They found the car and are on the way back to the clubhouse."

I felt a slight sense of relief at hearing they got his car, but we still had a lot of things to take care of before I could breathe easily. First and foremost was figuring out what we were going to do with Muzzle's body.

When we arrived at the clubhouse, Carbon parked the truck in the back, and we left the body where it was for the time being. "I don't see any reason to risk spreading his DNA around the clubhouse if we don't need to," Phoenix said as we followed him to church.

Once everyone was seated, Phoenix called the meeting to order. "Since everyone here is up to speed, I'll get right to the point. We need to decide what we want to do with Muzzle's body and car. I have some ideas, but I'm open to suggestions."

"Before we do anything with him, we need to remove the bullets from his body," Carbon said.

"Can you take care of that as soon as we're finished here?"

Carbon nodded. "Consider it done."

"Since we have a car and a body to get rid of, what about sending him off the side of a mountain? There are plenty of places that would be too hard to reach if anyone were to come looking," Dash suggested.

"Yeah," Duke agreed. "And we could rig up something to cause it to explode or catch on fire when it hits the bottom."

"Hell, we could just set it on fire before we push it over," Badger said.

"Yeah, but we need to be careful, so we don't accidentally start a wildfire," I added.

"Do any of you have a specific place in mind?" Phoenix asked. "I'd like to check it out and get this show on the road before that body starts stinking."

"I know a place," Shaker said. "It's rocky, so there's little chance of starting a forest fire. But it's on the outskirts of Croftridge, even farther away from Cedar Valley."

Phoenix leaned back in his chair and rubbed his chin thoughtfully. "I don't think that will matter if no one can get to the body. Muzzle went to Cedar Valley to get Evie. She's with a member of the Blackwings. It's entirely plausible that he drove to Croftridge to look for her."

"You don't think his car being found at the bottom of a ravine in Croftridge will be problematic for us?" Carbon asked.

"I don't think it matters if his car is found or not, let

alone *where*. We're going to have a problem with the Mad Dogs as soon as they realize he isn't coming back. The question is: do they know they're going to have a problem with us?"

All eyes turned to me. "I guess it depends on how they found her. It's entirely possible someone saw us together, but I haven't noticed anything suspicious or out of the ordinary when we've been together."

"What about that guy that got into it with the old guys at the diner?" Dash asked. "Do you think he's connected to this?"

"Even if he is, I wasn't there that morning."

"But we all were the next day," Badger pointed out.

"It doesn't matter right now," Phoenix said. "If they don't know, they'll figure it out soon. We need to stay vigilant and anticipate retaliation, but we'll get to all that later. Let's go take a look at the place Shaker suggested and see if it'll work for us."

To avoid drawing attention to ourselves, only Phoenix, Duke, Carbon, Shaker, and I went to scope out the location. It was in a fairly remote area near the top of one of the many mountains surrounding Croftridge. The curve in the road looked unsuspecting at first glance. However, the first section of the guardrail was missing, making it easy for drivers to misjudge the curve and go over the side.

"How in the hell did you find this place?" Phoenix asked Shaker.

"Keegan thought she saw a car one day when we flew over the area, so I circled back around to take another look. There are several vehicles down there."

"Really? I've never heard anything about accidents in this area," Phoenix said.

Shaker shrugged. "If that missing guardrail is any indication, I'm guessing no one knows. There are no skid marks or anything that would suggest accidents are happening here."

"Well, it's going to stay that way for a while longer because we sure as shit aren't reporting it."

"Agreed."

Phoenix stepped back and surveyed the area. "If we come up the other side of the mountain, we should be able to put him in the driver's seat and send him right over the edge without any trouble."

"And the fire?" Duke asked.

"We could toss a Molotov cocktail through the window before we send him over," I suggested.

Phoenix clapped his hands together and nodded once. "Yes. I like it. Okay, let's get back to the clubhouse and get to work. I want everything to be ready to go by eleven."

With that, we loaded into the SUV and drove back to the clubhouse with a solid plan in place. Before I got started on my assigned tasks, I went to my room to call Evie and check on things in Cedar Valley.

"Hello," she answered on the second ring.

"Hey. How's Irene?" I asked.

"She's doing okay. She was in a bit of pain earlier, but they gave her some medicine, and she's sleeping now. How are things there?"

"Fine," I said and took a moment to choose my next words carefully. I couldn't tell her exactly what was going on, but I didn't want to outright lie either. "I'll be at the hospital first thing in the morning. I'll fill you in on everything then."

"Oh, okay." I could tell she wasn't happy with my response, but I couldn't very well tell her over the phone that her father died and we were tossing his dead body and car off the side of a mountain.

Instead of trying to reassure her, I changed the subject. "Any news on Bart or Tony?" I asked.

"Neither of them has friends or family to speak of, and they both had Irene listed as their emergency contact. It took some doing, but we finally got one of the doctors to come in and talk to Irene. Tony has a broken arm and a concussion. Bart also has a concussion and a couple of broken ribs. They should be able to go home tomorrow and are going to stay at Tony's house to help each other."

"So, they're both going to be out of work for a while?"

"Sounds like it," she said. "Irene wasn't happy about it, but she agreed to keep the diner closed tomorrow."

"We'll get things figured out in the morning."

"That's what I told her, but you know how she is."

"Well, try to get some rest, and I'll see you in the morning."

"Okay," she said softly. "Be careful."

"Always," I promised and ended the call.

Leaning back against my headboard, I closed my eyes and sighed. Even though we had a handle on the situation for the time being, I knew there was more to come.

Since I didn't have time to dwell on it, I got to my feet and went out back to search Muzzle's car. I wasn't looking for anything specific, just doing a general search to see if there was anything that might be useful, particularly since we were expecting future dealings with his club.

"Gross," I grumbled to myself as I tossed yet another bag of fast-food wrappers onto the ever-growing pile. The man was a fucking pig. His car was filled with trash, and it smelled like sweat, smoke, and something rotten.

Other than a gun and some meth, I found nothing of significance inside the vehicle. The trunk, however, was another story. I opened it, saw what was inside, and immediately closed it before running back into the clubhouse.

"Prez," I said and tried to catch my breath. "Found something in the trunk you need to see."

Phoenix, Badger, and a few other brothers followed me out back to Muzzle's car. Without preamble, I opened the trunk and stepped to the side.

"Fucking hell," Phoenix grimaced. "Do you—?" he started and covered his mouth. "Do you know who that is?"

"I'm pretty sure it's Marcy, the waitress who works the evening shift at Irene's."

Phoenix gestured for me to close the trunk. "Well, I don't think that's coincidental."

"Me either," I agreed.

He pinched the bridge of his nose and exhaled

heavily. "I knew this had been too fucking easy. Give me a minute to think."

"I don't see how this changes anything," Badger chimed in.

"How so?"

"She's dead," he said simply. "We can't change that. She can go over the edge with Muzzle. Her death, or disappearance, will go unsolved or be linked to the attack at the diner. Either way, it has nothing to do with us," Badger explained.

"Yeah, I guess you're right," Phoenix said.

Badger grinned. "I usually am."

"Yeah, yeah," Phoenix said and shook his head. "Let's get this damn show on the road. I don't like having dead bodies on the property."

"It'd be weird if you did," Badger said.

Phoenix cocked his head to the side and gave him a strange look before he laughed.

"You can say it. I'm right again," Badger joked.

"Not happening," Phoenix chuckled and motioned with his hand. "Come on. We've got shit to take care of."

Much sooner than we initially planned, we were on the road and headed to Muzzle's final destination. I was driving Muzzle's car with his dead body in the passenger seat and Marcy's body in the trunk. Over the years, I'd done a lot of unusual things related to club business, but driving a stolen car with two dead bodies inside was by far the most disturbing. And it was *definitely* something I never wanted to do again.

Every time a pair of headlights approached, it felt

like my heart stopped, and I held my breath until the car passed and I could no longer see the taillights. By the time we reached the location, my heart was racing and I was covered in a light sheen of sweat.

"You okay?" Carbon asked.

I wiped the sweat from my forehead with my sleeve. "That fucking sucked."

"I bet," he said and slapped me on the back. "You did good though."

"Thanks, I think," I said and covered my mouth with my hand. Suddenly, I felt like I was going to vomit.

"Nope, not happening," Carbon said right before his open palm connected with my cheek. My head whipped to the side as a stinging sensation blossomed on my face.

"What the fuck, man?" I yelled and lunged forward to grab him.

He easily dodged me and held his hands up in surrender. "Anger and adrenaline supersede nausea. We can't have you spewing your DNA everywhere."

"You two knock it off," Phoenix ordered. "Let's get this shit done."

We got to work and placed Muzzle's body in the driver's seat while making sure the window was rolled down. Then I put the car in neutral and closed the door. When everyone was ready, I lit the end of the rag sticking out of our homemade fire starter and tossed it inside. "Now!" I yelled, cueing the guys at the back to start pushing. The car went over the edge with ease. We heard several loud crashing and banging sounds before silence once again filled the night air.

"Let's go," Phoenix said and clapped me on the shoulder as he passed.

I followed him to the SUV and climbed inside, sighing in relief when I took my seat. I knew it wasn't over, but getting rid of the two dead bodies made me feel a lot better.

17

EVIE

Edge walked into Irene's hospital room much earlier than I had expected, with a coffee in each hand. He handed one to Byte and one to me before leaning down to place a kiss on my cheek.

"Thank you," I whispered. Irene was still sleeping, and I didn't want to wake her.

"How is she?" he asked.

"She woke up twice during the night because of pain, but otherwise, she's doing okay. How are you?"

He smiled tightly. "Good. We'll talk later."

I glanced at my coffee and nervously toyed with the lid. I understood why he was putting me off, but I was dying to know what happened with Muzzle.

Edge cleared his throat to get my attention. "We need to figure out the details for the diner."

"We did that last night," I told him.

"You did?" he asked, sounding surprised.

"Yeah. It wasn't hard. Byte knows how to run the kitchen, and I know how to run the front. We just need a few people to help out until everyone's back on their feet."

"I need to touch base with Phoenix and see who's available each day, but yeah, we've pretty much got it covered," Byte said.

"It's too early now, but I need to try calling Marcy again. I haven't been able to get in touch with her since all of this happened," I said.

"Really?" Edge asked, but he had a strange look on his face.

"Yeah. I've left a couple of messages for her and sent a text, but she hasn't responded."

"Is that normal for her?"

I shrugged. "I have no idea. I've never talked to her outside of work."

"We'll plan on having someone there to cover her shift," Byte said. "If she shows up, great. I'm sure we'll be able to use an extra set of hands."

Edge shifted in his seat. "Do you want to go to your house to get a shower and a change of clothes before Irene wakes up?"

"Uh, sure," I said, slightly taken aback by his abrupt change of subject. "You'll be here with her until we get back?" I asked Byte.

He nodded. "Yeah. I'll head home for a bit when you get back."

"I don't need babysitters," Irene grumbled sleepily.

The three of us froze and watched with bated breath to see if she would go back to sleep. When her eyes remained closed for several minutes, Edge and I waved goodbye and quietly left the room.

I waited until we were in his truck, but just barely. As soon as he closed his door, I asked, "What happened with Muzzle?"

He grimaced. "I can't tell you the details, and honestly, it's better if you don't know them, but you need to know some of it for your safety."

He was rambling, which was completely out of character for him. "Just tell me what you can," I said gently.

"Muzzle's dead."

"Oh." I wasn't sure what I was expecting him to say, but the news took me by surprise. "Did I kill him?"

"Does it matter?"

Did it? In the grand scheme of things, I guess it didn't, but killing one's own father felt like something a person should know.

"Sort of," I admitted. "I mean, I don't care that he's dead, but if I killed him, I want to know. What if someone asks me if I've ever killed someone? I want to be able to answer honestly."

"You should always answer no to that question," he said seriously.

"Oh, yeah, I guess you're right," I said and laughed. Okay, maybe I was still in a little bit of shock.

Edge reached over and grabbed my hand. "Are you okay?"

I closed my eyes and inhaled deeply, trying to compose myself. "Yes, I'm okay. I suppose I've been concentrating on Irene, and now I'm starting to feel the impact of everything that happened." I hesitated briefly before repeating my question. "Did I kill him?"

Edge audibly swallowed and slowly nodded. "Luca said he died shortly after they picked him up."

The feeling of satisfaction that washed over me was completely unexpected. I nodded once. "Good. He deserved it, and I'm not sorry."

"Are you sure that's how you feel?"

"Yes. Why?"

He grinned. "Because I'm fucking proud of you. You walked into a bad situation and did what you needed to do to protect yourself and save your coworkers."

"I'm just glad it's over with, and everyone's going to be okay."

"About that," he said and pulled out of the parking lot. "I don't know how much truth there was to it, but Muzzle claimed his son knew where he was going and what he was doing and that his club would come looking for him if he didn't return."

"Are you serious?"

"That's what Luca told us. Even though there's no evidence connecting him to the incident at the diner or of us having anything to do with his disappearance, I think we should anticipate a visit from his friends in Fairbanks."

"What do you mean by 'visit'?" I asked, even though I wasn't sure I wanted to know the answer.

"I don't really know. Worst-case scenario: his son and their club show up to finish what he started."

"To kill me."

"That's not going to happen," he said vehemently.

"I certainly hope not, but that *is* what he came to do."

"Did he tell you that?" Edge asked.

"Sort of. He said he came to make me pay for trying to pin Randall's murder on him and Snarl."

"That's an odd choice of words. You didn't try to pin it on him. He did it, and you turned him in."

"Well, he wasn't the smartest man," I said and closed my eyes as I leaned back in my seat. I was hoping he would think I was tired, but the truth was I didn't want to talk about Muzzle anymore.

Even though I knew none of it was directly my fault, I still felt responsible for what happened to Irene, Tony, and Bart. They were hurt because of my presence. I briefly wondered if I should leave town before anyone else got hurt. Sure, they might come after me, but I could just keep moving to a new town every few months.

I shook my head. I knew that wouldn't work. The only reason I'd done as well as I had was because of Irene. The chances of me finding someone like her again were slim to none.

Not to mention Edge. The feelings I had for him were deep. I could see a real future with him. There was no way I could walk away from what we had together.

Somewhere along the way, both of them had wormed their way into my heart and made what was supposed to be a temporary refuge feel like home.

By the time Edge pulled up to my trailer, I had managed to get myself in a better frame of mind. There was no way I'd be able to handle the Mad Dogs on my own. I needed to stay put and deal with the situation while I had people willing to help me.

Edge insisted on going inside first to make sure my home was clear, and I didn't argue with him. When he deemed it safe, he opened the front door for me to come inside.

"You've been pretty quiet since we left the hospital," he said. "Are you okay?"

"Yes," I lied. "I'm just tired. I think a hot shower and a large cup of coffee will help."

It wasn't entirely a lie. I was tired, but I was *definitely not* okay. Everything that had happened could be traced back to me, and the guilt I felt was overwhelming.

"I'll start the coffee while you shower," he offered and placed a kiss on my forehead before gently nudging me toward the bathroom.

"Thanks," I replied with a weak smile.

I knew I needed to get my shit together, but I couldn't stop thinking about how everything was my fault. The intrusive thoughts continued as I stepped under the hot water.

Did Irene blame me for the attack? Would she kick me out and fire me? Would Tony and Bart refuse to work with me?

I almost screamed when the shower door opened, and Edge stepped inside. Before I could ask what he was doing, he grabbed a handful of my wet hair to hold my head in place while he covered my mouth with his.

"I can practically hear you thinking," he said against my lips. "Let me help you take your mind off things for a bit."

Before I could respond, his mouth was back on mine and his hands were exploring my body. He cupped my breasts and ran his thumbs over my nipples, making my knees feel like they were going to buckle. With one hand toying with my right nipple, he moved the other between my legs and started rubbing my clit.

"Edge," I sighed as my hips involuntarily moved toward his hand.

Before I could blink, he turned me around, hoisted me back by my hips, thrust his cock into me, and started fucking me in earnest. I braced my hands on the wall and groaned. The way he was roughly handling my body was exactly what I needed.

"Touch your pussy," he ordered.

I moaned in response and pushed back against him, meeting him thrust for thrust until I felt a sharp sting as his palm made contact with my ass.

"I said, 'Touch your pussy.'"

I didn't know if I could. I already felt like I was going to explode and collapse at the same time. Anything more might be too much. When he slapped my ass again, my hand moved between my legs of its own volition and gently pressed against my clit.

"Jamie," I breathed. "I, oh fuck, I can't," I said and started to move my hand back to the shower wall.

He reached over me, moving one hand from my hip to my breast, effectively keeping me from being able to put my hand on the wall. Then he did the same with his other hand, forcing me to lower my other hand as well. With his large hands wrapped around my breasts, he pinched both nipples and growled, "Play with your fucking pussy," as he continued to pound into me.

I did as he said and played with my clit, circling it with two fingers. The pressure was building inside of me, and it was going to be epic. "Jamie," I panted. "I'm going to come."

"Yeah, you fucking are," he said, punctuating each word with a thrust of his hips. "Give it to me."

I did. I came like I'd never come before. As waves of pleasure pulsed through me, he continued moving, wringing every possible ounce of ecstasy from me. I wanted to collapse into a pleasure-soaked noodle, but he didn't relent.

"Again," he demanded.

It took me a moment to understand what he meant. "I…I don't think I can."

"You can," he insisted and released his grip on my nipples to begin gently passing his fingers over the sensitive tissue.

I groaned at the sensation. My nipples had always been sensitive, and Jamie knew exactly how to toy with them.

"Play with your tits for me," he instructed, and gently nipped my ear with his teeth.

I moved my hands to my breasts and circled my nipples with my fingers.

"That's right," he said as one of his hands slid down my torso and pressed against my clit. He pinched and flicked, then massaged and circled until he had me worked into a frenzy. I was panting and grinding against him, desperate for another release. When he moved his hand from between my legs, I made a sound of discontent.

He chuckled at my displeasure and pressed his mouth against my ear. "Rub your clit for me, baby, while I play with your tight little ass," he said as his finger slowly slid inside of me.

The sound that left me was almost feral. The sensations were overwhelming and borderline disorienting. It didn't take long before I was once again exploding with pleasure and struggling to stay upright. Thankfully, Jamie's grip on me kept me standing while he found his own release moments later.

Bracing my hands on the wall, I took a few moments to catch my breath. Before I was finished, Jamie turned me around and wrapped his arms around me. We stood there for several minutes, taking each other in, as the water poured down around us.

"We should probably finish up before we run out of hot water," I said quietly. I had no idea how long we'd been in there, but the water heater was small, so we had limited time.

Once we were both dry and dressed, I gathered a few things I wanted to take to the hospital while he filled two travel mugs with coffee.

"Ready to go?" he asked and handed me a mug.

I took a sip and groaned. "It always tastes better when you make it. And yes, I'm ready."

He grinned. "It's because I put more sugar in it."

"La la la," I said loudly since I couldn't plug my ears because my hands were full. "Don't tell me your secrets."

After a quick stop at Irene's house to get her some clothes to wear home from the hospital, as well as her phone charger and her backup pair of glasses, we then drove back to the hospital in a comfortable silence.

"Took you long enough," Irene said as soon as we entered the room.

I quickly spun to the side to place her things on the bedside table and to hide the flush heating my cheeks. "I didn't realize you were timing us."

"The doctor said she could go home, and she's ready to leave," Byte explained.

"I've spent enough time here. I don't want to be here any longer than I have to," Irene griped.

"You have to wait for your discharge papers," Byte told her. "The doctor said it would be a few hours."

"They'll get me out of here a lot faster if I bug the piss out of them."

Byte chuckled. "I'll be happy to confirm with Gabby, but I'm almost certain you'll get the opposite result if you annoy the nurses."

"Fine," she huffed. "I'll wait patiently and hope I survive another horrendous meal. Seriously, what is this crap?" She lifted the warming lid covering her plate and pointed to the food masquerading as lunch.

I wrinkled my nose in disgust. "I have no idea but cover it up before more of the smell gets out."

"I'll go pick up whatever you want," Edge offered.

"I'll have a double cheeseburger meal from that place on the corner. No onions, add mayo, large fries, and Coke to drink," Irene rattled off without an ounce of hesitation.

"Do you want anything?" he asked me.

"I'll have the same thing she ordered."

"I'll be back soon," he said after getting Byte's order.

"Do you want me to help you get changed?" I asked Irene.

"I don't *want* you to," she grumbled, "but I do need help."

"I'll wait outside the door," Byte said, and quickly left the room.

"The fastest way to clear a room is for an old lady to threaten to take her clothes off."

"Oh, stop. You're still smoking hot, and you know it."

"Well, I've definitely held up better than others my age," she admitted. "Okay, let's get this over with."

I'm not sure what she thought she needed help with. I stood there while she did everything herself. "Glad I could help," I teased when she finished.

"I forgot about not being able to wear a bra. What the hell am I going to do for the next few weeks? I can't let the girls swing free. Someone might get hurt."

"Maybe you could wear a strapless bra," I suggested.

She narrowed her eyes. "I'm going to pretend like you didn't say that."

"What?" I asked innocently.

"Strapless bras come in two sizes—so tight you can't breathe or loose enough to breathe, but end up around your waist in a few hours."

I nodded in agreement. "Okay, I see your point. We'll figure something out."

"I'm sorry," she apologized. "I don't mean to be

cranky. I'm hungry, my entire body hurts, and I'm ready to go home."

"You don't need to apologize to me. You have every right to be cranky."

"I'm also pissed that son of a bitch got one over on me. And Byte refuses to tell me what happened after all was said and done. All he says is, 'we took care of it.' Now, I know what that means, but I want to know the details."

"I'll tell you when we get you home," I whispered.

"That's my girl," she said and patted my hand.

"I don't know if this will make you feel better, but you being injured on the floor is likely what saved all of our lives."

"How so?" she asked curiously.

"I dropped down beside you and was digging through my purse to find my phone when Muzzle started talking behind me. I was able to get my gun without him seeing because of how I was positioned."

A sharp knock caught our attention. "Ladies, let's save this conversation for later," Byte said from the other side of the door.

"I swear. I haven't been able to fart without one of those boys knowing," Irene grumbled.

"I'm not concerned about your farts," Byte retorted.

"Well, I am. Sometimes a lady wants to break wind in peace," she called back.

"We're finished. You can come back in," I interjected.

"You look like a new woman," Byte said with a grin as he resumed his seat.

“Flattery will get you nowhere.”

“You love me,” he said.

Irene grinned. “You love me, too.”

When Edge returned with lunch, Irene was packed and ready to go. We were just waiting for the nurse to bring her papers.

“Oh, thank you, you dear, sweet man. You get to be my favorite today,” Irene said as Edge placed her meal in front of her.

“Hey!” Byte said, pretending to be offended. “I’ve been by your side the whole time you’ve been here.”

“And not once did you bring me food,” Irene quipped before taking a huge bite of her burger. “Oh,” she groaned. “This is so good.” She had just taken her second bite when a nurse walked into the room with her discharge papers. “You have got to be kidding me.”

“I can come back later,” the nurse offered.

“Nope. Let’s get this done. But I’m going to eat while we do,” Irene said and continued devouring her food like she had been starving for days.

The nurse looked around the room and seemed to hesitate. Irene swallowed the food in her mouth and gestured for her to get started. “Go ahead, honey. They’re family.”

With that, the nurse started going over Irene’s discharge instructions. I tried to listen to everything she was saying, but she lost me in the first few minutes. “Do you have any questions?” she asked when she finished.

“Yes,” I said immediately. “Is everything you said written on those papers?”

She smiled knowingly. "Yes, everything you need to know is right here."

I relaxed a little at her words. I planned on helping Irene, and I wanted to make sure I was doing everything correctly.

"You can always call Gabby if you have questions," Byte said.

"Thanks. Will you text me her phone number? I don't think I have it."

He nodded, and my phone dinged seconds later.

"Finished!" Irene declared and wadded her wrapper into a ball. "Let's go." When I glanced at my untouched food, she laughed. "It'll keep until we get to my house."

I didn't argue with her. I had a feeling there was more to her urgent need to get out of the hospital and wondered if it had anything to do with the loss of her husband. She talked about him often, but not about his death. I got the impression he died suddenly and unexpectedly, though I'd never asked.

When the wheelchair arrived, Byte led the way to an SUV waiting for us at the curb in the patient pickup area with Dice behind the wheel. Somewhere along the way, Ink joined our group and helped Irene into her seat.

"Where did they come from?" I asked Edge.

He grinned. "They've been here the whole time."

"Is anyone else here?"

"Yep," he said simply. "You ride with Irene. I'll be right behind you."

"All right, now that we're behind closed doors, will somebody please tell me what actually happened?"

Dice chuckled, but it was Ink who answered. "Your girl put two bullets in the man who attacked you."

Irene huffed. "I know all that. Tell me what happened after."

"You know he was my father, right?" I asked quietly. At her nod, I continued. "Well, uh, he died, which sounds like a good thing, but he was the vice president of an outlaw motorcycle club in Georgia, and that's the reason for all of this," I said and waved my hand to indicate our security detail.

"Ah, now things are starting to make sense. So, y'all are expecting his club to come looking for him?"

Ink and Dice nodded.

"There's more to it than that," I said, and inhaled deeply. I didn't want to tell her the rest of it, but she deserved to know. "Muzzle came looking for me because he thinks I wronged him and his son. Supposedly, his son knew where he was going and why. When Muzzle doesn't return, it's very likely someone will come looking for him, and me."

"Your brother, right?" she asked.

I couldn't stop the look of disgust that formed on my face. "Technically, yes, but I never refer to him that way. We have different mothers and didn't grow up together. He's a piece of shit, and the world would be a better place if he wasn't in it."

Irene reached over with her good arm and patted my hand. "Noted. One down, at least one to go."

"I'm so sorry you got caught in the middle of my mess."

"Well, I'm not," she said vehemently. "You ended up

where you were supposed to be—with people who can help you. A broken bone and some bumps and bruises are a small price to pay for your safety and freedom."

Placing my hand on top of hers, I gently squeezed. "I don't know what I'd do without you."

"Let's hope you never have to find out."

Once Irene was settled at home, we started going over the details for the next few days.

"Has anyone heard from Marcy?" I asked. "I've called and left several messages, but she hasn't responded to any of them."

"I'll try calling her," Irene said and reached for her phone. Moments later, she lowered the phone and shook her head. "It went straight to her voicemail, which is apparently full."

"Crap. I could cover her shift, but I don't want to leave you here by yourself all day," I said.

"I'll be fine," Irene insisted.

"I'm sure you will, but you won't be by yourself," Byte told her. "Annabelle and Macy volunteered to keep you company tomorrow."

"I see," Irene said and gave him a pointed look. "And how many of your boys will be here?"

Byte shrugged. "A few, but they can stay outside."

"Oh, please. They're welcome in my house anytime."

"Okay. So Evie will work a double tomorrow while Annabelle and Macy stay with Irene. Ranger and Byte will man the kitchen while Dice, Ink, and me help wherever we're needed," Edge said.

"Sounds like a plan," I said.

18

EDGE

The first day running the diner was much busier than I expected. Several customers were waiting at the door when we opened, including two Evie introduced as Walter and Buck.

"What happened?" Walter asked as Evie poured them each a cup of coffee. "We came by for lunch yesterday, but the place was closed. Gus told us somebody broke in and attacked Irene the day before. Is that true? Is she okay?"

"It's true," Evie said. "She's pretty banged up and has a broken collarbone, but she'll be okay. It'll be a little while before she's back at work."

"Did they catch the son of a bitch who did it?" Buck asked.

Evie shook her head. "No. I was the one who found her, but whoever broke in was already gone when I got here."

"Well, you let us know if there's anything we can do," Walter said. "And give Irene our best."

Evie smiled. "I will and thank you."

The rest of the day was filled with similar conversations with Irene's regular customers. By the end of the day, I was exhausted.

"I don't know how you do this every day."

Evie chuckled. "I don't work doubles every day, and we had a lot more customers than we usually do. Tomorrow should be better."

She was wrong. The next day was just as busy as the first. The third day was slower, and I was thankful for the reprieve. Until two cops walked in shortly after the lunch rush was over.

"Have a seat anywhere you like," Evie said with a smile. "Can I get you a cup of coffee or something to eat?"

"We're not here to eat."

"Okay," Evie said slowly. "Is there something we can help you with?"

I got to my feet and rounded the counter to stand beside her while I waited to hear what they wanted. There were several possibilities, and none of them were good.

"We're looking for Marcy Wagner. We were told she works here," one of the officers said.

"She does, but we haven't been able to get in touch with her for several days," Evie told them.

"When was the last time you spoke to her?"

"She worked her shift the night before the break-in, so six days ago."

"What break-in?"

"Someone broke into the diner Sunday morning.

The owner and two staff members were hospitalized," I told them.

"Was this reported to the police?"

I wanted to roll my eyes. How could they not know? "Yes, it was. There was a large response."

One of them jotted something on a small notepad before tucking it back into his pocket. "So, the last time anyone had contact with Marcy was the night before the break-in?"

"Yes, that's correct," Evie said. "Is something wrong?"

"Her family said they haven't been able to get in touch with her and asked us to do a welfare check. She wasn't at her home, so we're trying to track her down. Do you know where she could be? Or anyone we could contact who might know?"

Evie shook her head. "I don't have a relationship with her outside of work."

"What about you?"

"I don't know anything about her. I'm filling in temporarily until the owner is back on her feet."

They both nodded, and one of them placed a business card on the counter. "Thank you for your time. If you think of anything we should know, or if you hear from Marcy, give us a call."

"Do you think something happened to her?" Evie asked worriedly.

"It's too soon to say, but not being able to get in touch with someone for a few days isn't usually a good sign."

"I hope she's okay," Evie said after they left.

She wasn't, but I couldn't tell her that, and I hated it. I just hoped they wouldn't link Marcy's disappearance to Muzzle and in turn link Muzzle to the break-in. I wasn't worried about the connections going further than that. We were very careful and made sure to leave nothing behind that could connect us to Muzzle's disappearance, but Evie already felt guilty for what happened at the diner and didn't need to add anything to it.

"I'm going to call Irene and tell her about Marcy," Evie said.

"Go ahead. I'll keep an eye on the front," I told her.

I was fighting the urge to close my eyes and take a short nap when the bell on the front door rang. I looked up to see Walter and Buck walking toward the counter.

"Hey, guys. What can I get for you?"

"Nothing," Walter said, scanning the diner. "Is Evie here?"

"She's making a phone call in the office. Do you want me to get her?"

"No," he said and lowered his voice. "We came to talk to you. We saw that asshole that started trouble in here last week. He was in the parking lot of that abandoned warehouse over on Highway Fourteen talking to a group of men on motorcycles."

"You're sure it was him?" I asked. I had a feeling they were right, but I didn't want to jump to conclusions.

"Absolutely," Buck said. "I got a good look at him through the binoculars Walter keeps in his car."

"What about the men on the bikes? Were they wearing cuts?"

Buck nodded. "Yeah, they were. I couldn't make out any of the words, because somebody doesn't know how to keep a car steady, but there was something that looked like an angry dog on the back."

"Don't blame your bad eyesight on my driving," Walter retorted.

"I see," I said and tried not to show any kind of reaction.

Walter gave me a knowing look. "We thought it was worth mentioning, and I can see that it was."

"Thank you. I really appreciate you guys looking out for Irene and Evie."

"We're happy to help," Buck said.

I waited until they were gone to stick my head into the kitchen and ask Byte to come out to the front. I wasn't surprised when Ranger came with him.

"What's going on?" he asked.

I quickly filled them in on what Walter and Buck told me, keeping my voice low so Evie wouldn't overhear us.

"Sounds like the Mad Dogs are in town," Ranger said.

"My laptop's in the office. I can check the traffic cameras and confirm," Byte said.

"They showed up sooner than I thought," Ranger said.

"You think it's really them?"

"Sounds like them. Men on motorcycles wearing cuts with a dog on the back. Who else could it be?"

Byte returned a few minutes later and confirmed our suspicions. "It's them."

"How many?"

"I saw five on the cameras, but I bet there's more," he said.

"I'll call Phoenix and let him know."

Byte held up his hand to stop me. "I already did. He's going to send Flint out to ride around and look for their bikes at hotels and campgrounds. They're a long way from home, so they'll have to stay somewhere. He's on his way with a few other brothers in case they show up here."

"In case who shows up here?" Evie asked in a way that made me think she already knew who we were talking about.

I sighed. I didn't want to tell her because I didn't want to upset her, but she needed to know so she wouldn't be caught off guard if something happened.

"The Mad Dogs," I told her. "We just got word that they've been spotted in town."

A look of surprise mixed with fear washed over her face before she hid it. "Do you think they'll come here?"

"We don't know," I said honestly. "They could be here looking for Muzzle, or they could be here looking for you."

"About that," Byte interjected. "Phoenix wants Ink to take you back to Irene's for the rest of the day. If they show up asking about you, we'll tell them you don't work here."

"Do you think that will work?"

"It's worth a try," I said. "Besides, I don't want you here if they come here and start trouble."

She opened her mouth like she was going to

disagree, but instead closed it and nodded. "When are we leaving?"

"Now," Byte said.

"I'll get my stuff," she said and headed to the break room. I followed along behind her.

"You okay, baby?"

She exhaled heavily. "Yes, and no. I knew this was a possibility, but I didn't think it would happen so soon. And I kind of feel like I'm running away to hide while you and your club clean up my mess."

"This is not your mess. You didn't ask for any of this, and you didn't do anything to cause it. Even if you and I weren't together, the club would still be involved because Irene is Byte's family."

"Yeah, but the only reason Irene was hurt is because of me."

"Wrong again. Irene was hurt because Muzzle was a piece of shit and chose to hurt her. He could've waited for you in the parking lot, but he didn't. He chose to be a monster, and his club will have to face the consequences."

"I'm not sure I agree with you, but you make a good argument," she said and kissed me softly.

Wrapping my arms around her, I held her against me for several long moments. "Try not to worry too much. We have plenty of experience dealing with situations like this, and they've lost the element of surprise."

"That's easier said than done."

"I know," I admitted and took a step back. "You should get going."

"All right but keep me updated."

"I will," I promised.

Ink appeared at the door. "Are you ready to go?"

"Yeah, I guess so," she said and gave me a quick kiss before she followed Ink through the back door.

I returned to the front to find Byte, Ranger, and Dice sitting around the front counter. "Well," I said and clapped my hands together. "What now?"

Ranger laughed. "Now we hope the dinner crowd doesn't show up before more help gets here. It's going to be a rough evening without Evie."

He was right. It took two of us to handle the same workload as Evie. She made it look easy and effortless when it most definitely wasn't.

Ink made it back to the diner a few minutes before Phoenix and the other brothers arrived. Everyone pitched in to help, and we made it through the dinner rush without too many hiccups.

Watching Carbon approach tables and take orders was quite comical. Some of the older customers were obviously terrified of him, while some of the middle-aged women stared at him with dreamy looks in their eyes. He didn't seem to find it as funny as we did, and I understood why after the last incident.

"I'm done," he said and tossed his pen and notepad on the counter. "I'll help in the kitchen, but I'm not waiting on any more tables."

"What happened?" I chuckled.

"Those women over there happened. One of them said she could see my nipple ring and reached out to touch it while her friend pinched my ass. They made me feel dirty, and not in a good way," he huffed. "Can you imagine what would happen if one of us did that to a random woman?"

"I'll be happy to kick them out," I said.

"Just have somebody else serve them," he said and started for the kitchen. He stopped and turned back to me. "But kick their asses out if they get handsy with anyone else. That shit is not okay."

I grabbed his discarded pen and notepad and walked over to the table. "Are you ready to order?" I asked politely.

"Yes, please," one lady said. "I'll have one of you with a side order of your friend."

"Actually, we're going to share," her friend said. "There's plenty of you to go around."

"Get out," I said calmly.

"What?" they asked in unison.

"You heard me. Get out."

The one lady huffed. "You can't be serious?"

"No, lady. You can't be serious. Why the hell do you think you can come in here and sexually harass the staff? It's inappropriate to make lewd comments to the employees, and it is *absolutely* not okay to touch people without their permission. Now, you can kindly exit the premises on your own or I can have the police escort you."

The woman slammed her palms onto the table and pushed to her feet. "You better believe Irene will hear about this."

"She probably already knows," I grinned and pointed to the cameras mounted on the walls. "They record audio as well as video, and she's been watching the feed from home all day."

As if on cue, Byte approached the table with his cell phone in his hand. "Okay, it's on speaker," he said.

"Gertrude, you get your ass out of my diner right now!" Irene yelled through the phone. "You, too, Hester."

They glanced from the cameras to the phone before they grabbed their purses and hightailed it out the front door.

"They're gone," Byte said.

"Good," Irene said. "I can't stand those bitches. I'm sorry they caused trouble, but I sure am glad to have a reason to keep them from coming back. It seems like you guys are doing okay otherwise."

"We are," I assured her. "How's Evie?"

"Pissy, because she's here and not there, but she's fine. I'll let you get back to it," she said and ended the call.

I shook my head and laughed. "She's something else."

"Yep," Byte agreed and shoved his phone into his pocket.

The rest of the evening went smoothly. It was busy, and we had to bust our asses to keep up, but we didn't have any other issues. The Mad Dogs didn't show up, and I wasn't sure if we knew where they were. I'd been too busy to ask.

"Did Flint locate where the Mad Dogs are staying?" I asked Phoenix while we were closing the diner for the night.

"Yeah. They're at some fleabag motel on the outskirts of town."

"How many are here?"

"Looks like only five," he said. "I've got him and Diesel keeping an eye on them. They'll let us know if they go anywhere."

"Is that the plan? To watch them?" I asked.

"For now," he said. "There's no sense in causing trouble or drawing their attention to us if we don't need to. It's possible they're here looking for Muzzle and will leave when they don't find him."

He was right. It was possible, but I had a feeling that's not what would happen.

My thoughts must have been written on my face. Phoenix clapped me on the shoulder. "But we're going to be here for a few days in case they don't."

"Where is everyone staying?"

He grinned. "Luca's place. He also offered his assistance if needed. Trust me. The Mad Dogs don't have a clue what they're up against."

The next morning, Evie stayed home with Irene while we opened the diner. I didn't like leaving her, but I knew it was safer for her at Irene's house. Dash and Duke were there with our two newest prospects, Falcon and Mason, as well as Annabelle and Macy. With Flint and Diesel watching the Mad Dogs, we'd have plenty of time to get more people there if they started moving toward Irene's place. But knowing all of that didn't stop me from worrying. It had been years since we'd had problems with another club, and the Mad Dogs had a reputation for being ruthless.

Phoenix pushed through the swinging door with his phone pressed to his ear. "They're on the move," he said quietly. "Stay vigilant."

The following fifteen minutes were a special kind of torture I hoped to never experience again. I wanted to follow Phoenix and demand to know more details. I also wanted to call Evie and warn her. Instead, I was forced to smile and make small talk with customers while taking their orders.

After what seemed like an eternity, Phoenix came back to the front. "It looks like they're leaving town."

"What?" I asked in disbelief. There was no way they were leaving town.

"Flint said they left the motel and got on the highway, heading south. I told them to follow them for a while to make sure."

"That doesn't make sense. Why would they leave so soon?"

Phoenix shrugged. "I don't know, but I can't say I'm sad to see them go."

"Yeah, I guess you're right." I was glad they were leaving town, but something about it wasn't sitting right with me. If they came to Cedar Valley to find Muzzle, why would they leave without answers? From what we'd been told, they hadn't really looked for him. I didn't want to look a gift horse in the mouth, but it seemed too good to be true.

Flint called two hours later to tell us they were still headed south and hadn't made any stops.

"We'll hang around for another day or two to

monitor things, but I don't think they're coming back," Phoenix said.

"Maybe we should talk to the guy who got into it with Walter and Buck," I suggested.

"I don't want to risk him telling the Mad Dogs we were asking about them, and I don't think he'd tell us anything anyway."

"Yeah, you're probably right."

I didn't like it, but there wasn't much I could do about it.

19

EVIE

A week had passed since the Mad Dogs left town, and it had been almost three weeks since anyone heard from Marcy. I briefly wondered if there was any connection between the two, but I couldn't figure out how. The police hadn't returned to the diner, but Byte found an update on her case, which remained open with no new developments.

I groaned when I rolled out of bed. I'd been back at the diner for three days and had worked open to close. The tips were great, but I was beyond exhausted. I knew Edge and the other guys were, too. They'd been working sixteen-hour days longer than I had.

After rushing through my morning routine, I found Edge in the kitchen with two travel mugs of coffee ready to go. "Morning, Sunshine."

"Morning," I mumbled and reached for my mug. I needed a few more minutes to myself before I would be ready to socialize. Thankfully, he understood and let me be.

We got into his truck and drove the short distance to Irene's house. She was standing on her front porch waiting for us.

"If I didn't know better, I'd think you were eager to get back to work," Edge said.

"Anything will be better than sitting around the house. I've been bored as hell all week," she said. I helped her into the back seat while Edge got the bag she had sitting by her feet. Her arm was still in a sling, but she was moving around much better than she had been.

When we arrived at the diner, Irene was greeted with cheers and applause from the guys who were already there. "Oh, stop," she said. "I should be clapping and cheering for you. Y'all stepped in and kept this place running. I can't thank you enough."

Byte smiled softly. "You're family. It's what we do."

"Yeah, yeah. You love me. I love you," she said and wrinkled her nose. "Emotions. Yuck."

Irene went to the office to catch up on paperwork while the rest of us got started on opening the diner. I was in the middle of rolling silverware when a strange feeling washed over me. I looked up and froze when my eyes landed on Snarl staring at me through the front window.

I stood frozen for several beats before my brain came back online. "Edge!" I shouted without taking my eyes off Snarl. He glared at me, mouthed something, and disappeared.

Edge was at my side seconds later. "What's wrong?"

"Snarl's outside. I just saw him looking through the window."

He pulled his gun from his holster and started toward the front door.

"You can't go out there!" I shouted.

"Go to the office with Irene," he said calmly.

Instead of following his instructions, I went to the kitchen to get Byte and Ranger. I had just told them what was going on when Snarl burst through the back door with a gun in each hand. Before anyone could react, he opened fire.

I tried to run but didn't make it very far before a burning pain ripped through my torso and stole the air from my lungs. Clutching my chest, I fell to the floor as gunfire and shouts of pain continued around me.

20

DICE

I was still half asleep when I walked into the diner, which is why I didn't think anything of the back door being open. I assumed Ink had gotten there before me and left it open, but I immediately realized that wasn't the case when I slipped and almost busted my ass.

"Son of a bitch," I cursed and looked down to see what made me slip. Blood. I slipped in someone's blood. Quickly scanning the kitchen, I saw Ranger and Byte lying on the floor with puddles of blood surrounding them. "Oh, fuck no," I whispered.

I don't remember reaching for my gun, but it was in my hand when I rounded the corner and found Snarl standing over Evie. She was holding her chest and gasping for breath.

"Why is this happening?" he asked in a way that made me think he was taunting her. "What's the matter, big sister? Bullet got your tongue?"

She wheezed and coughed in response.

"All you had to do was keep your mouth shut, but

no, not perfect little Evie. You thought you were so fucking smart. Trying to frame us for murder. But you're the murderer, aren't you?"

When she didn't answer, he kicked her in the stomach. She curled in on herself but barely made a sound. "Admit it!" he demanded. "You killed Randall!"

He lifted his foot to kick her again but stopped when she nodded.

"Say it!"

"I did it," she wheezed as tears streamed down her face.

"And that's why I did all of this," he said.

I didn't give him a chance to say or do anything else. I fired once, striking him in the head and dropping him where he stood.

As I ran to Evie, I noticed Edge's body crumpled by the front door. For a brief moment, I didn't know who to go to first—but she was moving, and he wasn't. I tried not to think about that too much as I dropped to my knees beside her.

"Help them," she gritted out as a tear slid down the side of her face. "I'm sorry."

I watched in horror as she closed her eyes and her body went limp.

"No!" I yelled and rolled her onto her back. "Stay with me!"

After checking for a pulse and not finding one, I started CPR. I knew I needed to call for help, but I couldn't stop what I was doing. "Help!" I shouted between breaths. "Somebody fucking help me!"

I wasn't expecting a response and almost sagged

with relief when I heard Ink's voice. "I'm here! What the fuck happened?"

"Snarl shot everybody. He's down. Call nine-one-one and start checking people. I don't know who's alive and who isn't," I told him as I continued to try to save Evie.

"Holy shit," an unfamiliar voice said. I continued pumping Evie's chest with one hand and pointed my gun toward the voice with the other.

Walter and Buck were standing just inside the front door with their hands raised in the air. "Tell us how to help," Walter said.

"One of you check him for a pulse. There are two more in the kitchen. And somebody needs to find Irene."

Walter dropped to his knees beside Edge while Buck ran toward the back. "He's got a pulse!"

Buck reappeared with Irene in his arms. "She's hurt, but alive," he said as he laid her on top of a table. "I'm going to help in the kitchen."

"Come on, Evie. Stay with us," I told her as I continued trying to resuscitate her. "What's going on over there, Walter?"

"Looks like a gunshot wound to the chest. I'm holding pressure. He has a pulse and is breathing on his own, but he's not conscious."

"You hear that, Evie? Edge is breathing on his own, and help is on the way. Now I need you to start breathing for me, okay? Please breathe," I begged.

"Cedar Valley Police," someone announced from the front.

"The shooter's down, and the scene is clear. Four people have been shot and need help," I said.

"Are you Dice or Ink?" the officer asked.

"Dice. Ink's in the kitchen with Buck and two victims."

"The scene's secure. Send the paramedics in," he ordered.

Within seconds, first responders filled the diner. Two paramedics rushed to Evie and took over CPR. When I stepped away from her, I looked around in confusion. I didn't know what to do next.

A hand landed on my shoulder and startled me. "Sorry," the officer said, and quickly withdrew his hand. "I'm Charlie, the Chief of Police. Can you tell me what happened?"

"I'm not sure how it started. When I got here, everyone was down. The shooter was standing over Evie. He was pointing a gun at her. He was yelling at her and kicking her. I shot him. I tried to help her," I told him. I knew I sounded disjointed, but I was having a hard time putting words together.

"Are you okay?" Charlie asked.

I glanced down at my hands and stumbled back a step when I realized they were covered in blood. "No, I don't think I am," I managed to say seconds before I leaned forward and vomited.

"Johnny, bring me some water and something he can wash his face with," Charlie instructed as he led me to a chair.

"Thanks, but I need to check on my friends. I don't know if—" More vomit interrupted the words I didn't want to say.

"Stay right here," Charlie said. "I'll see what I can find out for you."

When Ink appeared a few moments later, he was covered in more blood than me, and I almost threw up again at the sight of him. "Fuck, man," he said and collapsed into a chair beside me. He covered his face with his blood-stained hands and let out a gut-wrenching sob. With my hand on his back, we sat there silently, waiting for someone to tell us if we'd been able to save our family members.

Somebody brought two bottles of water to us and a couple of damp dishtowels, but neither one of us moved. I had a feeling Ink was just as lost as I was.

I managed to hold myself together somewhat until I heard Phoenix's voice. "You did good," he said as his hand landed on my shoulder. And I fucking lost it. Uncontrollable body-racking sobs overcame me as every ounce of pain, fear, and terror I'd kept pushed down bubbled to the surface.

Phoenix stood between the two of us with one hand on my shoulder and one hand on Ink's until we pulled ourselves together. "Luca brought some clean clothes for you. Go get changed, and we'll head to the hospital," he instructed.

As I made my way to the employee bathroom, I passed Walter and Buck. I started to extend my hand to thank them, but stopped when I remembered it was still covered in Evie's blood. Walter nodded knowingly.

"We'll catch up with you at the hospital," Buck said.

With a silent nod of acknowledgment, I continued toward the bathroom on autopilot.

I don't remember leaving the diner or riding to the hospital, and I don't remember how long we had to wait before we heard any news. What I *did remember* was the feeling of Evie's ribs cracking and breaking as I tried to make her heart beat again and the feeling of her chest depressing each time I pushed down. Trying to resuscitate her played on a loop in my head over and over.

Shaker and his family were the first to arrive at the hospital. Gabby almost had to be restrained when they wouldn't let her back to see Byte. She probably would have been escorted off the premises if Ink hadn't intervened. She was crying and demanding to see him when Ink calmly said her name. "I was with him," he said and patted the seat next to him. "I'll tell you what I know."

Before she left the front counter, she turned to Shaker and loudly said, "Call Gigi. If we have to buy this hospital so I can get back there, then that's what we're going to do."

"If they're not letting us back there, it means they're working on them. That's a good thing," Keegan said to her.

"Is that true?" I asked.

She nodded, then grimaced. "Well, it means they aren't dead. It doesn't mean they're stable."

"That's more than anyone else has told us."

She came over and sat in the chair beside me. "You found them?"

"Yeah. I got there first. Ink came in a few minutes later."

"What can you tell me?"

"Not much. Ranger and Byte were on the floor in the kitchen. Edge was by the front door, and the shooter was standing over Evie in the middle of the dining area. I'm not sure where Irene was."

"Do you know how many times they were shot?"

"Sorry, I don't. I think Evie was shot once, but I don't know about the others. Walter and Buck said they were coming to the hospital. They'll be able to give you some details if we haven't heard anything by then."

Shaker was tucking his phone into his pocket as he walked over to us. "Someone will be out to speak with us soon."

"Did you name drop?" Keegan asked.

"Yes, I fucking did. Gabby is losing her shit, and I honestly don't know how you're keeping it together so well."

"My grandfather is the toughest man I know. He's also stubborn and ornery as hell. He'll live through this on principle," Keegan said confidently.

"Marks family," someone called.

"Right here," Shaker said.

"If you'll follow me, we have a private waiting room for you."

"And so it begins," Keegan said quietly.

Once we were in the new waiting room, the doctor addressed us as a group. "I understand you have several family members that were brought in. We're still assessing and stabilizing, but I'll tell you what we know so far. First, I have Michael Fuller. He was brought in with three gunshot wounds."

Gabby gasped and fell back in her chair. Keegan grabbed her hand and gestured for the doctor to continue.

"He has one gunshot wound to the right upper chest, one to his right lower abdomen, and one to the left upper thigh. He is already in surgery."

"Did it hit his femoral artery?" Gabby asked.

"No, but I believe it hit his femur. I'll double check that. The bullet to his chest punctured his lung, but the gunshot to the abdomen is the one requiring surgical intervention. I don't have specifics on the damage caused at this time. He did not regain consciousness before going to surgery, but his vital signs were improving."

"What about Papa?" Gabby asked.

"Noah Norris," Keegan clarified.

"Mr. Norris has one gunshot wound to the right chest. The bullet hit one of his ribs but did not damage his lung. Our biggest concern with Mr. Norris is his head injury. He has a large laceration on the back of his head, a skull fracture, and a small brain bleed that does not require surgery currently, but we'll be monitoring it closely. He has not regained consciousness, but he should be able to have visitors soon."

"How did he get a head injury?" Keegan asked.

"He likely fell when he was shot and hit his head on something. It's more common than you might think."

"Thank you," she said. "Who's next?"

The doctor glanced at the tablet in his hand. "Jamie

Ellis. He was brought in with one gunshot wound to the chest. The bullet missed his heart but did some damage to nearby vessels, resulting in extensive blood loss. He is currently in surgery."

When the doctor paused, I gestured for him to keep going. "Irene Dawson was brought in with a gunshot wound to her right arm and right leg. The recent injury to her clavicle was worsened and will require surgery to repair, but it's not an emergency. Her surgery will likely be tomorrow, and she will be allowed to have visitors soon."

"And Evie?" I asked. I was anxious to know about her and didn't think it was a good sign that they saved her for last.

"Evie Sinclair was brought in with a gunshot wound to the chest. She was in cardiac arrest at the scene. EMS was able to restart her heart, but it stopped once more shortly after she arrived at the hospital. We were able to get it back again, and she was immediately taken into surgery. I don't know the extent of the damage, but I know the bullet hit her left lung and left kidney. They will likely have to remove part or all of her kidney."

"Her ribs are broken," I said quietly.

"I'm sorry. I didn't hear what you said."

"Her ribs are broken," I repeated louder. "I was the one doing CPR. I felt them break."

He nodded and tapped at the tablet screen. "Thank you. I'll make sure her care team is aware. Does anyone have questions for me?"

"Not at this time," Keegan said. "Just let us know when we can see the ones not in surgery."

After the doctor left, I looked around and realized more of the Blackwings had arrived. A lot more. Phoenix was standing off to the side, talking to Badger. It looked like they were having an intense conversation, and I had a feeling I knew what it was about. I also had an important piece of information that Phoenix needed to know before any decisions were made.

I pushed to my feet and crossed the room to where they were standing. "You doing okay?" Phoenix asked.

"I need to speak with you both privately," I said.

Since the hospital was packed with people, the three of us went outside to one of the club SUVs.

"What's going on?" Phoenix asked as soon as we closed the doors.

I exhaled heavily. I didn't want to tell him, but I knew I had to. "Before I shot Snarl, he was standing over Evie, yelling at her. He said everything that happened was her fault and insisted that she knew why. I don't know the details, but Evie killed her roommate and tried to frame Muzzle and Snarl for it. She admitted to it."

Phoenix drew in a sharp breath and rubbed his chin. "You're sure?"

"Yes, I'm sure. She was having a hard time breathing, but she managed to say, 'I did it.' That's when I shot him. I knew he was going to kill her after she confessed."

"Fucking hell. There must be more to the story, but the only people we could ask are in surgery."

"I really hope there is more to it," I admitted. "If there's not, I wrongfully killed their enforcer."

“No,” Phoenix said vehemently. “Regardless of what really happened with Evie’s roommate, their enforcer shot three of our club members and one family member. You had every right to take him out.”

“We need to wipe the camera feed,” Badger said urgently. “Or at least wipe the audio. No one else needs to know about her confession right now. Can Flint do it?”

Phoenix pinched the bridge of his nose. “I don’t know. He’s been working with Byte, but I don’t know if he has access to Irene’s system. I’ll text him.”

A few minutes later, Flint climbed into the back seat with his laptop in tow. “What’s going on?”

“Do you have access to Irene’s security cameras?” Phoenix asked.

Flint nodded. “Yeah. Byte gave me access after Muzzle attacked Irene in case—” he stopped abruptly and cleared his throat. “In case something happened to him.”

“What you’re about to hear does not leave this vehicle. That’s an order.”

“Understood,” Flint readily agreed and opened his laptop. “What am I looking for?”

“I need you to find the footage of Evie and Snarl in the main dining area. Save a copy that only we have access to. Then wipe the audio.”

“There are three cameras in the main part of the diner,” I added.

“Got it. Give me a few minutes,” he said and started typing. His fingers flew over the keyboard in a way that would make Byte proud.

We waited in silence until he finished. "Show me the one with audio," Phoenix said.

Flint handed his laptop to his dad. "Click right there when you're ready to play it."

"Prez," I said hesitantly. "I don't think I can do this."

Flint held out a pair of earbuds for Phoenix. "Here."

"Thank you," I said sincerely. Just the thought of having to see or hear that video was making me feel sick. I experienced all of it firsthand and would likely spend the rest of my life trying to erase it from my memory. I wasn't used to dealing with crises of such a serious nature because, thankfully, things like that didn't happen often.

After Phoenix watched the video, he passed the laptop and earbuds to Badger. When Badger returned the items to Flint, I exhaled in relief.

Phoenix turned in his seat. "First, I want you to know how proud I am to call you my brother. The way you and Ink handled the situation is beyond impressive. You neutralized the threat, provided lifesaving help, and maintained security."

I looked down at my hands, unsure of what to say. I didn't feel like the hero he was making me out to be.

"Evie's confession stays between the four of us until we can have church and make some decisions. Like I said before, whatever did or didn't happen with her roommate doesn't change the fact that Snarl shot three patched members. I'm sure we'll be hearing from the Mad Dogs when they get word of Snarl's death, but we have some time before they'll be able to do anything."

He paused and directed his attention to Badger. "I think we should lock up the clubhouse and send everyone in Croftridge to the farm. If it comes down to it, they can wait this out in one of the underground bunkers."

"Yeah," Badger agreed. "I think that's a good idea. If the Mad Dogs do come for retaliation, the first place they'll go is the clubhouse."

"I have something you might want to see," Flint said and handed his laptop to Phoenix. "It's a police report from Evie's roommate's murder."

Phoenix took the laptop and quickly read the report. "According to this, an anonymous caller reported the murder. The victim's throat had been slashed. The investigators found fingerprints belonging to Snarl and Muzzle in the apartment, and they found Snarl's prints on the murder weapon. Evie's fingerprints were also on the murder weapon, but it was a kitchen knife, so it makes sense that her prints were there." Phoenix turned in his seat and looked at me. "Didn't she say that she didn't have a relationship with her father or brother?"

"Many times," I confirmed.

"If she didn't have a relationship with them, then their fingerprints shouldn't have been in her apartment."

"What are you thinking?" Badger asked.

"She showed up in Cedar Valley with a busted-up face, right?" Phoenix asked me.

"Yeah. She had two black eyes and a swollen nose. She told people she'd just had sinus surgery."

"I'd bet money they made her do it," Phoenix said.

"Makes sense," Badger agreed.

The shrill ringing of Phoenix's phone abruptly interrupted our conversation. "Phoenix Black," he answered. "Okay. We'll be right there," he replied and ended the call. "The police are here."

With that, we went back inside to answer their questions.

21

EDGE

I opened my eyes and looked around in confusion. It only took seconds for me to realize I was in a hospital room, and then I remembered why. All of it returned to me in a single moment.

Pulling my gun and going out to look for Snarl.

Hearing the flurry of gunshots coming from inside the diner.

Running back inside and seeing Evie fall to the ground.

A bullet ripped through my chest before I could fire a shot.

My gun fell to the floor seconds before I did.

Watching Evie's brother kick her as my vision faded to black.

"Evie," I rasped and tried to move.

"He's awake," someone said.

"Evie," I repeated.

Dice's face appeared in my line of sight, and he looked like hell. "Hey, man," he said. "Welcome back."

"Evie," I said again.

He grimaced, and my heart sank.

"No," I groaned.

"Oh, no, no, no," Dice rushed out. "She's alive."

Any relief I felt quickly disappeared when he continued. "It's been touch and go with her, and she hasn't woken up yet."

I wanted to ask for more details, but my mouth was so dry I could barely talk. "Water," I croaked.

"Oh, sorry, man," he said and pressed a straw to my lips. "Here you go."

I took two small sips and groaned in pain. Everything fucking hurt.

"I'll get the nurse."

"Wait," I gritted out. "Tell me everything first."

"It was bad, man. When I got there, everyone was down, and Snarl was about to kill Evie. I shot him and tried to help her. Ink, Walter, and Buck showed up a few minutes later and jumped in. Byte was shot three times, and Ranger was shot once. Byte was awake and talking right after surgery, and Ranger came to the next morning. He also has a head injury, but he's doing good. Irene was shot twice and refractured her collarbone. She's been released from the hospital but refuses to leave Evie. You and Evie were hurt the worst. He barely missed your heart, and you lost a lot of blood. And Evie—" He halted and turned away from me.

I tried to reach for his hand but couldn't make my arm move. "Tell me," I pleaded.

"He performed CPR on her until the paramedics arrived," Phoenix said from the other side of the room. "Her heart stopped twice before they got her to surgery. They had to remove one kidney and the lower part of her lung. The surgery went well, but now she has an infection they're dealing with. She's not out of the woods yet, but she's slowly improving."

"How long?" I asked and tried to reach for the water.

"I got it," Dice said and once again put the straw to my lips.

After a few sips, I tried my question again. "How long has it been?"

"Four days."

"What?" I blurted, followed by a burst of pain. "Ow, fuck."

"How are we doing in here?" a female voice I didn't recognize asked.

"He's awake, but I think he could use something for pain," Phoenix said.

"Oh, good. Welcome back, Mr. Ellis," she said. "Can you rate your pain on a scale of zero to ten for me?"

"Fifteen," I breathed.

"Got it. I'll be right back."

"We need to talk about something before that pain medicine knocks you out again," Phoenix said quietly.

"What is it?"

"Dice, watch the door and let me know when she's coming back," Phoenix said and lowered his voice. "This is going to be unexpected, so try not to tense. Who killed Evie's roommate?"

He was right. His question was completely unexpected, and I greatly appreciated the warning. "Muzzle or Snarl. They were both there, but I don't know which one specifically did it. Why?"

"Incoming," Dice said.

The nurse entered with my pain medicine. She injected it into my IV, pushed some buttons on one of the machines, asked me a few questions, and left the room in record time.

"Why are you asking about Randall?"

"Right before Dice shot him, Snarl said Evie was the one who did it and demanded that she admit to it."

"What?" I asked. There was no way. I tried to remember the conversation Evie and I had about her roommate's death. She told me about everything leading up to the night Randall died and how Muzzle and Snarl showed up at her job when she got off work. I somehow kept myself from gasping when it hit me. "She never said who did it. She was telling me what happened and had to stop because she got choked up. I finished for her saying, '…and they killed him.' She didn't correct me. Wait. Did she admit to it?"

Phoenix nodded. "She did, but I don't think it's as simple as that. Evie doesn't strike me as the type of person who would kill someone, unless she had to."

"You think they made her do it?" I asked. My eyes were starting to feel heavy, and I knew I wouldn't be awake much longer.

"Yeah, that's exactly what I think."

"I remember her saying something about Muzzle being mad at her for trying to frame him and Snarl. I pointed out that it was a weird thing for him to say since they actually did it. She brushed it off by saying he wasn't a smart man. But his choice of words makes sense if they made her do it. It all makes sense. The reason she was so scared at first, how she wouldn't talk about them or Randall, and why she ran away. It all makes sense." My voice faded as my eyes closed. There was more I wanted to ask, but I couldn't stay awake long enough to do it.

* * *

I DON'T KNOW HOW LONG I SLEPT, BUT WHEN I WOKE UP, it felt like I'd been hit in the chest with a battering ram that was on fire.

"Holy fuck," I grunted.

"What's wrong?" Dice asked.

"Hurts."

"I'll get the nurse."

When he came back, he picked up the cup of water. "Want something to drink?"

"Yeah," I said and tried to breathe through the pain. I'd never felt anything like it before, and I desperately wanted some kind of relief.

Thankfully, my nurse arrived quickly with the pain medicine. "Now that you're waking up, we're going to put you on something called a PCA pump. You'll have a button you can press to instantly deliver pain medicine when you need it. It will have limits set, so you won't be able to overdose."

"Thanks," I said. I didn't care what they did as long as it took the pain away.

"Evie?" I asked when she left the room.

Dice shook his head. "No change, man."

"Who's with her?"

"Irene, Duke, and Carbon are in the room with her, and there are always at least two brothers outside her room. Phoenix and Badger go back and forth between the rooms."

"How are Byte and Ranger?"

"They're both doing good. Ranger should get to go home tomorrow. They were going to release Byte today, but Gabby convinced them to keep him until tomorrow so they can take them both home at the same time."

"What about the Mad Dogs?" I asked quietly.

"They know what happened. Phoenix called their president to arrange a sit down, and Hound told him to fuck off. So, we're keeping an eye on them, and we'll be ready if they make a move before we do."

"Who's watching them?"

Dice chuckled. "Apparently, Flint put trackers on the five bikes that were in Cedar Valley. It was a fucking genius move, but Phoenix didn't know whether to be pissed or proud."

"Wait until you have a kid in the club," Phoenix said as he entered the room.

"Prez," I started, but stopped when he held up his hand.

"I don't want you worrying about this shit right now. We've got things under control for the time being. We'll know if they head this way, and we'll have plenty of time to get the Devil Springs chapter and the Manglers here."

"What about Croftridge?"

"We're on a light lockdown. The clubhouse is empty, and everyone who isn't here is staying on the farm.

Copper sent a few guys to Croftridge to watch over things, since most of our crew is here."

"I'm sorry for all of this."

"If you weren't laid up with a gunshot wound, I'd smack you across the back of your head. This isn't your fault. Just like it isn't Evie's fault. There's nothing for you to apologize for."

"I should've stayed in the diner instead of chasing after Snarl," I admitted.

"You did exactly what anyone would have done. And you don't know what would've happened if you'd stayed. You could've been killed instead of injured. Same goes for Evie. It happened the way it did for a reason. We might never know that reason, but I'm thankful as fuck that you're all still here with us. Like I said before, you focus on getting better, and we'll deal with the rest."

"Thanks, Prez," I said and closed my eyes. I meant to only close them for a moment, but it was hours later when I opened them again.

22

EVIE

Sounds were the first thing that registered to me. I could hear several, but they were all unfamiliar to me. I tried to open my eyes but couldn't. Then I unsuccessfully tried to move my arms. When I couldn't move my legs, I started to panic. Something was wrong. I just knew it.

"It's okay, Evie," Irene said. "You're okay."

I felt someone take my hand in theirs as Irene continued talking to me.

"There's a tube in your throat helping you breathe," she said. "Try not to fight it."

As soon as she mentioned the tube in my throat, I became hyperaware of its presence. It was touching all kinds of things that shouldn't be touched, making me want to cough and gag.

"Try to relax, Ms. Sinclair. We're going to take it out," a voice I didn't recognize said.

I had no idea what was going on, but I couldn't relax. Whatever was in my throat had to come out immediately. Somehow, I managed to move my hand to my mouth and yanked the offending tube from the depths of my body. Unfortunately, it did not bring me the relief I thought it would. Instead, it made me cough, which caused pain to explode in my torso. It took me a moment to realize the guttural moans were coming from me.

"Do something!" Irene shouted.

"We're giving her something for pain now," someone said.

What in the hell was going on?

"Irene," I croaked.

"I'm right here, baby," she said. "Try to calm down so you don't hurt yourself. You're in the hospital."

"Hospital," I mumbled.

"Yes, the hospital."

"Edge?"

"He's in the room next door," she said.

"Why?"

"It's okay, honey. Just rest. We're not going anywhere."

"Okay," I said and drifted back into oblivion.

* * *

I OPENED MY EYES AND IMMEDIATELY CLOSED THEM WHEN the bright white light pierced my skull.

"Lights," I rasped.

"She's awake!" Irene shouted. "What was that, Evie?"

"Lights. Bright."

I heard shuffling, followed by a click. "Okay," she said. "They're off."

I hesitantly opened one eye to make sure the offending light was gone before I slowly opened both eyes and looked around the room. Irene and two big scary guys were staring at me. I recognized one as Carbon, but I wasn't sure who the other one was.

"Um, what happened? Where's Edge?"

"Oh, honey, we've been so worried about you," Irene said and reached for my hand. That's when I realized she was in a wheelchair.

"What happened?" I repeated and tried to clear my throat. My voice sounded weird, and my throat was really sore.

"Do you want some water?" Carbon asked. At my nod, he brought the straw to my lips. Those first sips of water were amazing.

"Thank you," I sighed. "Now, will one of you please tell me what happened? And where the hell Edge is?"

"Snarl showed up at the diner and shot everyone there, including you and Edge," Carbon said.

I closed my eyes at his words. "No," I whispered. "No, no, no."

"Everyone's okay," Irene quickly added. "Well, they will be. Edge is in the room next door."

"What about Snarl?"

"He's dead," Carbon said. "Dice took him out."

"Please thank him for me." The relief I felt was overwhelming, and tears started to stream down my face.

"You can thank him yourself," Carbon said.

I turned my head toward the door to see Dice entering my room. He came directly to me and took my hand. "It's so fucking good to see you awake and talking."

"Thank you," I said softly.

"You don't need to thank me. I did what anyone else would've done," he said.

"She was thanking you for Snarl," Irene clarified.

"Oh," Dice said. "Um, you're welcome."

"What did you think I was thanking you for?" I asked.

"Saving you," Irene answered for him. "You stopped breathing, and he did CPR until the paramedics got there."

"Dice," I whispered and squeezed his hand. "Thank you."

He blew out a slow breath. "I'm just glad you're doing better. You gave us quite a scare."

"Okay, will one of you please tell me everything that happened?"

"I will," Dice said and pulled up a chair. As I listened to him talk, parts of that morning started to come back to me. I remembered seeing Snarl staring at me through the front window, and I remembered telling Edge not to go after him. And then I remembered Snarl standing over me and yelling at me.

"I need to talk to Phoenix," I blurted when he finished.

"Is something wrong?" Dice asked.

"No, I just really need to talk to him."

"Okay, we'll get him for you."

Phoenix appeared moments later. I looked around the room and hesitated. I didn't want to be rude, but I needed to speak to Phoenix privately.

He seemed to understand what I was thinking. "Can y'all give us a minute?"

He waited until the room was clear to ask, "What's going on, Evie?"

I had intended to maintain my composure, but I burst into tears the moment I opened my mouth. "This is all my fault."

"What do you mean?"

I told him everything that happened with Randall, just like I told Edge, but then I told him the rest of it. "They told me I had to do it. They said they would pass me around their clubhouse and then kill me if I didn't. I knew they were making me do it to keep their own hands clean, but I didn't want them to get away with it. I asked Snarl to hand me a knife so his prints would be on the murder weapon. Knowing he was left-handed, I used my left hand to slit Randall's throat and dropped the knife to the left of the body. Thinking that would be enough evidence to prove they did it, I packed my shit and ran. I made an anonymous phone call to the police and told them what happened, but that obviously didn't turn out the way I thought."

"You are not the one at fault here. You did what was necessary for survival. I'm sorry you had to go through something like that, but I must admit, that was a clever fucking plan you came up with."

"Thanks, I think."

Phoenix chuckled. "Thank you for telling me the

truth. I'll be honest and tell you we'd already figured that part out, but I truly appreciate your honesty."

"You're not mad?"

"Of course not. Like I said, you did what you had to do to survive. And frankly, it would've been foolish of you to tell us the truth when you first met us. That's not something you share with people until you know you can trust them, and that takes time. Muzzle and Snarl fucked up when they decided to make innocent people collateral damage in their quest for revenge. Since those innocent people are my people, this is now my problem, not yours. You worry about getting better, and we'll take care of the rest."

"I still feel responsible."

"That's because you're a good person. Trust me when I tell you that no one blames you for what happened."

"Thank you," I said sincerely. "For everything."

He smiled kindly. "You're welcome. I'll come back to check on you a little later." He started to leave but turned back to me. "The police will want to get a statement from you now that you're awake. Tell them the version of the story where Muzzle and Snarl killed your roommate. You ran because they threatened you, and Snarl came after you because you turned them in to the police. Make sure you don't say anything about Muzzle being behind the break-in at the diner. You got there after the assailant was gone and don't know who was responsible."

"Got it," I said. The thought of having to talk to the

police did not sit well with me, but I knew it couldn't be avoided.

Before I could get myself too worked up about talking to the cops, Irene returned to the room with Carbon pushing her wheelchair and the man I didn't know following along behind them.

"Who are you?" I blurted.

He came over to my bed and extended his hand to me. "I'm Duke, Reese's husband."

"Oh," I said and pointed between the two men. "So, how did I end up with you two as my bodyguards?"

Carbon grinned and gestured to Duke with his thumb. "I don't know why he's here, but I'm the biggest and the scariest."

I laughed and immediately groaned. "Crap, that hurts."

"I'll call for the nurse," Irene said. "I'm sure you can have something for pain."

"Okay," I sighed. I knew the medicine would make me sleepy, and I'd just woken up after being out for days, but the pain seemed to be getting worse by the second.

"It's okay. We'll be here when you wake up," Irene assured me.

"You haven't left, have you?"

"Nope, and I'm not going to until you do."

"Do we know when that will be?"

"They haven't said, but I'd guess at least a few more days."

"What about the diner?" It sounded like none of us would be able to return to work anytime soon.

"It's just going to have to stay closed for a few weeks.

I'm going to have some overdue repairs done while we're closed."

"I'm sorry," I whispered.

"Nope. We'll have none of that."

"Okay, okay," I acquiesced. "So, how are we going to do this?"

"Do what?"

"Take care of each other." From what they had told me, it sounded like we were all going to need help for a while.

"Phoenix took care of that. There's a vacant house on their farm that's big enough for all of us and a few people to help out," Irene explained.

The nurse came in with my pain medicine before I could ask anything else. She asked me a bunch of questions that I thought were absurd but answered anyway. Then she checked my incisions and all the tubes and wires connected to me. By the time she finished, I was exhausted, uncomfortable, and drowsy.

"Tell Edge I love him," I mumbled before I drifted off to sleep.

* * *

Two days later, Edge and I were discharged from the hospital. They were going to let him go the day before, but Phoenix told his doctors he wouldn't leave until I did, so they kept him an extra day.

As soon as they said I could leave, I was ready to go. Despite him being in the room next door, I hadn't seen

Edge since the shooting and was anxious to see how he was for myself.

"When are we leaving?" I asked Carbon as he packed up my room. Even though I didn't bring anything to the hospital, there was plenty to take home.

"Later tonight. I'm not sure of the exact time."

"What? Why?" I asked and grimaced from the pain caused by my body tensing.

Carbon whirled around with a look of concern on his face. "You okay?"

I took a few slow breaths before I answered him. "I'm good. I just…I'm ready to go home, and I want to see Edge."

"We're leaving at night as a safety precaution. We have no reason to think that anyone has been watching the hospital, but just in case someone is, we're leaving after dark and through a different exit."

Something about the way his voice changed at the end made me ask, "What kind of exit?"

He sighed. "It's the one the morgue uses when they come to pick up a body."

"Oh, well, okay then," I stammered.

"I know it sounds weird, but it's well concealed, for obvious reasons, and the chances of anyone monitoring that exit are very slim."

"I get it."

"And like I said, Phoenix is being extremely cautious. Our club has never been attacked like this before."

"That does not make me feel better," I said dryly.

"Don't get me wrong. We've had our fair share of incidents, but we've never had this many with critical injuries before. None of us like it when our people get hurt, so we're going to do whatever we can to make sure it doesn't happen again."

"I appreciate everything you guys are doing, and I'm truly sorry for my part in all of this."

He stopped what he was doing and turned to face me. "I'm going to ignore that because I know Phoenix told you to stop apologizing, but I would like to make a suggestion."

"Suggest away."

"You seem to be carrying a lot of guilt. I've seen what that can do to people when it's not dealt with. My wife is a licensed clinical therapist. If you want help to process all of this, give her a call. Most of us have been in her office at one point or another."

"Even you?"

He laughed. "I live with her, so I don't have to go to her office. Actually, neither do you. She'll come to you."

"Thanks. I'll keep that in mind." And I would. Considering everything I'd been through, I probably needed therapy.

When Duke and Irene returned from the cafeteria, there was nothing left to do but wait, and it felt like the time passed at a snail's pace. Finally, when it was almost eleven o'clock, Carbon announced it was time to leave.

"It's been eighty-four years," I said in an old lady voice.

Irene laughed while Duke and Carbon had matching looks of confusion.

"It's from a movie," I explained. "It's not important. Let's go."

Surprisingly, I was able to get out of bed and into the wheelchair with little assistance.

"Take it easy, and let them help you," Irene said. "You don't want to overdo it."

"I know, but I'm so ready to get out of here, and I'm dying to see Edge." I realized what I said immediately and slapped my hand over my mouth. "Sorry, that was a poor choice of words."

Irene chuckled. "We know what you meant."

I was almost bursting with excitement as Duke and Carbon pushed our wheelchairs down the hall.

"How much would I have to pay you to get you to run?"

Carbon laughed. "We're trying to not draw attention to ourselves, remember?"

"I never would've pegged you for a rule follower."

"No one pegs me. Ever."

"Oh," I groaned and crossed my arms over my stomach. "Don't make me laugh."

"You started it," Irene pointed out.

We came to a stop in front of a sketchy looking elevator. "This doesn't seem safe."

"It's fine," Carbon assured me. "I used this elevator when I took your stuff down to the car."

"Just because you didn't get hurt doesn't mean it's safe."

"Do you have a fear of elevators?"

"No, I have a fear of falling elevators, but only when I think about it. And, well, I thought about it."

Irene leaned closer to me and whispered, "I think

the pain pills have a different effect on you than the IV medicine."

"I think you might be right," I whispered back. "I feel a little loopy."

"You're acting a little loopy."

Between Irene and the pain pills, I didn't realize we'd gotten on and off the elevator until we were rolling down the basement hallway. "I don't think I like it down here. It feels creepy."

"We're almost there," Carbon said.

Moments later, we were outside in a small alcove surrounded by brick walls on three sides. One black SUV was parked in the loading area with two more idling behind it at the curb.

Phoenix opened the rear door, and Carbon pushed my wheelchair as close to the vehicle as possible. "Do you need help getting in?"

"I want to say no, but the truth is probably yes."

Ever so gently, Carbon scooped me up like a small child and placed me in my seat. I opened my mouth to thank him, but the words disappeared when I saw Edge sitting in the seat beside me. "Edge!" I gasped and practically fell into him.

"Evie," he breathed as his arms circled around me. "I've missed you so much."

"I've missed you, too. I hated not being able to see you." We'd been able to talk on the phone a handful of times, but seeing him settled something inside me.

Carbon got in and took his seat in the row behind us. "Ready when you are, Prez."

"Wait!" I blurted. "Where's Irene?"

“I’m right here,” she said from the front seat.

“If we’re all riding together, what’s with the other SUVs?”

“It’s another layer of protection. We’ll pull out together, change positions a few times on the road, and turn in different directions. If anyone was trying to follow us, they won’t know which vehicle to follow,” Carbon explained.

“That’s clever,” I said, followed by a yawn. “Sorry, the pain medicine makes me sleepy.”

“If you’re tired, go to sleep,” Edge said. “I’ll wake you when we get there.”

I was already closing my eyes by the time he finished his sentence.

23

EDGE

We'd been home from the hospital for a few days when I jolted awake and quickly surveyed the room. Evie was sound asleep next to me, and nothing seemed out of place. After glancing at the time, I groaned. Six-thirty was earlier than I usually got up, but I knew I wouldn't be able to go back to sleep. Something seemed off. After a few minutes of internal grumbling, I started the slow process of getting out of bed and trekking to the bathroom. Then I went out to the kitchen to make some coffee.

Ranger was sitting at the kitchen table sipping his own coffee. "What are you doing up so early?" he asked.

"I woke up and couldn't go back to sleep."

"Something wrong?"

"I've got a weird feeling, but I don't know why," I admitted.

"Fucking hell. I hate weird feelings."

A few minutes later, Carbon walked into the kitchen, followed by Shaker and Byte.

"Well," Ranger said expectantly. "What in the hell's going on?"

"We don't know yet. Phoenix called and told me to get the guys up. He said he'd be here soon," Carbon said.

"This can't be good," I mused.

Thankfully, it didn't take Phoenix long to arrive at our temporary home. "Where are the girls?" he asked when he joined us in the kitchen.

"They're still asleep," Carbon answered.

"I got a call from Walter about twenty minutes ago. He and Buck were driving past the diner and saw smoke. When they pulled into the parking lot behind the diner to see what was going on and call nine-one-one, they saw a man coming out of the diner carrying a gas can. He saw them and started to run, but they were able to stop him. Turns out, it was the guy they got into it with and saw talking to the Mad Dogs. Walter asked if he should hold the guy for the cops or bring him here. I told him to bring the piece of shit to us. They'll be here in fifteen minutes or so."

"What about the diner?" I asked.

"I don't know how much damage was done. They called it in but couldn't hang around. I'm sure Irene will get a phone call soon."

"I should give her a heads-up," Byte said.

Phoenix gave him a sympathetic look. "You can't. Technically, none of us should know anything about the fire."

Byte sighed and reluctantly nodded in agreement.

"We're going to meet them at the gate and go to one

of the storage sheds at the back of the property. I'll let you know what we find out."

"I'm going with you," I said.

"Me, too," Byte added.

Phoenix rubbed his chin and studied us. "I don't think that's a good idea."

"We can sit there just as easily as we can sit here," I pointed out.

"Fine, but that's all you're going to do." He turned to Ranger. "What about you?"

Ranger nodded to his rifle propped against the wall beside him. "I'll stay here with the girls."

"Sounds good. Dice, Ink, and Patch should be here any minute. Let's roll."

I slowly made my way out to Phoenix's truck without going back to my room to kiss Evie goodbye. I didn't want to chance waking her and having to tell her I was leaving without being able to tell her why.

"If y'all hadn't been through hell, I'd give you shit for how slow you're moving," Phoenix teased.

"I'm pretty sure that counts as giving us shit, Prez," I retorted.

"Well, I sure am glad both of you are here to give shit to."

When we arrived at the storage shed, everyone was already there, including Walter and Buck with their special delivery.

Phoenix got out and shook their hands. "I really appreciate you doing this for us."

"We were happy to help," Walter said.

Buck grinned and held up one finger. "Since we're

already accomplices in this kidnapping, can we stay and watch?"

"Are you going to be able to lie to the cops if necessary?"

"I don't think we'll have a problem with that. We've already lied to them once today," Buck said.

"All right. Follow me."

Once inside, Walter and Buck sat with me and Byte while the rest of the guys set up a makeshift interrogation area and secured the guy to a chair.

Phoenix didn't waste any time getting started. "Your responses and willingness to cooperate will determine how this goes. I didn't have disposing of a dead body on my agenda today, but I'm a flexible man. I'm also reasonable. Keep that in mind and choose your answers wisely." He stepped forward and ripped off the tape covering the man's mouth. "What's your name?"

The man looked around the room before returning his attention to Phoenix. He shook his head defiantly.

Phoenix sighed in exasperation and gestured to Carbon. "You're up."

Carbon stepped forward almost gleefully as he rubbed his hands together. "Hot damn! I've been waiting forever for an opportunity to try this." He pushed a small table in front of the man and started placing things on top of it.

"What's he doing?" Walter whispered.

I leaned closer to him to answer. "I don't know, but judging by the smile on his face, it's nothing pleasant."

When Carbon was set up, he sat in a chair beside the man and freed one of his hands. Then he held up a fishing hook for everyone to see. "Let's try this again. What's your name?"

"What are you going to do with that?"

Carbon made a sound similar to the one game shows used to indicate an incorrect answer. "Wrong answer." Then he quickly pushed the fishing hook through the tip of the man's finger. The guy tried to pull his hand away, but Carbon didn't relent until the hook popped through his fingernail.

The guy screamed and stared at his finger in horror. "What the fuck are you doing?"

"Try not to move next time," Carbon said calmly. "If it doesn't go through the fingernail, it'll probably rip through the skin when we hang you from the ceiling."

"Are you fucking serious?"

"Do I look like I'm kidding? Now, what's your fucking name?"

The guy was breathing heavily and sweating. His eyes darted around in panic, but he didn't answer the question.

Carbon grabbed his hand and pierced another finger with a fishing hook. The guy looked like he was going to puke, and I couldn't blame him. Between the pain medicine, lack of breakfast, and the morbid manicure I was watching, I felt like I was going to be sick as well.

"What's your name?" Carbon repeated.

The guy hesitated but blurted his name when Carbon picked up another hook. "Gary Doyle."

Carbon dramatically stuck out his lower lip and dropped the hook to the table. "You're no fun."

"There's still time," Phoenix assured him. "We need to know a lot more than his name."

"What do you want to know?" Gary asked.

"Why did you start a fire at the diner?"

"I can't tell you that."

Carbon picked up a hook. "Can't or won't?"

"I was hired to do it," he rushed out.

"You know what we want to know. Keep talking or I will literally pull it out of you," Carbon said and yanked on one of the hooks in his finger.

"They'll kill me if I tell you," he squealed.

"Do you think we're going to just let you walk out of here if you don't tell us what we want to know?"

"Fuck, man," he whined. "This isn't fair."

"Life isn't fair," Carbon grumbled and slammed his hands on the table. "Start fucking talking."

"All right. All right," Gary blabbered. "The Mad Dogs paid me to burn down the diner."

Carbon rubbed his hands over his face. He was losing his patience by the second. "This is your last chance. Start from the beginning and tell us everything." To emphasize his point, he tugged on the hooks in Gary's fingers.

"Okay! Okay! Please stop!" Gary begged. Carbon gave him a moment to catch his breath. "I'm a private investigator. Well, I was. I lost my license a while back, so I take what jobs I can get, which are usually the ones licensed PIs won't take. A while back, Carl Sinclair hired me to find his daughter, Evie Sinclair. There wasn't much to go on, and it seemed like she disappeared into thin air. I used traffic cameras to track her to Tennessee, but I lost her shortly after she crossed the state line. I tried tracking her phone and her debit card, but didn't have any luck. Finally, I got a hit on her license plate. Her car was on the back of a tow truck. I traced the tow truck to the Blackwings garage."

"Son of a bitch," I blurted. He didn't have to say it. I knew I was the one who led him to Evie.

"I went back through the traffic cameras and tracked the tow truck to Cedar Valley. I didn't know exactly where it went to pick up Evie's car, but I had it narrowed down enough to make a trip to Cedar Valley. It didn't take me long to find her at the diner."

"Keep going," Carbon ordered.

"I watched her from a distance the first day. The next day, I planned on having breakfast at the diner to get more information, but the two old guys fucked that up."

"You fucked that up yourself, buddy," Buck said. "I would've thought not drawing attention to yourself would've been lesson number one in PI school."

"I didn't fucking see you!"

"All you had to do was apologize or say, 'Excuse me' but you wanted to fuck around and find out."

"Fuck you, old man!"

Carbon slapped Gary across the face. "We respect our elders around here."

"We're not that old," Walter said under his breath, causing Byte and me to laugh.

"Apologize so we can continue," Carbon said.

Gary huffed, but did what he was told. "Sorry."

Buck covered his heart with his hand. "Your sincerity touches me."

"Let's get back on track," Phoenix said. "What happened after you left the diner that morning?"

"I told Carl where he could find Evie," he said simply. "He paid me and that was that."

"If that was that, we wouldn't be here. What happened next?"

"The president of the Mad Dogs contacted me and told me Carl was missing. He wanted me to find out what happened to him. I traced Carl's car to two areas in Cedar Valley. One area was an apartment complex, and the other was somewhere in the vicinity of the diner."

"What apartment complex?" Carbon asked.

"The one where the missing waitress lived."

I tried not to gasp when he mentioned Marcy. Obviously, we knew Muzzle killed Marcy, but I don't think any of us realized anyone else knew there was a connection between Muzzle and Marcy.

"I gave Hound the information I had, and he said they would be in Cedar Valley the next day. I met up with them at an abandoned warehouse. They paid me and said they didn't need anything else from me. I asked why, and Hound told me they'd seen the Blackwings at the diner and he didn't think Evie was worth the trouble." Gary paused and swallowed. "Can I have some water or something?"

Carbon produced a bottle of water and opened it before handing it to him. I found Carbon's hospitality to be quite comical, considering the situation.

"They came to Cedar Valley to get Evie?" Phoenix asked.

"That's what Hound said. It wasn't my job to question what he did."

"Then what?"

"They went on their way, and I went on mine. A few days later, I got a call from Carl's son, Ken. He wanted all the information I'd collected for his dad. For a small fee, I gave it to him. I thought that was the end of it until Hound called and told me about the shooting. He wanted me to keep an eye on things and let him know where y'all went when you left the hospital. You guys must have snuck out of there in the middle of the night or something because y'all were there one day and gone the next. Hound was pissed when I told him, and he told me to find you. So, I started looking, but y'all were nowhere to be found. I checked Irene's house, the diner, the clubhouse, and anywhere else I could think of. Yesterday, Hound said he wanted to draw you out and told me to burn down the diner. And that's it. I swear. There's nothing else to tell."

As I sat there trying to absorb his words, I was incredibly grateful for the extra precautions Phoenix insisted we take when leaving the hospital. Leaving at night kept him from knowing about our departure, and taking the back roads kept him from tapping into traffic cameras to find us.

When Phoenix's phone rang, he looked at the screen and uttered a curse under his breath before he stepped away to answer the call. He returned moments later, and his demeanor had completely changed. "That was Flint.

They're on the move. They've been headed north on the highway for thirty minutes. I think it's safe to assume they're headed our way."

"What's the plan, Prez?" I asked. I knew he had one. Knowing Phoenix, he probably had at least three.

"You and Byte are going to sit this one out. I know you don't want to, and I get it. This involves your girl, but it also involves my brothers. We came close to losing the two of you once, and we're not doing it again so soon."

"There's no shame in staying behind and protecting the families," Byte added.

"I'm happy to do whatever you need me to do," I said honestly. Yes, I wanted to be a part of the action, but I also knew I wasn't at my best, which could inadvertently put others in danger.

"We'll move everyone to the bunker under the main office building. You, Byte, and Ranger will be on guard duty. I'll assign some others to help once we get the details figured out."

"We can help protect the families," Walter said.

"Are you sure? I don't know how long this will take. It could be anywhere from several hours to a few days."

Walter shrugged. "We don't have anywhere to be."

"Thank you. We appreciate the help. Stick with Byte and Edge. They'll show you where to go and what to do."

"What about me?" Gary asked.

Phoenix rubbed his chin. "Yeah, I don't know what the fuck to do with you."

"Come on, man. I told you everything you wanted to know."

"And there's nothing stopping you from going back and telling the Mad Dogs about everything that happened here today. I think you're going to have to hang out with us until this is over."

"No!" Gary shouted and started flailing in his seat. "You can't hang me from the ceiling for days!"

Phoenix crossed his arms over his stomach and doubled over with laughter. "For fuck's sake. I didn't mean it literally."

"What was I supposed to think? I've got fishing hooks in my fingers!" Gary held up his hand to show us, as if we'd all forgotten.

"Byte, can you arrange for Patch to take those hooks out?"

"I'll take care of it."

"All right. Let's get him set up in one of the holding rooms. Then I want the officers to meet me in the conference room on the first floor for church. I'll have the prospects start calling the families to let them know they need to head to the bunker. Byte and Edge, Walter and Buck can help you get Ranger, Irene, and Evie over to the bunker. Take Flint with you and send Dice and Ink to the conference room."

"What do you want us to tell them when they ask what's going on?" I asked.

"Tell them the truth. I want everyone to be aware so that no one is caught off guard. Let's get moving. I want to be ready and waiting long before they arrive."

Byte and I rode back to the house in Walter's truck.

"I hope someone's called Irene by now. I don't want to be the one to break the news to her."

"I can do it," Buck volunteered. "She'll know something's wrong as soon as she sees us."

When we walked into the house, it was clear that they had already heard the news. Evie and Irene were sitting on the couch with their arms wrapped around each other, though I wasn't sure who was comforting who.

Irene looked up and her eyes immediately went to Walter and Buck. "What are you two doing here?"

"Do you know what happened?" Walter returned.

"Yes," Irene said slowly. "How do you know what happened?"

"We caught the son of a bitch who did it," Buck said proudly.

"You what?"

"We saw the smoke when we were driving by and pulled into the back parking lot to see what was going on and call nine-one-one. As Walter was parking, this jackass comes walking out the back door carrying a can of gas. Turns out, it was that bozo with the bad manners from a few weeks ago."

"They didn't say anything about a suspect when they called to tell me about the fire."

"That's because they don't know about him," Walter explained.

"What's going on?" Evie asked.

"It's a long story, which I will tell you, but I'm going to give you the short version right now for the sake of time. The Mad Dogs hired someone to set fire to the diner, hoping to draw us out. Walter and Buck were in the right place at the right time and caught the guy, which is how we know the Mad Dogs were behind the fire. It looks like they're headed in our direction, so we need to get everyone moved to a safer location," I explained.

"Where is this safer location?"

"There's an underground bunker on the farm property. Phoenix wants everyone to stay there while they intercept the Mad Dogs. Walter and Buck are here to help. What do you need to take with you?"

"How long are we going to be there?"

"I don't know. It could be anywhere from a few hours to a few days."

To my surprise, she didn't balk at my answer. "Okay. I'll need my medicine, my phone and charger, the two books on my nightstand, a change of clothes, and my toothbrush."

"Is that all?"

"I don't know. I've never done this before."

"You won't need anything else," Gabby assured her. "The bunker is well stocked with anything you might need, other than your medications and your phone. I'll put your stuff in a bag and meet you in the car."

"Thank you," Evie said.

"Yes, thank you," I added.

"No problem. I'll grab your medications and a change of clothes for you and Irene, too."

Within twenty minutes, we were loaded into the car and headed toward the bunker.

24

PHOENIX

As we were getting Gary settled in the holding room, his phone rang. I didn't think anything of it at first, but when it continued to ring, I reached into his pocket and pulled out his phone to see Hound's name on the screen.

Holding up the phone for Gary to see, I gave him a pointed look. "You're going to answer and pretend like everything's fine. Do not even think about doing anything to tip him off."

Gary swallowed thickly and nodded. "Okay."

When Hound called again, I accepted the call and put him on speaker so we could hear what transpired.

"Hello," Gary answered shakily.

"It's about time," Hound snapped. "I've been trying to call you. Did you do what you were supposed to?"

"Sorry, I was in the bathroom. Yeah, I went by there this morning. I did what I had to do and left. No problems."

"Good. We're heading that way now. Keep an eye on things and call me when they show up."

"Will do. There's no sign of them yet."

"It's only a matter of time. I'll call you when we're close so you can meet us at the same place as last time." With that, Hound ended the call.

"Where does he want you to meet him?"

"It's an abandoned warehouse on Highway Fourteen in Cedar Valley. I don't know the exact address, but I can show you where it is."

"Show us on a map," I said and turned to Byte.

Byte placed his laptop in front of Gary with a map already on the screen. "Is this it?" he asked and pointed to a warehouse and empty parking lot.

"Yes, that's it," Gary confirmed.

"All right, let's get over to the conference room to make some plans."

Church was short and simple. We were going to meet them at the warehouse and work things out one way or another, but we were going to have some precautions in place in case things went sideways.

Before I knew it, I was hugging my kids and kissing my wife goodbye. "Be careful," Annabelle said.

"I always am, doll face. I love you," I told her and kissed her once more.

"I love you, too."

I knew she was worried. I was too, but there was no way around it; we had to meet with them face-to-face.

When we arrived in Cedar Valley, we parked behind the warehouse and got set up while we waited for them to arrive. As he said he would, Hound called Gary to let him know when they were thirty minutes away.

We waited until they pulled into the parking lot and turned off their engines to make our appearance from behind the building. The look on Hound's face was priceless. In a different situation, I would have laughed.

Hound stepped forward and crossed his arms over his chest. "What the fuck are you doing here?"

"You know exactly what we're doing here. You forced my hand when you refused to talk to me after the shooting. Then you ordered the fire at the diner to draw us out. Well, here we are."

"You killed two of my members and are harboring a girl who tried to frame us for murder. Why the fuck would I want to *talk* to you?"

"We killed one of your members—after he shot three of mine and two family members."

"You killed Muzzle," Hound insisted.

"No, we didn't. I'm not sure why you would even think that."

"Muzzle came up here looking for his daughter, the one your club is hiding. He disappeared, and then your club is staked out at the diner where his daughter works. You really expect me to believe that's a coincidence?"

"The diner is owned by a family member. She was injured during a break-in, as were two of her employees. My club was there to help run the place until they were back on their feet. Our presence had nothing to do with you."

"That's bullshit, and you know it!" Hound shouted.

"I don't have any reason to bullshit you. If I killed Muzzle, I'd tell you."

Hound narrowed his eyes. "Fine. Hand over Evie, and I'll let it go."

I snorted a laugh and shook my head. "No fucking way. She didn't do what you think she did, but that doesn't matter because she's a Blackwings old lady."

"She tried to frame Muzzle and Snarl for murder," Hound insisted.

I sighed in exasperation. "I read the police reports. Snarl's fingerprints were on the murder weapon. He's left-handed. The victim's throat was cut from right to left, and the knife was on the ground to the left of the body. There's video evidence of Muzzle kidnapping Evie from the hospital parking lot the night of the murder. There's photo evidence of Evie's bruised and swollen face right after she was taken. Yeah, she may have reported it, but there was no framing. They did it. The only reason they wanted to find Evie was to tie up that loose end by permanently silencing her. You had to know that."

"What the fuck is he talking about, Prez?" the man beside Hound asked. A quick glance at his cut told me he was the new vice president, Mange.

"Not now."

"Yes, now. You said Evie stole the money from Randall's sales, killed him, and set Muzzle and Snarl up for the murder before she took off. Now you've got us in a war with the Blackwings because Muzzle and Snarl were too stupid to not kill her when they killed Randall."

"I said not now!"

"Fuck that! They're dead. Whatever Evie does or doesn't do doesn't matter anymore."

"We don't know that Muzzle's dead," Hound argued.

"You just accused the Blackwings of killing him. What are you trying to pull here?"

"Shut the fuck up, Mange! I should end you for disrespecting me!"

"And I should end you for disrespecting our club!"

I knew what was about to happen and took a few steps back as each one produced a gun and pointed it at the other.

"If we can wrap this up, you guys can handle your shit without us here," I said calmly.

They turned, and suddenly both barrels were aimed at me. Slowly raising my hands, I pointed to the roof of the warehouse where Shaker, Badger, Copper, Judge, Boar, and two other Manglers were positioned with sniper rifles. "I wouldn't do that."

Hound lowered his weapon while Mange redirected his back to Hound and fired. Hound fell to the ground in a heap while Mange raised his hands and let his gun dangle from one finger. "I think we're done here."

"I'm going to need more than that."

He sighed and returned his gun to its holster. "Hound, Muzzle, and Snarl have been problematic for the club for a while. As far as I'm concerned, whatever issues they had with you died with them."

"What about Evie?"

"Evie is no longer our concern. This is over. You have my word," he said and extended his hand.

"It's not completely over. Evie was listed as a person of interest in Randall's murder after the charges were dropped against Muzzle and Snarl. Now, I'm not an expert in murder investigations, but it seems like things weren't on the up and up, and we're going to have to clear Evie's name, which might bring trouble to your door. I'm not interested in stirring up shit where shit doesn't need to be stirred."

"Not a problem. I'll make sure Muzzle and Snarl are blamed for the murder, and Evie's name is cleared." When I arched an eyebrow, he added, "We have a nice setup in Fairbanks. We don't need any outsiders sniffing around and changing things."

Knowing that was as good as it was going to get, I shook his hand. Evie was safe, no one was hurt, and they were leaving. I was satisfied with those outcomes.

25

EVIE

I was doing my best to hide it, but I was a nervous wreck. I couldn't imagine how I would feel if Edge had gone with Phoenix and the others to meet with the Mad Dogs.

"Are you okay?" Ember asked.

"How do you do this?" I blurted. "You guys are so calm, and I'm over here completely freaking out."

She laughed. "Trust me. We're all freaking out, too. We've just gotten better at hiding it over the years."

"Do you really think they'll be okay?"

"Anything can happen, but my dad is the president for a reason. He doesn't head into situations blindly. He makes plans and takes precautions."

"Mom!" Raven called from across the room. "Come look at this."

Ember sighed and got to her feet. "Excuse me while I go see what my grown-ass child needs."

She'd barely made it halfway across the room when

Harper dropped into the seat she'd vacated. "How are you feeling?"

"I'm tired and a little sore, but it's getting better every day. How are you?"

"Nervous. Worried. Pretending like I'm fine."

"Yeah, I was just telling Ember I don't know how y'all do this."

"Stuff like this doesn't happen too often, but I think it helps to have others to commiserate with."

"You guys are lucky to have each other."

"It probably doesn't feel like it yet, but you're a part of this group, too."

"I'm surprised you guys don't hate me," I said and immediately covered my mouth. I hadn't meant to say that, but there was no way I could take it back.

Harper's face softened. "The club has had to handle stuff for a lot of us. Some of us asked for their help, and some of us didn't. Sometimes people got hurt, sometimes they didn't. But every time, they helped because they wanted to. Because their family needed help. You're family now. This is what they do. No one's going to hate you for that."

"I'm not family," I corrected.

"Oh, yes, you are. You're Edge's woman. Even if you weren't with him, I'm pretty sure Irene would claim you as her daughter. Since she's more or less Byte's mom, that'd make you Byte's sister. It doesn't matter how you slice it, you're family now."

I wasn't sure how to respond, so I nodded in acknowledgment while I let her words sink in.

"They were talking about watching a movie to pass

the time, but I think story time would be better," Harper said. "I'm going to get some snacks and round up the old ladies. Don't go anywhere. I'll be right back."

She came back several minutes later with a bag full of junk food. Reese was trailing along behind her carrying a bag filled with various types of drinks. While they were arranging the snacks and drinks on the table, Ember, Annabelle, Macy, Keegan, Gabby, and Irene joined us.

"What's going on?" I asked.

Harper smiled. "I thought it might be helpful for you to hear our stories. Somebody could probably write a book about each one of us."

I listened intently as each woman shared their story. Irene had told me a good bit about what happened with Gabby, but I had no idea about the others.

"Thank you," I said sincerely. "Hearing your stories really did make me feel better."

"We just wanted you to know that we've all been through stuff, and we understand how you're feeling right now," Harper said.

"Did your husband put you up to this?"

She smiled. "He may have dropped a few not-so-subtle hints."

"Please thank him for me. I don't know that I would've reached out on my own."

"That's completely understandable. We're new to you, but now you know you can," she said and clapped her hands together. "So, how about a movie?"

"Sounds good to me." Even though I hadn't been doing anything other than sitting, I was exhausted. The doctors told me I would feel tired even with light activity for several weeks, and they were right.

"Do you need anything?"

"A blanket, if there's one around."

She lifted the top of the ottoman and pulled out a blanket for me. "You're going to fall asleep, aren't you?"

I grinned. "It's highly likely. Will you wake me if there's any news?"

"I will," she promised.

Shortly after the movie started, I was sound asleep.

* * *

"Evie, wake up," Edge said softly next to my ear.

When I opened my eyes, it took me a few seconds to remember where I was and why. "What happened? Is everyone okay?"

He smiled. "Everything's fine. I'll tell you what happened when we get back to the house."

"Fine," I grumbled and slowly got to my feet. After waiting all day for news, I didn't want to wait any longer.

"I can tell you now, but we might miss out on dinner."

"Dinner? What time is it?"

"Almost seven. Since everyone was busy all day, we're having dinner delivered. It'll be here any minute."

When we reached the stairs, I wanted to cry. After struggling to walk down them that morning, I didn't think I'd be able to climb them.

"I got you," Dice said from behind me. He gently

scooped me into his arms and carried me to the top of the stairs.

"Thank you."

I turned to see Edge halfway up the stairs with Ink following along behind him. He was taking his time, but didn't seem to be struggling.

"I bet people in their nineties move faster than we do."

"You're probably right," Edge agreed when he finally reached the top.

We pulled into the driveway as the delivery driver was walking back to his car. "Looks like we're right on time," Ink said.

By the time everyone was seated and served, I was ready to burst. Thankfully, I wasn't the only one. "All right. We're all here. We all have food. Somebody start talking," Ranger said.

"The Mad Dogs were surprised to see us. Phoenix and Hound started talking. Hound's vice president, Mange, got pissed when some things Hound told their club didn't match up with what was being said. Things got heated. Guns were pulled. Then Mange shot and killed Hound. He said Muzzle, Snarl, and Hound had been a problem for a while and they were happy to be rid of them. He said the issues they had with us died with them," Carbon said.

"Does that include me?" I asked.

"Yes, it does. Phoenix specifically mentioned you, and Mange said you were no longer a concern for them."

"It's over?"

Carbon nodded. "It's over."

"What about the murder investigation? I was named as a person of interest."

"Mange said he would take care of that."

"He what? How?"

"He said they didn't want people asking questions and upsetting the crooked system they've got going on in Fairbanks, so he would make sure Muzzle and Snarl were named as the murderers and your name was cleared."

I looked down at my plate and struggled to hold back my tears of relief. I could start living my life again without the threat of the Mad Dogs hanging over me. But what did that mean? I had no interest in moving back to Fairbanks. I could stay in Cedar Valley and continue working at the diner when it reopened, or I could look for a job as a phlebotomist.

Edge placed his hand on my thigh and leaned over to whisper, "You okay, baby?"

Swallowing thickly, I exhaled slowly and nodded. "I'm good. It's just a lot to process."

After dinner, I moved to the living room, hoping to distract myself with some television before bed. I couldn't stop thinking about my future, and the uncertainty of it was driving me crazy.

A few minutes later, Irene joined me on the large sectional sofa. "Please tell me you're planning on watching something ridiculous and trashy because my mind needs a vacation from today."

"I was going to put on *Hot in Cleveland*. It's one of my comfort shows, but ridiculous and trashy works for me."

"Go ahead with *Hot in Cleveland*. I love that show."

I barely made it past the theme song before I asked, "Have you heard anything else about the diner?"

"Nothing official, but it sounds like the place is going to be a total loss."

"No," I gasped. "Oh, Irene, I'm so sorry. What does that mean for you?"

She sighed. "Insurance will cover everything, so that part isn't a problem. I just don't know if it's worth it."

"Why wouldn't it be worth it?"

"I'm not as young as I used to be. I was going to have to retire at some point. Maybe now is a good time."

I was at a loss for words. Irene and the diner had become a huge part of my life, and I couldn't imagine what my days would be like if she didn't reopen. The thought of not working with Irene put things into perspective for me. I was free to move on with my life and return to my previous career, but I didn't want to. I wanted to stay exactly where I was.

"Instead of rebuilding in Cedar Valley, you could move to Croftridge and open a diner here," Byte suggested.

Irene opened her mouth to respond but closed it without saying anything.

Byte grinned. "Give it some thought. You've got plenty of time before you need to make any decisions."

We watched a few more episodes before I was ready to call it a night. It was just as well; my mind had been reeling the entire time.

Edge turned to his side, facing me. "You've been

pretty quiet tonight. What have you been thinking about?"

"Everything. What's going to happen with the diner? Is Irene going to reopen or stay closed? Will I have a job? Will I have to move? I don't like the uncertainty of it all."

"No matter what happens with the diner, Irene isn't going to kick you out. And now that you don't have to hide from the Mad Dogs anymore, you could get a job as a phlebotomist at a hospital or doctor's office or find a job doing something completely different."

"Yeah, I guess you're right."

"You don't sound so sure."

"I really enjoyed working at the diner with Irene. I guess I'm not ready for things to change."

"I know it's easier said than done, but try not to worry about it too much right now. Irene may decide to rebuild, and then things will go back to the way they were. If she decides not to, we'll cross that bridge when we come to it."

"You're full of old people sayings tonight," I teased.

"They're called idioms."

"What?"

"Phrases like that. They're called idioms."

"How do you know that?"

He chuckled. "We do the Dirty Santa gift exchange at the clubhouse every year for Christmas. Last year, I ended up with a word of the day calendar."

"I love that you actually use it."

"While I find some words newfangled, my

propensity for learning has made my vocabulary quite copious."

"If you keep talking like that, I might be forced to find your calendar and hide it from you."

He grinned. "Go ahead. I'm sure there's a word of the day app I can download."

"Who are you?"

"Your man, and I'm full of surprises."

26

EDGE

The next morning, I woke up before Evie and went to the kitchen to make a cup of coffee and get a muffin for her. I really wanted to bring her breakfast in bed, but with my limitations, coffee and a muffin were the best I could do.

When I returned to our room, she was awake and sitting up in bed. She smiled when she saw me. "Morning. What are you doing?"

"I brought you coffee and a muffin. You like the blueberry ones, right?"

"I do, and thank you, but you didn't have to do that."

"I know, but I was hoping we could talk about something."

"We can," she said slowly, "but judging by the look on your face, I'm not sure I want to."

I sat down beside her and made myself comfortable. "It's about Randall."

"Oh. What about him?"

"Well," I started and cleared my throat. I knew what needed to be said, but I wasn't sure how to say it. "After everything happened in Fairbanks, you had to keep the truth to yourself. Now that the truth is out, I was wondering if you wanted to talk about it."

She exhaled heavily and started picking at the muffin wrapper. "I'm not sure there's much to talk about. It happened exactly the way I told you, except for the last part. Honestly, I don't really remember much of those few moments. I can recall everything in detail right before and right after I did it, but not the actual act itself. I think my mind went somewhere else or blocked it out to protect me."

"Yeah, that's understandable. If the memories come back or you find yourself thinking about it a lot, I want you to know you can talk to me about it. You've been through so much over the past few months. You don't have to keep it all inside if you don't want to."

"Thanks," she said softly. "I felt bad about killing Randall to a degree, but I also knew it was the only way to save myself. They would have killed both of us if I didn't cooperate with them. I reminded myself of that every time I started thinking about that night. It's kind of the same with Muzzle. It was me or him, and I chose me. For the record, I don't feel any guilt for shooting him. In fact, I wish he would've gotten what was coming to him much earlier in life. It would've saved me a lot of trouble."

"Yeah, but then you might not have met me."

She gave me a small smile. "I hadn't thought about

it like that, but you're right. I likely wouldn't have ended up in Cedar Valley."

"How did you end up there? I know why you left Fairbanks, but why did you choose Cedar Valley?"

"I didn't choose Cedar Valley, per se. That's where I ran out of gas," she said simply.

"Seriously?"

"Well, I had a little bit of gas left, but I didn't have enough money to put more in the tank and eat, so I stopped there and started looking for a job. If the guy at the gas station hadn't told me about the diner, I don't know what I would have done."

"You would've figured something out. You've proven to be resourceful."

"I'm glad you think so. I felt like a hot mess most of the time. It seems like it's always been like that for me. As soon as I get settled and think things are going my way, life comes along and flips everything upside down. Even now. I moved to a new town, found a job and a place to live, made some new friends, and started making a life for myself. Everything was fine. Then, boom! Me and my new friends are almost killed, and my place of employment is burned to the ground, leaving me wondering what will happen next."

"Nothing's going to happen. The threats to you have been eliminated."

"That's not what I meant. I was referring to my job and my living situation. Irene and I had a deal. Instead of paying me an hourly wage, she let me live in the trailer on her property for free, and I got to keep my tips. If she doesn't reopen the diner, that deal will change, and I'll have to find another job."

"Have you talked to Irene about any of this?"

"No. She's got enough on her plate without worrying about my stuff, too. She needs time to think, and I don't want my needs to influence her decisions."

"For what it's worth, I want you in Croftridge." Cedar Valley wasn't far from Croftridge, but at the end of the day, I wanted her with me.

"Yeah, it is nice here," she agreed.

"Really? You'd move to Croftridge?"

"I can't think of a reason I wouldn't."

Well, that was easier than I thought. I expected some resistance from her, but I wasn't going to complain about not getting any.

"Good," I said and leaned over to capture her lips with mine.

Things were getting heated when we were interrupted by a knock on the door.

I broke the kiss and leaned back against the headboard with a sigh. It was just as well. Neither of us was in any shape to do more than kiss. "Come in."

Dice opened the door but didn't come inside. "Phoenix wants us over at the conference room."

"Why? Is something wrong?" Evie asked.

"Everything's fine," Dice assured her.

"He probably wants to go over everything and make sure we don't have any loose ends to tie up," I told her. "I shouldn't be long."

"Okay." I didn't care for the look of concern on her

face, but there wasn't much I could do about it other than try to reassure her.

"It's just a standard meeting. Everything will be fine," I promised and placed a kiss on her lips.

"Do you know what this is about?" I asked Dice once we were on our way over to the conference room.

"Exactly what you told Evie. Going over everything and tying up loose ends."

"What loose ends?"

"Gary," Byte said.

"He's still around?" I asked. I was more concerned about what happened with the Mad Dogs and hadn't given Gary a second thought.

Dice chuckled. "Yeah, he is. When we got back yesterday, Phoenix told Gary he was too tired to figure out what to do with him and that he'd have to wait until today. I thought the man was going to shit himself right then and there."

It didn't take us long to get over to the conference room, but I wasn't surprised that we were the last ones to arrive.

As usual, Phoenix didn't beat around the bush and got started right away. "We need to decide what to do with Gary. Killing him isn't an option I want to entertain but letting him go or turning him in for the fire are possibilities. Thoughts?"

"If we turn him in, we run the risk of him telling the cops everything we did to him, as well as everything that happened with the Mad Dogs. That could bring unwanted attention to Muzzle's disappearance and

Hound's death, which would muddy the already choppy waters between us and the Mad Dogs," Dash said.

"Yeah, but if we let him go, he could go straight to the Mad Dogs and tell them we made him tell us everything, which ultimately led to a confrontation between us that resulted in their president's death," Duke countered.

"We didn't kill their president. Their vice president did," Shaker said. "I don't think there's much he could tell them that would warrant a response from them. Everything he was hired to do wasn't sanctioned by their club. If you get down to it, Gary's loose lips turned out to be beneficial for their club."

"So you think releasing him is the way to go?" Phoenix asked.

"I think it's the better of the two choices."

"Gary has been scared shitless since he's been here. I think he'll agree to whatever we ask of him if he gets to leave here in one piece," Carbon said.

"Of course he will. The question is: will he keep his word once he's gone?" Badger said.

Carbon chuckled and cracked his knuckles. "I'm sure we can come up with a way to guarantee his silence."

"We already have one," Byte said. "We have video evidence of him starting the fire at the diner. We also have a voice recording of him admitting to accepting money for a job he wasn't licensed to do and illegally tracking down Evie."

"That should work," Phoenix said. "Does anyone disagree?"

When no one did, Phoenix told Carbon to bring Gary into the room. "We've come to a decision on what to do with you," Phoenix started.

"Please, man, don't kill me," Gary begged. "I'll do whatever you say."

"Good. So, here's the deal. You are on video starting the fire at the diner. We also have a recording of you admitting to starting the fire, hacking into traffic cameras to track people, and continuing to work as a PI after your license was revoked. We're going to let you go, but if you so much as breathe a word about any of this to anyone, I'll make sure the evidence we have falls into the right hands."

"I won't say a word. I promise."

"Yeah? What are you going to tell Hound when he asks why you didn't show up at the meeting yesterday?"

"I don't know. I'll tell him I got arrested or something. Yeah, that's it. I was arrested and had to spend the night in jail."

"And when he asks you to continue working for him?"

"I'll tell him I can't. That it's too much of a risk. I'll cut ties with him. I'll do whatever you want me to do."

"What happened to your hand?"

"Fishing accident."

Phoenix nodded. "Let me be very clear. Don't mistake this for an act of kindness. I'm letting you go because it's what's best for me and my club. If you cross me, I won't hesitate to eliminate you."

"I understand. I will happily go on my way, and you'll never hear from me again," Gary promised.

"All right. Carbon, get him out of here."

Gary's face paled, and I almost laughed.

"Where are the old dudes? Can't they take me back to Cedar Valley?"

Carbon laughed. "I'm not taking you back to Cedar Valley. I'm taking you to the bus station in Croftridge. Is that a problem?"

"Nope. Not a problem at all," Gary blurted.

Once they were gone, Phoenix took a seat and leaned back in his chair. "I think that takes care of everything. Does anybody have anything else we need to discuss?"

"Can we resume regular activities at the clubhouse?" Duke asked.

"Let's give things another day or two to settle before we do. I think Gary will keep his word, but I'd rather be safe than sorry. Anything else?"

When no one had anything else to discuss, Phoenix banged his gavel and dismissed us.

On the way back to the house, I finally had the opportunity to talk to Byte about something that had been on my mind. "Evie's mother and stepfather live in Fairbanks. Can you do some research on them? Evie went no contact with her mother well before anything happened with Randall, but I want to make sure there isn't anything that might cause them to suddenly reappear in her life."

"Sure. Is there something specific I should look for?"

"Not that I know of. Just anything that seems like it could be a reason for them to contact her, like money trouble or health issues."

"Okay. I'll see what I can find. Anything else?"

"Yeah," I admitted. "Can you do a little digging into Muzzle, too? He was cheating on Evie's mother with the woman who gave birth to Snarl. I'd like to know if he has other kids who might try to find Evie."

"Say no more. I'm well versed in the hell secret siblings can cause."

"Thanks, man. And, um, can we keep this between us for now? I haven't mentioned any of this to Evie. I don't want her to feel like I'm going behind her back and invading her privacy when I really just want to make sure she's safe."

Byte nodded. "I won't say anything, but if you don't want her to feel that way, you should tell her what you're doing."

"I don't plan on keeping it from her. I just haven't had a chance to talk to her about it yet."

"Oh, good. I thought I was going to have to knock some sense into you with my crutch."

I laughed. "You sound like Ranger."

"I'm equally flattered and offended."

Evie was still in our room, resting in bed, when we got back to the house. She looked up when I entered the room and smiled. "That didn't take long. Is everything okay?"

"I told you it wouldn't, and yes, everything's fine."

"Is that all I'm going to get?"

Climbing into bed beside her, I got situated before I answered. "There will be times when I can tell you things, and there will be times when I can't. If I can't tell you something, it's not because I don't want to or because I don't trust you. It's for your safety and well-being."

"What do you mean by that?"

"Plausible deniability, for example. You can't be held accountable for something you truly knew nothing about. This doesn't really apply to us, but a lot of motorcycle clubs keep their women in the dark to keep them from being targeted for information."

"So, whatever you guys discussed this morning is something I don't need to know about?"

"I didn't say that," I chuckled. "You know Walter and Buck caught the guy who set the diner on fire. They brought him here, and we questioned him, which is how we knew when and where to meet the Mad Dogs. Phoenix called the meeting this morning so we could decide what to do with him."

"Oh," she said and stayed silent for several moments. "What did y'all decide?"

"He agreed to keep his mouth shut, so we let him go."

"What?"

The look of utter disbelief on her face almost made me laugh. "We have the video of him starting the fire and a voice recording of his confession to the fire and other crimes. He'll keep his mouth shut or go to prison. Either way, he won't be a problem for us."

"You guys really do have a different way of handling things."

"We do. It might not always be within the lines of the law, but it's usually the right thing to do. And speaking of the right thing, I need to tell you something else."

"No," she almost whined. "I don't want to hear any bad news."

"It's not bad news. At least, I don't think it is."

Picking up a pillow, she carefully hugged it to her chest. "Fine. Let's hear it."

"On more than one occasion, you've mentioned how things will be going good for you when something comes along and flips your world upside down. I don't want that to keep happening to you, so I asked Byte to check into your mother, father, and stepfather to see if there's anything that could be problematic for you in the future. He hasn't started yet, so if it's not okay with you, I'll tell him to forget the whole thing."

Her reaction was not what I expected. "Oh," she smiled. "That's kind of sweet."

"Really?"

"Yes. I appreciate you being proactive and looking out for me, but it will probably be a waste of time. Muzzle is dead, and even though they're assholes, my mother and stepfather are pretty boring people. I can't think of anything that would possibly be a future problem for me."

"I can. Unknown siblings are the first thing that comes to mind."

"Are you serious?"

"Yes. You know what happened to Gabby and Patch. There are several people in the club who have discovered a sibling later in life, though most of those didn't have a bad outcome, but that's not the point. Is it possible that Muzzle fathered other children?"

"I never thought about it, but I'm sure it's possible," she said and wrinkled her nose. "Does it make me a bad person if I hope there aren't any?"

"If it does, I'm a bad person, too," I admitted. "Not that I don't want you to have other family members, but there's no way in hell I'd trust one of Muzzle's kids."

"I'm one of Muzzle's kids."

"You know damn well I wasn't referring to you."

She grinned. "I know."

"So, it's okay for Byte to poke around in your family's business?"

"Yes. It's completely fine and thank you for thinking of it."

"Well, now that we have that settled, do you have any big plans for today?"

"If I thought it wouldn't hurt you or me, I'd slap your chest."

"Oh, come on. We have so many options to choose from. Will we be binge-watching television shows or having a movie marathon? Are we watching in bed or on the couch? Should we schedule naps or let the pain pills decide when we sleep?"

She closed her eyes and clutched her pillow. "Oh, don't make me laugh."

"Laughter is the best medicine."

"I swear, one day I will beat you and your idioms with this pillow."

"One day, but not today."

"Edge," she groaned.

"Okay, okay. You decide on a movie franchise while I get some snacks. Bedroom or living room?"

"Can we get someone to push the ottoman in to make the sofa a huge bed so other people can watch with us if they want?"

"I'm sure that can be arranged."

"Then I choose the living room," she said and started working her way out of bed. "Go ahead and get the snacks. I can make it to the couch by myself."

I knew she could, but I wanted her to have help if she needed it. Since I was on the same weight and activity restrictions as her, there wasn't much I could do to assist her. As luck would have it, I ran into Dice in the hallway. "Can you help Evie get to the couch? She wants to have a movie marathon in the living room."

"Sure, man. Is she ready now?"

"She is," Evie said from the doorway.

"She'll need her blankets, too," I said before I continued down the hallway, wishing I was able to walk faster. Evie didn't like asking for help, and she didn't like me asking for her, but she was always gracious about accepting it.

So that's how we spent the rest of the day—snuggled on the sofa, watching back-to-back *Pirates of the Caribbean* movies, snacking on junk food, and intermittently napping alongside our friends.

27

EVIE

The next few days were filled with a whole bunch of nothing and dragged by slowly. I was itching to know what Irene was going to do with the diner, but I couldn't bring myself to ask her. She was facing a big decision, and I didn't want to pressure her in any way, but I also didn't want her to think I didn't care. I cared a lot. Maybe too much.

Edge moved closer to me on the couch and placed his hand on my thigh. "What are you over here thinking about?"

I nodded at the book in my hand. "I'm reading."

"Try again. You haven't turned a page in over thirty minutes."

Sighing, I placed the book in my lap and glanced at Byte, who was resting comfortably on one of the recliners.

"Should I go?" he asked.

"No," I rushed out. He was doing well with his leg injury, but I would have been an asshole to ask him to leave. "It's nothing you can't hear. I was just thinking about the diner and wondering what Irene is going to do."

"Have you asked her?"

I shook my head. "No. I didn't want to pressure her."

Byte snorted. "You can't pressure Irene."

"That's true," I admitted.

"I haven't talked to her about it since I suggested she open the diner in Croftridge instead of Cedar Valley. I figured I'd give her a few days to think about it before I brought it up again. It's been a few days, so we'll ask her about it when she gets back from her appointment."

"Ask me about what?" Irene asked as she entered the living room.

"How was your appointment?" I asked.

"Nice try. I'll tell you about it after you tell me what y'all were talking about."

"We were wondering if you'd made any decisions regarding the diner," Byte said.

She walked to the sofa and took a seat. "I've given it a lot of thought, but I haven't made a final decision yet."

"What have you been thinking?" I asked.

"Oh, I'm definitely going to reopen. I just haven't decided where that will be yet."

I exhaled in relief. "If it was easier, I'd get up and hug you!"

She gave me a strange look. "You sound like you were worried."

"I was. I didn't want to pester you, but not knowing what you were going to do was driving me crazy."

Her forehead wrinkled in confusion. "You still want to work at the diner?"

Her reaction wasn't what I expected, and I suddenly felt unsure of my answer. "Yes, if that's okay."

"Oh, honey, it's perfectly fine. I assumed you'd want to go back to being a phlebotomist once you're all healed."

"I thought about it, but I really like working at the diner. Even with everything going on, I was much happier there than I ever was at the hospital."

She smiled softly. "Well, you'll have a job and a place to live when I reopen, regardless of where that is."

"Thank you," I breathed. It felt like a weight had been lifted off my shoulders. Just knowing she was going to reopen was enough for me. I didn't need to know all the details. "Is there anything I can help with?"

"Actually, yes, there is. I need to see what commercial properties are available in Croftridge. There's no point in considering Croftridge if I can't find a good place for the diner. You can help me look for properties online if you want. I should probably look at some residential properties, too."

"There are several vacant houses on the farm. If you can't find something you like, you can always stay in one of those until you do find something," Byte said.

"Thanks, I'll keep that in mind."

"I'm happy to help you search, but I don't know what I'm looking for," I told her.

"Preferably something in town or close to it, with an existing building around the same size as the one in Cedar Valley. It doesn't matter what kind of business was previously there. Pretty much anything can be gutted and transformed into a diner."

"Couldn't a real estate agent help with this?" Edge asked.

"Yes, but I'm not ready for that yet," Irene said. "I want to see what's out there first."

With that, we started scouring the internet for commercial properties in Croftridge. It was refreshing to have something purposeful to do. By dinner time, I had a list of several properties I wanted to show Irene.

"I think this one is promising," I said and passed the laptop Byte had loaned me to her.

"You're right. And I wouldn't have to do a lot of renovating since it used to be a restaurant. But I wonder why it closed."

"Let me see," Byte said and looked at the listing on the screen. "Oh, if I remember correctly, that place closed when the owner passed away. His kids weren't interested in running it, so they closed it and put the property up for sale."

"How long was it open?"

"I'm not sure. It was open when I moved to Croftridge, so at least twenty years. Do you want me to find out when it opened?"

"No, that's not necessary. If it was around for over twenty years, that tells me location and accessibility weren't an issue."

"It's in a great location," Edge added. "It's downtown, but not in the middle, so traffic isn't an issue, and it's not far off the exit ramp, so you can catch highway traffic as well."

"Sounds like you know something about business locations," I said.

He shrugged. "Not really. I remember eating there with my family not long after it opened. The owner came over to talk to my dad, and that's what he said about the location."

"It seems like a great location, but it's been on the market for a while," Irene said. "I wonder if there's a reason why."

"Like what?" I asked.

"It could be anything from ridiculously high taxes to a problem with mold," Irene said.

"Or it could be that no one has wanted to open a restaurant in that location," Byte added.

Irene narrowed her eyes. "If it seems too good to be true, it usually is."

Byte chuckled. "Usually, but not always."

I reached over and gently squeezed Irene's hand under the table. "I have to agree with him." She was too good to be true, and we all knew it.

"I guess it wouldn't hurt to send the agent a message," she said.

"If you want to go look at it first, I can drive you over after dinner," Gabby offered.

"That's not a bad idea," I said. "It might look completely different in person. And it'll give you a better idea of where it is."

"Yeah, I think I'd like to see it," Irene said. "If you're sure you don't mind."

Gabby smiled. "Of course not. We can go whenever you're ready."

"Do you mind if I tag along?" I asked. "I'd like to see it too."

"We can all go," Edge said. "Road trip!"

After dinner, Gabby, Byte, Irene, Edge, and me slowly, and somewhat painfully, piled into Gabby's SUV and rode downtown to look at the property. Gabby pulled into the parking lot and circled the building before she came to a stop near the front door.

"Do you want to get out and peek in the windows?" Byte asked.

Irene laughed. "It'd take over thirty minutes just for us to get out and get back in. I've seen enough to know that messaging the agent and making an appointment to see inside is worth it. Thank you, Gabby."

* * *

A FEW DAYS LATER, DICE DROVE US TO MEET THE REAL estate agent at the restaurant.

"I never thought I'd say this, but I could get used to being chauffeured around," Irene said.

"Me, too," I laughed. "I've never been a huge fan of driving. I'd happily become a passenger princess for life."

"Once I get my driving privileges back, that can be arranged," Edge said.

"Don't make promises you don't want to keep," I teased.

"I'm not," he said.

"We're here," Dice announced.

"Are we early?" Irene asked. "It doesn't look like anyone else is here."

As soon as the words came out of her mouth, another car pulled into the parking lot. The woman stepped out of her vehicle and smoothed her outfit before she straightened and started walking toward us. Dice got out to greet her while the rest of us unloaded.

"You'll have to excuse us," Irene said. "We're recovering from a recent accident, so we're moving a little slower than usual. I'm Irene Dawson."

"Hi, Irene. I'm Daphne Clark," she said and extended her hand to Irene.

"These are my kids, Byte and Evie. This is Evie's boyfriend, Edge. And this is their friend, Dice."

"It's nice to meet you all," Daphne said nervously and shook hands with each one of us.

Irene gave her an appraising look. "You must be new around here."

Daphne looked surprised by her observation. "Yes, I am. What did I do to give myself away?"

"You look scared of the boys. The Blackwings are the good guys in town."

"My apologies. I hope I didn't offend you."

Irene waved her good arm dismissively. "Not at all. It's good to be cautious and aware of your surroundings. I just wanted to put your mind at ease."

"Thank you for that," Daphne said sincerely. "Would you like to go inside?"

"Yes, please."

We followed Daphne inside and trailed along behind her while she gave us a tour of the restaurant. She did a good job of moving slowly through the building so we weren't struggling to keep up with her. When she was finished, Irene gestured to one of the tables. "Can we sit for a few minutes?"

"Of course. Make yourselves comfortable."

Irene pulled out a notepad and pen and started making notes. After a few minutes, she asked the question I'd been curious about since she first brought it up. "Why has this place been on the market for so long?"

Daphne cleared her throat. "From what I've been told, the seller is picky."

"What?" Irene and I asked at the same time.

"The previous agent told me the last three offers weren't accepted because the seller didn't like the buyer. He said the seller was in no hurry and wanted to wait for the right buyer to come along."

"Well, I doubt they'd consider an old lady wanting to open a basic diner to be the right buyer," Irene said.

"Can you tell us who the seller is?" Byte asked.

I almost laughed. He'd be able to find out if Daphne couldn't or wouldn't tell us.

She nodded and tapped the screen on her phone. "Yes, the seller is Luca Peccati."

Byte chuckled. "Well, I don't think buyer approval will be a problem."

"Oh, do you know Mr. Peccati?" Daphne asked.

"Yes, we do," Edge said. "He's a family friend."

Irene made some more notes and walked around the building one more time before she was ready to go.

"Are there any other properties you're interested in seeing?" Daphne asked.

"Not at this time, but if this works out, I will need help finding a place to live. Do you show residential properties as well?"

"Yes, I do, and I'd be happy to assist you," Daphne said and handed Irene her business card.

"Great. I'll be in touch."

They shook hands, and we got back in the SUV to go home.

"Are you okay?" Edge asked.

"Yes, but I think I've reached my limit of physical activity for the day." It was a little depressing. Everyone else was getting better and moving around while the slightest bit of activity exhausted me.

"It'll get better."

"I hope so."

"It will," he insisted. "Your injuries were much more substantial than everyone else's, so it's going to take you a little longer to bounce back."

"I know. It's just frustrating. I probably shouldn't have gone to tour the restaurant, but I really wanted to get out of the house." Since being released from the hospital, I'd been to the bunker, Patch's office for an appointment, and the restaurant.

"Did Patch give you a timeline of what to expect?" Irene asked.

I hadn't realized she was listening to our conversation and felt slightly embarrassed about complaining. She noticed my discomfort and shook her finger at me. "We'll have none of that. Answer the question."

"Yes, Mom," I said and stuck out my tongue. "He said most people feel tired and are easily exhausted after having part of their lung removed for six to eight weeks, but it would probably be a little while longer since I also lost a kidney."

"What else did he say?"

"He said I should take it easy and listen to my body, meaning I should rest when I felt tired."

"You went out and walked around a little. You got tired, and now you're going home to rest. Sounds like you're right on track to me."

"Yeah, I guess you're right," I admitted.

"If it's any consolation, I'm tired, too."

"Me, too," Byte said.

"Same," Edge added.

"I could go for a nap," Dice said, causing the rest of us to laugh.

Back at the house, I had a quick snack and took something for pain before Irene and I got comfortable on the couch and started looking at floor samples and diner furniture online. We'd moved on to industrial kitchen appliances when Phoenix arrived at the house.

"Mind if I interrupt?" he asked.

"Of course not," I said cheerfully. "What can we do for you?" My pain medicine had kicked in and I didn't have a care in the world.

Phoenix chuckled. "I spoke with Luca Peccati. The restaurant is yours if you want it."

My mouth dropped open in surprise. I wanted to

jump up and dance around the room, but Irene had a different reaction. She crossed her arms as best as she could with one in a sling and cocked her head to the side. "What's the catch?"

"There's no catch. He knows who you are and was familiar with your diner in Cedar Valley. I told him you were thinking about relocating to Croftridge after the fire. He mentioned his available property before I had a chance to tell him you were interested," Phoenix explained. "He also said he would come down on the price. He listed it high to 'weed out the undesirables.'"

"I have to wait for the insurance payout before I can do anything."

"He knows. He said to take your time and think it over. If you decide you want to buy the property, he won't sell it out from under you while you're waiting for the insurance company."

Irene leaned forward and lowered her voice. "By doing this, I won't be getting in bed with the Mafia, will I?"

Phoenix leaned back and laughed. "Luca's association with the Mafia has never been confirmed."

Irene rolled her eyes. "That just means he hasn't been caught. And it doesn't answer my question."

"No, you wouldn't be agreeing to anything with the Mafia. This would be a business transaction, just like any other."

I raised my hand and wiggled my fingers. "I have a question."

"Go ahead."

"Does that 'no ties to the Mafia' thing apply to me, too?"

"I'm not sure what you mean."

"Luca's the one who helped me that morning," I whispered. "Do I owe a Mafia boss for getting rid of a body for me?"

Phoenix continued to laugh. "Technically, that was a favor for me, so you're good."

"You used a Mafia favor for me? That's sweet, and kind of scary."

"How much have they given her?" Phoenix asked Irene.

"Just one. She's a lightweight." Irene gently patted my thigh. "Evie, baby, stop talking."

"Oh, sorry. The pain pills make me yappy. I don't like it either."

"Shhh," Irene reminded me.

"Right. Zipping the lips. Carry on," I said and used my fingers to zip my lips.

"If I decide I want to buy the property, how should I proceed?" Irene asked.

"Give me a call, and I'll give Luca a heads-up. Then call the agent and let her know," Phoenix said.

"Thanks. I need some time to think about it, but I'll let you know as soon as I decide."

"Oh, I almost forgot. We have a few vacant houses here on the farm. If there's one you like, you're welcome to it."

"Thank you. I might take you up on that while I'm looking for a new place."

"That's fine, too. But I meant that you're welcome to live here for as long as you like."

"Like a rental?"

Phoenix chuckled. "No, not a rental. I have more houses than I know what to do with. They sit here unoccupied. Just like this one. So, if you find one you like, you're welcome to occupy it, free of charge, no strings attached."

"You're serious?"

"I am."

"Well, that's definitely something to think about."

"She's wondering what she'll do with the people she rescues," I stage whispered.

Irene gave me the same look mothers give to their children when they want them to shut up, but Phoenix didn't miss a beat. "The same thing she's always done—give them a job and a place to stay. Like I said, we have plenty of room around here."

"I think you should say yes," I told Irene.

"I think you need to take a nap," Irene retorted.

"Right. Re-zipping the lips," I said, leaning back against the couch and closing my eyes. Irene knew what she was talking about because I was asleep in a matter of moments.

28

EVIE

Three Weeks Later

With the exception of Ranger, we were all still staying at the house on the farm. Byte was walking without crutches, Edge seemed almost back to normal, and Irene only had minimal limitations with her arm. Meanwhile, my incisions and broken ribs had healed, but I was still moving around slower than a sloth and getting exhausted with minimal activity. It was frustrating, but I was trying to take it in stride. Irene had plenty of administrative things I could do while sitting in front of a computer.

I looked up from the laptop when I heard her enter the kitchen. "Are you ready for today?" I asked.

She sighed as she poured herself a cup of coffee. "As ready as I'll ever be."

"Are you having second thoughts?"

"No, not at all. I'm just dreading packing up all of my shit. And then unpacking it. There's a reason I haven't moved in years—because I hate it."

I laughed. "I know what you mean. I'm not a fan of it either."

"Neither of you will have to do anything other than supervise," Edge said.

I raised my hands in surrender. "You don't have to worry about me. I don't have much to move anyway."

"Are you two ready to go?" Edge asked. "Ink will be here to pick us up soon."

"I am. I just need to pour some coffee into a travel mug. Irene, do you want one?"

"Have I ever said no to coffee?"

"Got it. Three coffees to go."

When Ink arrived a few minutes later, we were standing on the front porch waiting for him.

"Am I late?" he asked as we got into his truck.

"No, we were just ready to leave ahead of time. We must be getting better if we're moving faster. Well, they are anyway," I said.

"You're doing great. Patch even said you were doing better than he expected," Edge reminded me.

Smiling, I gently squeezed his hand. "I know."

When we arrived at Irene's, Ink dropped her off at her house before continuing to the trailer. While Ink unloaded the boxes and packing supplies, I went inside for the first time since the shooting. I'm not sure what I was expecting, but everything looked the same as it always did. However, it didn't feel like home anymore.

"Where do you want to start?" Edge asked.

"I guess we can start in the bedroom and work our way to the front."

Since most of my clothes were already in Croftridge, I really had little to pack. We finished in less than two hours. It was almost embarrassing.

"What about the furniture?" Ink asked.

"It all belongs to Irene. I don't know what she wants to do with it. We'll have to ask her."

Once the truck was loaded, we went up to Irene's house to help pack. There were several vehicles parked in her driveway, including a moving truck. As we were walking up to the door, Falcon and Mason came out carrying a sofa. I peeked inside the back of the moving truck to find it was almost halfway full.

"Holy crap. They've got a lot done."

Edge chuckled. "Moving isn't so bad when you have a lot of help."

He wasn't wrong. Several hours later, Irene's house was empty, and we were headed back to Croftridge.

"While we were at Irene's house, Byte told me he hasn't been able to find anything concerning regarding your family," Edge said. "As far as he could tell, Muzzle didn't have any other children. Snarl has a four-year-old daughter, but he wasn't involved in her life. The child's mother got married two years ago and moved to a different state."

"What about my mother and stepfather?"

"Like you said, they're pretty boring. He said everything seemed to be in order with them."

I exhaled in relief. "Thank you. I guess knowledge is power."

He laughed. "Good one."

When we arrived at the farm, Ink turned into Edge's driveway while everyone else continued driving to Irene's house, which wasn't far from Edge's house.

I didn't think much of it and got out when Ink and Edge did.

"Where do you want the boxes?" Ink asked.

"You can stack them along the back wall in the living room," Edge said.

"What is going on?" I asked.

"What do you mean?"

"Why are we unloading my stuff here?"

"Because you're moving here," Edge said slowly.

"Yes, to Irene's house."

"When did you change your mind?"

"Change my mind about what?" He wasn't making any sense, and I wasn't sure which one of us was confused.

"Moving in with me."

"What? When did we even talk about moving in together?"

"What did you think I meant when I said I wanted you in Croftridge?"

"I thought you meant you wanted me to live in Croftridge, as in the same city, not the same house."

"Oh." He quickly hid his disappointment, but not before I saw it. "I thought you agreed too easily. It's okay. I'll get Ink to bring your stuff back out, and we'll take it to Irene's place."

"Wait!" I blurted before I had a chance to think about what I was doing. "Are you sure about this?"

"Yes, but this isn't about me. It's about you. Are you sure? And it's okay if you're not."

Surprisingly, I didn't need to think about it. I didn't have any feelings of trepidation regarding Edge. "Yes, I'm sure."

He fisted my shirt and pulled me to him, covering my lips with his. When he broke the kiss, he rested his forehead against mine. "I love you," he said softly.

"I love you, too."

EPILOGUE

EVIE

Three Months Later

"Surprise!" we collectively shouted when Irene arrived at the diner.

"Which one of you came up with the idea to tell me a pipe burst the night before our grand opening?"

"That was me," Dice said sheepishly.

Irene narrowed her eyes and pointed a finger at him. "No cake for you."

"My apologies," Dice said.

Irene stared at him for a few more seconds before she smiled. "See? It doesn't feel good when someone you trust messes with you."

"Are you mad?" I asked.

"Of course not. I mean, I could've done without the stress of the last thirty minutes, but this is definitely a welcome turn of events. Honestly, I should've known. You people don't miss an opportunity to throw a party."

"Only when there's a reason to celebrate," Phoenix said. "Congratulations on your new diner. It's a welcome addition to our town."

"Thank you," Irene said and clasped her hands together. "Well, enough of that. Let's have cake. There is cake, right?"

I laughed. "Yes, there's cake."

"Have a seat. I'll get you a piece," Edge said.

"Give me one second. I need to get something from the office." She returned a few minutes later with a large envelope in her hand. "This is for you," she said and handed it to me.

I stared at the envelope while everyone else started enjoying their cake. "What are you waiting for?" Irene asked. "Open it."

Carefully opening the flap, I pulled out a stack of what appeared to be legal documents. I quickly scanned the first page, but I couldn't make sense of the words I was reading. "What is this?"

"It's the legal paperwork necessary to name you as co-owner of the diner. All you have to do is sign on the pages marked."

My mouth dropped open, and my eyes widened in shock. "What?" I finally managed to ask.

"You heard me. Half of the diner is yours." While I tried to process her words, she looked around the room and found Byte. "Don't worry. I didn't forget about you. You get the other half when I retire."

"Irene," Byte started, but she held up her hand to stop him.

"If I've learned anything over the last few months, it's that I'm not invincible, and I'm not going to live forever. You and Evie are the son and daughter I've never had. It makes sense to leave it to you."

"You are definitely the mother I wished mine would have been. You've done more for me in the time I've known you than she did for my whole life. This means so much to me, and I can't thank you enough." Wrapping my arms around her, I hugged her and used those few moments to get my emotions under control.

Irene leaned back and smiled. "Okay, enough of this. There's a perfectly good cake that needs to be eaten."

Once the cake was served, I sat back and looked around the room. It was filled with friends and family. Tony and Bart were off to the side, quietly talking to each other. Walter and Buck were laughing with Phoenix and Ranger while the rest of the Blackwings were milling about. And Edge was by my side, smiling at me with love-filled eyes.

ABOUT THE AUTHOR

Website/Newsletter Sign-up

Facebook Reader Group

Signed Books/Merchandise

ALSO BY TEAGAN BROOKS

Blackwings MC

Dash

Duke

Phoenix

Carbon

Shaker

Badger

Blackwings MC Box Set

Blackwings MC - Devil Springs

Copper

Judge

Savior

Batta

Bronze

Bear

Coal

Game

Devil Springs Box Set Volume One

Devil Springs Box Set Volume Two

Blackwings MC - Devil Springs

Byte

King Mountain Shifters

Slade

Standalones

Beached

Christmas in Tinsel Town

Printed in Great Britain
by Amazon

57601049R00185